"The world is dying, Dannoc," he said finally.

"Kor—"

"I am serious. All the world is being chipped away. I can see it happening, the salmon less each year, and the doves; no weasels seen in three years, or herons in six. There were gannets when I was a boy, and gair fowl darkened the cliffs with their numbers. None now. Where have the wolves gone, the mountain lions, the bears? If one of them came now, I would not care if it killed me: I would die happy to have seen any one of them."

I said, "I have often thought the same, and so has every hunter of our tribe—"

"But there's more. A wanderer told me that the six tribes between the sea and the plains are the only ones he'd ever found. Anywhere. Even we are being chipped away, Dan.

"There are no other people in the world."

Look for these Tor books by Nancy Springer

MADBOND
WINGS OF FLAME

NANCY SPRINGER

MADBOND

A TOM DOHERTY ASSOCIATES BOOK

MADBOND

Copyright © 1987 by Nancy Springer

First printing: June 1987

A TOR BOOK

Published by Tom Doherty Associates, Inc.
49 West 24 Street
New York, N.Y. 10010

Cover art by Kevin Eugene Johnson

ISBN: 0-812-55486-8
CAN. ED.: 0-812-55487-6

PRINTED IN THE UNITED STATES OF AMERICA

0 9 8 7 6 5 4 3 2 1

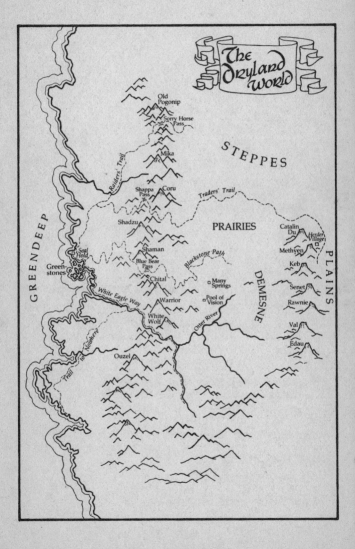

The Dryland World

Old Pogonip
Sorry Horse Pass
Mika
Raiders' Trail
Shappa Pass
Coru
STEPPES
Shadzu
Traders' Trail
PRAIRIES
GREENDEEP
Seal Hold
Greenstones
Shaman
Blue Bear Pass
Chital
Blackstone Path
Many Springs
Catalin
Du
Herder Village
Methven
Keb
Senet
Rawnie
DEMESNE
PLAINS
White Eagle Way
Warrior
White Wolf
Pool of Vision
Otter River
Val
Edau
Trail of Nowhere
Ouzel

Two there were who came before
To brave the deep for three:
The rider who flees,
The seeker who yearns,
And he who is king by the sea.

Two there were who came before
To forge the swords for three:
The warrior who heals,
The hunter who dreams,
And he who is master of mercy,
He who has captured the heart of hell,
He who is king by the sea.

—TASSIDA'S SONG

Prologue

I am a madman, a murderer, a mystic and some say a god.
But before I was any of those, and even before I was a
fool, I am a storyteller.

Let me tell you the tale of the sea king, at first as the
eye of sky saw it.

He waited alone in the midnight shadows. No body-
guard for the young sea king that night, no Birc, no
faithful Rowalt. Once each fortnight, at the time of the
highest tides, when the moon was at the full or at the new,
it was required of him that he should keep vigil alone in
the darkness of the great lodge. He, his tribe's most precious member, waiting to fend off death, alone—no one
clearly knew why. The practice reached back beyond
memory into the times of legend, into ages even before
the time of Sakeema, he-whom-all-we-seek, he who would
come again. The young king could not call even on
Sakeema for help. Pacing the shadows with his long
knife of flint in hand, every nerve at the ready, or
standing and hearkening for the approach of the unknown
enemy in the black night, the footfalls masked by the
soughing of the surf . . . Seven times challengers in
disguise had come to meet him and he had bested them,
not without wounds, but in grim silence, holding fast to a
cutting point of honor: that the king in vigil beset must not
cry out. Of necessity he had become a canny fighter,
though never an eager one. And three times the devourers
had come, the cold, swaddling, life-sucking demons from

the stormy western sea, or certainly as cold as that greendeep, though they came at him out of wind and shadowy air. They had beaten him to the rocky floor with the corpse-cold folds of their winglike flesh. Their teeth had torn at his chest. They seemed to mind his knife no more than seawater would, and still he had not shouted out for help. And somehow he had driven them off.

But no such foe had ever come upon him as that which attacked him the night of the late winter's new moon.

The sea was raging in bitter storm, so that there could be no warning. Lightning in the night sky, even at the time of year. Thunder like that of the surf, and then—hoofbeats, it was a maddened horse, the rider burst right in at the door! Half the wall came down with him—he was a man well thewed to be a warrior, one of the wild Red Hart hunters from the vast mountains that loomed eastward, half naked even in the freezing cold, his hair, braided, flying, the color of the lightning. Bearing down at the gallop he came—and in his upraised hand, lifted to strike, a long knife such as had never been seen, a knife of more than a forearm's length! The blade was as smooth as ice, made of some strange substance that bore an edge sharper even than chipped obsidian, and it glinted as pale as the horseman's hair. But the long knife-thing, the sword, was not the worst weapon the rider bore, not to the young sea king who sucked in a single breath and faced him. Far worse was the battering force of the stranger's heartbroken rage, the grief that skewed his face, the pain that gave mountainous power to his blow.

Ducking, parrying that first mighty blow—the knife of flint broke off in his hand. The mounted attacker towered over him. Falling back, circling, the sea king screamed aloud for his followers.

He who came in the lightning, he of the long weapon, the pale hair, it was I whom folk called Dannoc, I the storyteller, Sakeema's fool.

Chapter One

It was like coming up through black water, awakening. I thrashed and flinched, for my enemy stood at the surface, I knew that, stood waiting with knife poised to stick me in the gullet when I gasped for breath. I would die. I gasped anyway, and struggled, striking out with my fists to protect myself, and I felt an oddly quelling touch take hold of them, a touch as strong as my fear but far gentler. I awoke:

Dark, but not as dark as the black water—I was in a sort of cave. A young man, as young as I, had hold of me. He was no one I knew. I grew still with surprise, and he let go of my arms and looked down at me where I lay, his gaze unsmiling but not harsh. He seemed grave, as a deathbed vigilant might be grave. Beyond him white winter light slanted down like snow through the only entry—overhead. A pit, a prison!

The long arrow of fear darted through me, for all my life I had roamed the uplands and the highmountain meadows where the deer leap, and prison seemed the worst of torments to me. Or nearly the worst . . . I wanted to leap up like a deer, whurr away like a partridge, but instead I flopped about where I lay, like a great fish. My legs and wrists were tied with thongs. The young man at my side put a hand on my chest to restrain me.

"Gently. You will hurt yourself," he said to me, speaking my own language of the Red Hart tribe with only a slight hesitation. I grew still again and stared at him. His hair was dark brown, his eyes also of some dark color—it

3

was hard to see what color in the dim light. He wore a
plain tunic of rough wool such as the Herders weave. He
was not of the Red Hart.

"What place is this?" I demanded of him.

"You are in a pit for the keeping of roots or prisoners—
most often roots. Near the Hold of the Seal Kindred."

"What?" I shouted. I struggled again, but in a more
centered way. The youth took hold of me by my bound
arms and helped me to sit up.

"But how can that be?" I exclaimed. How could I have
come to the sea over the snowpeaks, and in the wintertime, yet? I had never ventured so far from the Demesne
of my people. Yet I could not disbelieve him. Even as I
spoke I could hear the cat-snarling of the surf.

"Why am I imprisoned?" I asked next. "For what
misdeed?"

The young man sat back at a small distance and faced
me. Even sitting, I overtopped him somewhat, for I was
long of limb, rawboned and loose-knit, taller than most
men. But I did not feel tall, sitting bound and helpless as I
was.

"You are no prisoner. You are my guest," he told me.
"I have but to call, and they will let the pole down for us
from above."

He was not, then, a captive like myself? Perhaps not.
He moved about freely, while I sat bound, and there was
nothing of a captive's despair in his look.

Or did they treat prisoners so well, here? My glance
dropped to my hands. The rawhide thongs that bound the
wrists were padded heavily with wrappings of fleece, as if
to spare me discomfort. I sat on a thick bed of linden-bark
matting and pelts—sealskins, they were, and they made a
warmer, thicker bed than I had ever known. Someone had
taken care for me, as if indeed I were an honored guest.

I could see that my companion had slept nearby. His
bedding lay beside him, but it was only a single sealskin
and a fleece for his head. Sitting half in shadow, he gazed
at me steadily, as if waiting for something. "What is your
name?" I asked him, for in my own silence I was beginning to feel the pressure of a blackness—I did not want to

comprehend that blackness more threatening than the prison pit.

"Rad."

It was a name of the Seal Kindred and told me little. "Is there a meaning to it?" I hazarded. "If you would care to tell me," I added for courtesy's sake.

He shrugged. "It is the foolish name my mother gave me, 'sea otter.' She often told me the tale, how on my infant naming day when she carried me down to the shore to ask the sea for a name, an untoward wave knocked her off her feet so that I was hurled into the greendeep. She dived after me but could not find me, and she raised the lament for the dead, for she felt sure that I had been drowned." The youth who called himself Rad looked at me with straight-lipped amusement. "Babes of the Seal Kindred in their first moon do not swim, no matter what the Otter River Clan may claim. So the entire tribe lamented me loudly. But a month later a man searching for glimmerstones after a storm found me in a sea cave, being suckled by a seal, and he bore me home rejoicing."

I listened, not knowing whether to believe him, or how much to believe.

"I was too scrawny to be called the little seal, my mother said. So she called me Rad. I had the look of a sea otter, she said, slender and handsome." I saw his straight mouth twitch, as if he mocked himself, and I decided that the tale was not meant to be believed, though I should have known it was too foolish not to be true. "Also, my father was of the Otter clan. Though as for sea otters, she could not have ever seen one. Children watch the kelp beds, but none have been seen for generations."

At once I felt my heart yearn. Another of Sakeema's creatures, gone, like the wolves. Like the great red catamounts. My grandfather had seen such a mountain cat once, my grandfather now dead, but even in his dying age manly and proud in his bearing, his long braids, once as yellow-brown as mine, gone bone white—

"And what might your name be?" Rad asked me, and in the space of a quickly drawn breath it was as if my grandfather had disappeared beneath—the thing I would not remember. I could no longer see him, any more than I could truly see myself, and I stared at the one who asked me the question.

"Your name," he repeated, as if perhaps I hadn't understood him. But my name lay hidden in the—deep, deep, glinting darkly like a weapon of sharp edge.

"I do not know," I told him.

"But you must have a name," he pressed me gently.

"I do not remember." I truly did not, and I was not dismayed. In fact I felt glad, as glad as a captive of war might feel, excused from torment. My companion peered at me and nodded as if understanding something.

"We'll call you Archer, then," he said, "after those calluses on your hand."

I looked down at the hand as if it were a stranger. Indeed, the marks of the bowstring roughened my fingers and thumb.

Then the one who called himself Rad came over, and, pulling a knife from its leather sheath at his belt, he began to cut my bonds.

It was a blackstone knife, probably traded from my own tribe, quite ordinary; but I watched it closely, feeling a queasiness I could not name. The youth released my wrists first, then my legs, which had also been thickly wrapped. In spite of the wrappings, I saw, there were bloody cuts on my limbs, in plenty, from the thongs. But the cuts had been treated with grease and did not hurt me. My prisonmaster offered his hand and helped me to my feet. If I had been myself I would have scorned his help, but I knew more than ever that something was wrong, for I could barely stand at first. He had to support me, and I swayed on my feet.

"You have not eaten," he explained. I placed my palm against the stony wall, and he left me and went to stand under the entry.

"Birc!" he shouted. "The pole. And he'll need a rope, I think." I was able to understand most of this. The language of the Seal Kindred differed from mine in rhythm— the wash of a lulling sea was in it. But many of the words were the same.

I did not need the rope to cling to. I scorned it, centered my strength and climbed the pole—a pine log with foot notches, creaking but solid—I managed. My folk had always said of me that I was as strong as a bison. Then they would add, nearly as clumsy. I stumbled out into the light to find a young guardsman warily eyeing me, spear in hand. Rad came up behind me and nodded at his tribesfellow.

"Run down ahead of us, now, and see that there is some food ready."

Birc looked frightened. "My king," he blurted, making obeisance, "let me walk with you."

I saw him bow his head, saw his upraised hands, heard the word, "king," and I staggered anew in my astonishment. But this—this youth wore no headband, nor even the armband of a warrior, no fur-tipped cloak, no ornament of any kind. And he was of no great height, being shorter than I. And his name—no fitting name for a warrior—but as he was of the Seal, he would have earned another name in vigil, an honored name . . . could it be? He caught at me with both hands to support me.

"Korridun son of Kela?" I whispered. "Seal king?"

He did not answer me except to nod. "Birc," he said, annoyed, "there is no need to be afraid. Go do as I told you—oh, blast it to Mahela, I suppose you had better help me here."

Birc was scarcely more than a boy, and plainly terrified. Of what, I wondered. Only later did I discover how truly loyal and courageous he was. He came to do his king's bidding, and with one of them on either side of me we walked down the steep mountainside to the headland where the lodges stood.

Long, low huts of pine timber they were, thatched with reeds. I stared at them all the while we approached them. This was the strangest of tribes to me, these Seals who ate fish and lived in fixed dwellings within sight of the snarling sea. My folk were upland hunters, woodsfaring with the wandering of the deer. . . . The lodges were built atop the rock, overlooking the sea cliff where the waves beat themselves to foam. In a high storm, spray might have clawed the log walls. Nothing else stood atop that cliff but a few contorted pines, and it was all, rocks, trees, and huts, thickly greenfurred with moss from the damp. The sky hung fishy white, breathing a cold, white fog. It chilled me—I, who walked bare-chested in the eversnow. I wondered why anyone would live within reach of that fog, that surf, so much under the eye of sky. But perhaps there was nowhere else to camp. The mountain slopes came down sheer to the sea.

"Look," said Korridun to me with a slight quirk in his voice. "My cousins are hauled out."

Even though he pointed down toward the sea I could not tell what he meant. I saw no people, only rocks mottled with lichen and weed. Then one of the rocks moved, and I blinked: there were seals lying at the base of the sea cliff, a throng of them, half a hundred or more.

"So many," said Korridun. "My cousins prosper."

Of all the tribes, only his people, the Seal Kindred, claimed such kinship with a creature of Sakeema. We of the Red Hart cherished the deer, but we knew our shortcoming, that we could not like them leap out of bowshot with a single bound. . . . But the Seal Kindred claimed a seal ancestor, Sedna, from whom sprang their royal line. They called seals "cousins," as I had many times heard my people grumbling around a campfire—my people of the Red Hart, but I could not remember their faces. Danger, if I remembered their faces.

Korridun guided me by the arm. We were drawing near the lodges, threading our way along steep shelving rock, and the chill air had braced me so that I walked more strongly, without much help. But we did not enter any lodge. Instead, Birc left us and, running ahead, brought back a torch. Rad Korridun guided me under an overhang, and I stood in such a cave as I had never seen.

Eerie, it seemed to me at the time, the smoothness of the rock walls, as if a sleek giant of an otter had made the place to slide in, had made tunnels everywhere running off at all levels, no pattern to them that I could discern. And the floor, if it might be called a floor, lay all in swells, like the surface of a quiet sea. I had experienced the jagged mountain caves where the mountain cats once denned, but this was of a different sort of stone, brown and polished, and far more open, so that a man could walk upright in it. But what man could have built it, or would have fashioned it so askew?

"The sea made this Hold, we think, ages past, and has since withdrawn," Korridun said, as if I had asked him. "Perhaps one day it will take a notion to surge up again. There is no telling."

I did not understand him, how the sea could make caves. Still less, how its level could change. I knew but little then of the ways of that vast, cold greendeep.

We came to a room, or rather a large hollow, which glowed warm and red with fire. There was a stone firepit built against an upward crevice, which made a smoke hole for it. Much food stood by the fire, and there were places for many people, timber stumps topped with thick pelts for sitting on and long, flat, timbers laid between supports for the placing of food. But there were no folk. Birc threw his torch in the fire and left the place, nearly running, and Korridun motioned me to a seat on one of the fur-topped stumps. But I settled myself cross-legged on the floor instead, as is the Red Hart custom, picking with my hands at the rushes that strewed it. Korridun dipped me food out of a basket of spruce roots, tight-woven and sealed with pitch to make a vessel fit for cooking in. It was a thick soup made of fish, boiled in the basket with stones heated in the fire, much as my folk would have made a venison stew and used the stomach of the deer to hold it. Korridun brought the food to me in a bowl of red clay, and I felt all the honor of that. Vessels of clay had to be traded from the Herders, from the far plains beyond the thunder cones. Most Seal folk, I thought, would eat from dishes of wood or shell. But perhaps Korridun himself was accustomed to clay. He was the king.

He handed me the bowl and a bone spoon. "Eat slowly," he cautioned me.

I was ravenous, as hungry as I had been after the days of my name vigil, but I was not much accustomed to fish, and the odd, oily taste kept me from gulping it too quickly. Korridun got some of the stuff for himself and sat on a sort of bench, setting his bowl on a flat timber. I eyed him, holding my own bowl on my lap, and we ate in silence. There were many questions I was not asking—how I had come into the prison pit, and when, and why I had been bound, and why were the marks of the thongs on my limbs, as if I had fought most fiercely, and why was he, Korridun King, attending me. For the most part, I did not want to know the answers. But when I had taken the edge from my hunger, silence began to press on me again, and I spoke.

"If you are king here," I said to Korridun, "how is it that no one waits on you?"

He gave me a look so wry it might have been a smile, though in fact he did not smile. "It is the custom of the Seal Kindred to humble their kings," he said.

I ate, and regarded him curiously. He was half a head shorter than I, and perhaps too slender to be very strong—so I thought at the time. But he was trimly thewed in a way that I never would be, with a centered look about him, a control. It was in his face, too, a quietness. Something about the glance of his eyes, as if Sakeema's time looked out of them, deep time, creature time, the always now. And his face comely enough so that no woman, I thought, would scorn him. But for all that, he hardly seemed a proper king to me. A young shaman, perhaps, but a king should be thewed for war. I bore in my mind the image of a king—

And as I thought it, the fell arrow of fear pierced me again, and all seemed black.

"Archer?" Korridun inquired, seeing pain in me. So I supposed.

"Nothing. A cramp in my gut." I straightened and faced him. A smoldering, reasonless anger started in me because he dared to be kind to me, so quaint are the ways of petty pride. And I decided that he might be king to others, but he was no king of mine. I would not call him by the king's name, Korridun, an ancestral name of his royal line. Nor would I call him Rad, as his loved ones might. I would take his kingly name and make it smaller, as I felt myself lessened. I would call him Kor.

"Kor," I tried it on my tongue.

His head turned to me, his face grave, courteous. "Yes?"

He was all comity, the courtesy so inborn that he was likely not himself aware of it. I ducked my head in angry discomfort, blundering for something to say. "Does—does no one call you Kor?"

"You may, if you like." He got up and found me a slab of jannock, a sort of oatmeal bread. "Do you yet remember your own name?" he asked as he handed it to me.

"No."

"A terrible loss. Your very self."

It troubled me no whit, as it kept the blackness at bay. I did not answer.

"What do you know of yourself, then?"

I shrugged. "I am of the Red Hart." Of course, with my hair as yellow as bleached prairie grass, the braids of it lying long on my bare shoulders—men of my people seldom wore much above the waist. Deerskin below, lappet and leggings. Boots of thick bison leather on my feet. These were gear such as Red Hart hunters wore. "I have shot the deer in the highmountain meadows, and I shoot them well." Deer were the food and warmth of my people, but I hated to cause them pain, deer or any of the creatures of Sakeema, so I had shot my bolts at deer of straw through the hot suns of many summers until I had learned to kill cleanly with a single swift arrow to break the neck. This mercy lay close to my heart, and I remembered it. "I have hunted with the hawk also, and the hawks fly well for me. I have fought against the Otter River Clan when they held the Blackstone Path." Again, I had tried always to kill with mercy, and I remembered that I had not liked that killing. "I have ridden against the Fanged Horse Folk when they raided us, and I have fought against the Cragsmen."

"Do you remember your tribesfellows who fought at your side?"

"I remember in a general way only."

"What are you doing in my Holding?"

"I do not know."

"Did you come here to fight?"

For the first time I felt some small qualm, not knowing who I was or why I was there in the land of his people. As a shield, I turned the question back on him. "Have you given me reason to fight you?"

"No." Soberly he studied me. "You look not much older than I," he said after a moment. "Twenty, twenty-two . . . Of what age were you when you made your name vigil?"

Days alone on the crags where only the wild sheep came, my straight, yellow hair newly braided, waiting for the vision that would give me my name—that much I remembered. But even the thought of a name of my own hurt me with a black pain, and I could not answer. I felt my shoulders sag, and I could not look any longer at Kor. My eyes shifted; I stared beyond him. And there, in the shadows of one of the several entrances, stood a stocky old woman, listening. Her head jutted forward from her stooped shoulders, her jaw thrusting at me like a weapon. Even as I saw her she strode toward me, hands knotted as if she would strike me, and I stiffened where I sat, for her creased and weathered face bore a look of such outrage as I had never seen.

Korridun turned on his seat to look where I was looking and saw her. "Istas!" he barked at her.

His tone must have served to warn her off, for she stopped. She spat at me some word I could not understand— such fury was in her, it twisted her speech as it twisted her face. I think even one of her own people might not have been able to understand her that day. Then she swung around and strode out with the hurried, scuttling stride of a strong old woman, and I heard her huffing as she left.

"That is Istas," Kor told me, "my most valued counselor." His voice seemed low, and there was no smile on his face, such as there might have been if her rage were a matter of no moment. I chose not to ask what it was that Istas had called me, for I felt very tired, and there was a deadness in me. Kor saw it at once.

"Come," he said, rising, "let us find you a place to sleep."

The place was a small chamber in the hollowed rock. A

reed wick lighted it, burning dimly in a shallow stone lamp. I wrinkled my nose at the smell of fish oil, but only for a moment, for I had not been daintily reared. Moreover, the sweet rushes strewn on the floor offset that odor nicely. On a sort of wooden platform lay my linden-bark mat and a thick bed of pelts—I recognized them from the pit. Birc, perhaps, had brought them in here. I made for them wearily.

"Wait but a moment," Korridun said, and he left me.

I lay down but did not close my eyes. A chamber of my own to sleep in—I could not help but feel honored. In the deerskin tents of my people we slept six and eight together, jostling each other, and only the king . . . but I would not think of the king. I got up, pacing like a spotted wild dog. Perhaps the wolves had once paced in that same way. I had never seen any.

Korridun came back, carrying things for me: a furred doeskin by way of covering—or perhaps to make me feel at home, a clay basin of water for washing or drinking, a wooden cuckpot.

Perverse anger welled up in me. "Why are you nursemaiding me?" I demanded. "You are supposed to be a king! Do you not have people?"

He set the load down—he must have been stronger than I had thought, to carry the heavy cuckpot, the pottery, the water. Then he stood and faced me, seeming not at all taken aback.

"I will not order my people to go where I would not go myself," he said. I scarcely heard him. I was raving.

"Do you not have servingfolk? A king who carries a cuckpot!"

"The cuckpot is an improvement," he said mildly. "I cleaned your ass many a time, up there in the pit."

I doubled over as if I had been hit in the gut and sank down on my bed, the anger gone with my wind. Voiceless, I stared up at him.

"I will not command my folk to do the thing they fear unless I am willing to do it as well. . . . You do not remember why they are frightened of you?"

I shook my head, remembering nothing of the days, the

weeks before I had awakened under his care. It seemed very quaint that folk should be afraid of me when I was myself so terrified—no, I would not think of that fear. I had to speak, quickly.

"Why was I kept in the prison pit?" I whispered.

Thongs binding my wrists, padded, the cuts of them on my arms even so . . . He stood silent for the span of a long breath, and I would not look at him for fear that I should see pity in his eyes.

"I do not call you madman, Archer," he said finally, "but there are those who do."

Madman! I was no madman—but how could I say that, I who could not remember my own name?

"Is that what Istas called me?"

"No."

Silence. A merciful exhaustion had numbed me, so that silence no longer troubled me.

"Will you sleep now?" Kor asked at last.

"I think so," I muttered, still not meeting his eyes.

"Rest in Sakeema, then," he said, and he went out and left me.

Chapter Two

Sometime after the lamp had started to flicker and smoke I awoke and used the accursed cuckpot, and scowled at it. Then I blundered out. Sometime past dawn, for faint daylight filtered down into the passageway from fissures and from weapon slots fashioned in the rock where the walls were thin. Birc lay dozing just beyond the entry to my chamber. He jumped up when he heard me and pointed his spear at my gutknot, shaking so badly he could not hold it steady—the shaft wobbled crazily. But the flint head was chipped to a keen edge, fit to tear my innards out, not to be meddled with. And a scared man who stands his ground is as dangerous as a frightened horse. I stopped and leveled a look at him.

"I am going to get something to eat," I told him, speaking slowly and hoping he could understand me. "I will no longer have your king playing the manservant." I waited, watching the spearhead waver. "What, am I a prisoner after all?"

Losing patience, I sidestepped and pushed the spear away with my hand, then shoved past him. He could have attacked me from behind, but he did not. Instead, he trailed after me as I found my way back to the room with the cooking fire. It was full of people taking their morning meal, and for the first time I saw how the folk of the Seal Kindred looked. I liked them at once, for something about them made me think of Sakeema's creatures, of trim-thewed animals with gentle dark eyes. Their faces were round and smooth, shell-brown with a pink tinge, their

15

hair brown and soft and cropped short, man and woman alike, except that the maidens wore theirs in a long cloud. I saw several maidens whom I fancied, even at a glance, though they were clothed too modestly for me to see much. These people chose to keep warm, it seemed, and they had been trading with the Herders, for they all wore woolens as well as furs. This much I saw in a breathspan, and then they spied me and scattered with a noise and rush like that of startled quail, snatching up their babies and young children and crowding out of the several entries.

One of them did not run: Istas. She stood her ground and glared at me with a look of black hatred. But she did not speak, and in a moment she turned and followed stiffly after the others. I was left alone except for Birc, behind me. I looked around at him. He was keeping a cautious distance.

"Kor spoke to her, bidding her hold her tongue," I said to him, guessing, and after a long pause he curtly nodded.

It gave me a peculiar feeling, that she hated me, that the others ran from me. But I shrugged and went to the fire. There was millet gruel. I got myself some in a clamshell, picked up an oat cake as well, nodded at Birc, and sat down on the rush-strewn floor to eat. Plying a shell spoon, I took my time, ignoring the half-finished food spilled or abandoned all around me, feeling, without looking up, Birc's scrutiny and that of others who peeped from the entries. If they did not want to abide me, then they could well-come-hell wait until I was done. I ate stolidly. There was a heavy, knotted feeling in me that I did not yet recognize as anger. But I had to force the food down around it, as if a stone sat in me, and after all I could not eat much. I left it finally and went outside, hearing footfalls fleeing before me.

It was a foggy morning, with a fine rain drizzling out of a fishbelly-white sky hanging so low over the mountains that the steep flanks of them, dark with spruce and fir, faded into cloud and seemed to rise forever. I hearkened. Words echoed in the fog, and voices carried.

"Not fog. Smurr," a fisherman said somewhere down on the narrow beach below the cliff. I could not see him, but from his tone he must have been instructing a young-ster. "Smurr, when it makes small rain. Brume, the gray fog. Mist, the thin fog. Haze, thinner yet. Scarrow-fog, the high, white haze that makes a blurred spot of the sun."

I smiled, feeling a goodness, as if something had cen-tered for me. So the Seal Kindred knew many names for fog. And the Otter River Clan named the salmon with many names: the tiny fry struggling out of the gravel, then parr, the length of a man's small finger, then smolt, turning from brown to graysheen before going to the sea. And then the great salmon, returning, the grilse, the peal, turning from graysheen to red and the jaws of the males growing into great hooks. A trader from the Otter had told me those things once, sometime when I was small. . . .

Blurred memories, hazy as the sun through scarrow. Myself, a child, my hair yet hanging loose, sitting cross-legged by someone far taller, reciting the many names of the mountains, north from the Sorry Horse Pass on south. Old Pogonip. Mika, the cold maiden. Coru, Shadzu, Sha-man, Chital, Warrior, White Wolf, Ouzel. And the passes between them, the Blue Bear, the Shappa, the White Eagle Way along the Otter River. And the parts of mountains, as if they were great sleeping horses, dun or gray, furred with pine, maned with eversnow, their polls and crests, their brows where the icefields fell like forelocks, the high passes we called nagsbacks, where the trade trails wound through.

I stared eastward. Mountains stood there, somewhere, behind the fog—no, smurr, blast it. There, the great peaks, not even so far away, but I could not see them. I could not—remember my own name. . . .

I strode off at random, fleeing my thoughts, scouting the strange place where I found myself.

Some distance downshore I found the inlet where folk emptied their cuckpots, and I went back to fetch mine. No king was going to do that chore for me if I could prevent it. When I had returned the foul thing to my chamber I walked toward the sea. The tide was out. Waves crashed and foamed against the rocks far below me, and wind blew hard in my face, such wind as an eagle would joy to front.

Once the ernes, the great white sea eagles, had lived on rocky headlands such as this. But that was in Sakeema's time. . . . There was a dark, homely, long-necked bird, a cormorant, the glutton among birds, perched to dry its wings on the rocks bared by the tide. There were people down there as well, some of the middling children, gathering mussels or sea lettuce or whatever they could find among the rocks. Nearly naked, their furs and woolens left in a lump on the shore, they splashed in and out of the sea, not minding whether they were wet or dry or doused by waves, though I shivered as I watched. Seawater looked very cold to me, gray beneath white wintry sky, and the day was chill. But the children shouted and left work for play, plunging into the surf and chasing each other out again just as quickly, running along the beach, their wet bodies shining brown, rubbing their numbed arms and legs with driftwood sticks.

Far out on the sea their elders fished from coracles, pitiful little boats made of sealskins stretched over willow frames, tiny with distance, on waves that looked high and tossing to me. I shivered again and turned away.

Wandering, I took stock of Kor's Holding. People had been going about their work, but they hid from me as I walked, darting into Seal Hold or skulking within lodges. I paid no attention. There were several lodges, one twice as large as the rest but damaged, perhaps by some storm. Out in the open there were stones for the sharpening of shells into knives, for women of the Seal used such knives to prepare food. There were stones for the grinding of oats or millet into meal. I saw the lodge where the spearmaker worked, where shafts lay in readiness for tips of bone or shell, or of flint or blackstone traded from my own people, inland. I saw many racks for the drying of fish, most of them empty and waiting for summertime. There were even pens for the keeping of fowl. It was strange to me, this settled way of living in one place, the men doing one thing, women another, and everyone eating together for the most part. In my tribe each pair, man and woman, fashioned their own bows of stagshorn and sinew, fletched arrows by the wintertime campfire, and hunted and gath-

ered and fended for themselves and their little ones. The
Seal Kindred's ways were very different. Still, these Seals
did not lack for toughness, not when their children frol-
icked in the wintertime surf.

Back among the stunted spruce trees, behind and above
Seal Hold, I found the place where Kor's folk got their
drinking water. Springs ran in cascades down the steep
mountainside, lying on the rocks like a net, but fine as
spiderweb. Basins had been carved in the stone to catch
their flow. Many years must have gone into the carving of
those pools. I stared a long while before I walked on, for
my people wandered and never left their mark anywhere.

At the farthest distance of the headland from the Hold
there stood a sort of pen with tall walls built sturdily of
large spearpine. So densely were the timbers pegged together that only a handsbreadth of space showed between
them. Something large and dark was moving in there,
larger than the great maned elk that had once grazed the
upland valleys in the time before my grandfather's time. I
walked over to see what it was—

Before I could put my eye to a gap between logs there
was a scream louder and more wild than the scream of a
goshawk, and a thundercrack blow against the inside of the
pen that shook the walls. I glimpsed a hoof flashing nearly
in my face. My eye would have been gone if I had come
closer, or my skull smashed. The thought made me peevishly more determined—by Sakeema, I would see inside!
I ran to a corner, where the logs jutted out, overlapping,
and like a young bear, so my grandfather would have said,
I climbed them.

By the mighty peaks.

It was a wild horse with fangs longer than my finger,
fangs stained brown at the base but keen white at their
chisel tips, fit to tear a heart out. A mare, it had to be a
mare. Nothing else is as fierce as a fanged mare. Warriors
value them above all other mounts for their staying strength
and their will to kill—though when they are in heat they
will kill their own masters as readily as they will an
enemy. And there, glaring up at me, stood an ugly, hammer-
headed, straight-necked, slab-hipped mare the dun gray

color of the short-grass steppes in winter, sparse black
mane and tail, and even as I saw her, saw the deep circle
she had worn in the narrow pen with her spinning, saw the
heavy bones showing gaunt through her scarred hide, she
attacked me, rearing to strike at me with her deadly
forehooves. Her prison was built high enough to keep me
out of her reach, but she startled me so that I fell back
anyway, hearing her crash into the log wall as I landed on
my ass on the rocky ground.

I could not get up at once—the breath was knocked out
of me. Confound it, and someone had seen me. It was
Korridun, coming up the headland with a large willow
basket on his arm and, of all things, children, six or seven
very small children swarming around his heels like so
many weanling pups. Strings of limpet shell hung around
their pudgy necks to ward off ill luck, the demons that take
children in the night. Kor walked slowly for the sake of
the children, and he looked as if he was going to ask me
whether I had hurt myself. I hated him. Forgetting the pain
in my nates, I jumped up and strode to confront him.

"Kor!" I shouted at him. "Why is that horse in that
miserable pen?"

"Lower your voice," he told me without raising his
own. "You'll frighten the little ones."

They did look frightened of me, somewhat, but deemed
that Korridun provided sufficient protection and clustered
behind him, clinging to his legs, looking up with large
eyes of dark brown. I lowered my voice.

"She has worn herself to the bone with her frenzy in
there. It is too small. She was born to have the breadth of
the steppes for running on."

"I know it," Kor said with a faint note of sorrow in his
voice but no shame. "We built the enclosure as ample as
we could. We had to go far inland for the logs."

It was true, all the trees on coast and headland were
blown into shapes as of tattered cloaks by the constant sea
wind. Some crouched and crept along the very rock, like
the spruces at the tree line up on the highmountain passes.
Rampicks, we of the uplands called those half-dead trees

broken off by wind. There was another thing with a name. Unlike me.

The fanged mare squealed out an angry challenge.

"She is never let out of there, I suppose," I said curtly.

"Never. No one can go near her without being attacked."

"But of what use is the steed to you, so wild?"

"None whatsoever."

"Then why not make shift to set her free? Failing that, even killing her would be kinder." My voice was rising again. Kor's quietness maddened me.

"Pajlat would take offense," he said.

I stood and stared at him. Pajlat was the fierce king of the Fanged Horse Folk.

"Pajlat thinks more of his own scheming than of the creatures of Sakeema," Korridun added. "The poor beast is his gift to me."

"Why would Pajlat give you such a gift?" I burst out.

"To humiliate me," said Kor. "He knows I cannot ride it."

He spoke quite levelly, and he was right, of course. There seemed to be something in him that spoke truth always, that did not sway to winds of pride or anger, a sureness that stunned me.

Seeing that I was done with him for the time, he loosened the children from around his legs and sent them back down the headland toward the lodges. The little ones rolled about like ducks as they walked, their legs were so short. A thought came to me, why the children might be with him. Kings were expected to augment the numbers of their people.

"Yours?" I asked.

He shook his head. "I am not yet pledged."

No more was I, but I suspected I had fathered a few such scantlings. . . . Great Sakeema, what sort of a king was this one? I watched silently as he walked the rest of the way to the fanged mare's pen. The horse shrilled and kicked the logs as he approached. Paying her no heed, Korridun climbed up the corner as I had done and emptied his basket of fish into the feeding trough ten feet below.

"On the high plain, I know, they eat snakes," he

remarked to me. "But she has taken to the fish well
enough. She would be fat if she did not wear it all off with
her fretting."

The horse's charge set the barrier to shuddering, and
Kor climbed down, unhurried. I watched him in a sort of
despair.

"Are there no servingfolk to feed the horse?" I asked,
nearly imploring. My tone made him grin. If I had known
how rare such smiles were from him, I would have felt the
gift of it.

"No more than there are for you."

Well hit. It was true, I felt a sympathy with the maddened mare. I turned away from Korridun and watched her
whirling around her prison while her food lay untouched.
No, more than sympathy. A hidden kinship, a stirring of
some dark understanding.

"I will—" I stopped, swallowed, and started over again.
Though I did not call Korridun "king," I would remember
that I was a guest in his household and owed him courtesy.
"I would like to have the tending of her."

"To feed her?"

"To take a long, strong rope and drop a loop of it over
her head and give her freedom if only to the rope's extent.
I will need a stick also, to fend her off. But I think she will
want mainly to run."

Korridun gave me a startled look. "You are so willing
to risk your life?"

"Yes!" Though I could not say why, I who did not
know what had happened to send me to his side, I who did
not know my own name. I felt the jolt of something
shadowed, some feeling almost as nameless as I, and I
quickly quelled it. Korridun was staring at me. I stared
back.

"Once you have regained your full strength," he said at
last.

"I am strong enough!" I protested.

"By Sedna's bones, I believe you are nearly strong
enough to wrestle the blue bear of Sakeema." He did not
smile, and I thought I heard something taut in his voice.
"But I have my people's well-being to think of, you

know, should the mad thing escape you. Ask me again in
three days.''

He picked up his wicker basket and turned away. I
found myself staring at his back, at the brown wool of his
tunic. Very well, three days did not make so long a
time. . . . ''Does the horse have a name?'' I called after
him. He glanced back at me, a curious look taking hold of
him.

''No. It is as nameless as you.''

I turned back to the mare, looking at her through the
bars of the pen but keeping well back from hooves and
tearing teeth. Her angry eyes met mine. Large, the largest
eye I had ever seen in any beast, white-rimmed, with a
dark center the color of cloudy water, brown with a bluish
tinge. Sorrows of ages seemed to be hidden in that murky
eye. I felt a sudden surge of compassion for her, the wild
creature in her confinement.

''I will undertake vigil for a name for you, daughter of
the hot winds,'' I promised her.

As I had once done vigil for a name for myself.

Chapter Three

"Archer," Kor protested, "you have not yet eaten even three full meals!"

"So much the better. The trance will all the sooner come to me."

He puffed his cheeks at me in exasperation and urged me toward a seat by the firepit, fed me chunks of fish and some bitter-tasting green stuff from the sea. I sat at trencher this time, but ate with wrinkled nose.

"Do the Seal Kindred not know the worth of red meat?" I demanded. "Is there not enough game on the slopes?"

"Red meat? We feed it to yon fanged mare." Kor faced me soberly, and I could not tell whether he was jesting with me.

After I had eaten I took my place by "yon fanged mare" and ate nothing more for the days of the vigil, waiting for a name to come from Sakeema.

He is legend, Sakeema, he-whom-all-we-seek. Yet more than legend, for he is god. Yet less than legend, for he is living man, and my grandfather's grandfather once spoke to an old man who knew him as a friend.

Sakeema was born in a cold cave far up on the snowpeaks, my folk say, and all the creatures came to look at the naked babe. The little shivering pika came and the mighty catamount, the otter, the white fox, the tall antelope of the crags, the badger, and the wolf standing next to the shy hare, and the peregrine perched in the blue pines alongside the wren. They all kept silent vigil. And when his human mother left him he was suckled by a deer. Or so the Red

Hart people say—the Seal Kindred say he was born in a seaside cave and suckled by a cow seal, held to her breasts with her flippers and taken to swim in the sea. No one knows surely whence he came.

Sakeema, the king who will come again. He did not quickly come to me, and I shivered through that first day in the smurr.

Kor brought me a deerskin to sit on, and a woolen cloak to ward off the chill, and a sort of cape woven out of the inner bark of cedar to fend off the damp and the rain. I put the things on, for day was darkening into dusk and I was miserable with the weakness of the vigil starting already to come on me. He looked at me a moment, then nodded and left me.

Sometime during the first night the mare grew weary of screeching and striking at me. She went to stand against the farther wall, and after that all was silence and blackness until dawn. There was something cruel and nameless gnawing at my heart, and it was hard to empty my mind for the sake of Sakeema when the silence oppressed me, making me feel crushed by blackness, as if I would drown. Nor could I run away. So I sang. Years later Seal folk told me how they lay awake and cursed me through the night of that singing.

Nonsense, mostly, I sang, my voice no more melodious than that of the craking rail. "Mare, dare, what about this mare. . . . What a shame, the lady has no name. . . . Name, shame, where is her name. . . . I give it up, Sakeema, send a name. . . . King, sing, what sort of creature is a king, Sakeema, I beg of you. I give it up, what king, what a thing . . ." On and on. And sometimes snatches of the old songs with words no one understood:

"The hart wears a crown but Sakeema wore none.
    Sakeema the king, where have you gone?
    Badgers have setts and the bears have their dens.
    Sakeema the king, where is your throne?
    What wantwits we are, what wanhopes all . . ."

Wantwit and wanhope, indeed. I did not know what were a crown, a throne, nor had I ever seen a bear.

I felt bereft.

With dawn I saw barnacle geese feeding along the shore-line, and teetertails running, and seals swimming in the waves beyond the surf. The fanged mare snorted and struck at me, whirling about her pen, but mostly for show, I think—the blow lacked zest. I watched her and blinked with pity. Whirling . . .

Even before the men had come out to launch the cora-cles, the day had blurred into dreaming for me.

I was a warrior in the midst of battle, disgraced because I had let my horse be killed under me, but I fought on, afoot. Myself in an earlier body, perhaps, in the time when my grandfather's grandfather was a lad. Though I was a yellow-braided Red Hart, much as ever. Who we fought, I cannot remember. It seemed as if we fought the whole world. There was a heavy-bearded Fanged Horse raider trying to run me down, and also I recall those bellowing giants of Cragsmen, and the narrow-eyed Otter with their female leader were in it somehow. But none of that seemed important, afterward: for he came.

Riding on a massive stag he came, the antlers shielding him to either side, and he bore no weapon, but let his leaping mount take him into the thick of the combat. Great wolves ran snarling all about him, a black wolf by his left side and a white wolf by his right, and gray wolves and wolves of all colors, two tens of wolves, surging at his fore or crowding after him. And spotted wild dogs ran with him as well. Tall on his stag in the midst of the battle he raised his hands, and those who fought were flung into confusion by his coming, for their bolts and spears stalled in their flight and fell to earth as softly as feathers. And in every warrior's hand the stone knives sagged to earth as if they were heavy as mountains. Even the Cragsmen could not lift their cudgels any longer. And Sakeema spoke, and there was a splendor about him so that even the striving kings fell to silence and listened.

"This land, this vast dryland demesne, is rich in food and wandering room for all," Sakeema averred. "Kings of the peoples, why do you battle with each other?"

No one answered him, for no one seemed able to remember.

"Go hence," Sakeema told us all. "Roam in families and clans as the wolves do, find your food. Strive no longer after mastery."

And we common warriors felt bemused and glad enough to go. Most of us left at once, taking pause only to tend our dead or wounded. The kings withdrew to a distance and muttered with their counselors as the wolves watched them warily. But I strode up to speak with the one who sat on the great maned stag.

"Give me a name," I begged him.

Sunset light banded his head in fire. I could not see his face as he looked down on me, only that skybright glory.

"But has not your mother named you?" he asked me.

"I have no mother."

"Your father?"

"I have no father."

He slipped down from his mount, the stag lowering its head in a sort of bow as he did so, swinging its antlers out of his way. He crouched by the stag's shoulder, sank his fingers into the earth, stood and offered me cupped hands full of loam.

"Father and mother of us all," he said.

Seeing him wholly, I gazed at him, full of wonder and love, forgetting the matter of the name. "I will follow you forever," I told him.

"But, son of earth, I can lead you only into sorrow."

"No matter."

"You do not know. What if I ride away from you? What if I leave you here?"

"I will search for you until the world's end."

The gaze of his eyes never left mine, but his fingers worked the loam in his hands, stroking it, fondling it as if it were a living thing—it was. A tiny bird as blue as any mountain harebell fluttered up, warbled like a bubbling stream and flew, gone in sky. Sakeema's gaze left mine at last to follow it.

"Blue wren," I whispered.

"You have named it, son of earth."

It was a dream. I knew even as it happened that it was all a dream, too sweet to be real. Yet it was all true, as things dreamed are sometimes more true than things real, very truth, a truth I would have put my hand in fire for, and taken oath.

Indeed I did travel with him. He sent his stag away, and we walked. Creatures came to him wherever we walked, and people, for there was healing in his touch. Battle's wounded, made well. A woman dying of childbed fever, standing up to tend her baby. A small girl's twisted leg made straight. Scrofula in a young man, gone as if it had never been.

And there was that marvelous power in his hands, which I first had seen. If he took a bit of earth in his hands, or even a brown pine flower or a twig, and if he dreamed . . . The wonders that came of Sakeema's hands and Sakeema's dreams. Great-eared foxes called fennecs. Small burrowing bears. The crested jay, each of its feathers a different color from the others, and each brighter than the last. The tiny blue deer of Sakeema with antlers the clear color of ice. All these things I saw.

That was the time of wonders, Sakeema's time. There were a twelve of sorts of deer in those days, as many sorts as there are bodyguards in a king's retinue, and I saw them all. Great maned elk, and the swimming deer with tines, small spotted deer, musk deer, the yellow deer with flattened antlers, black-tailed deer, many others—all gone, afterward, except the red. And the wolves, the foxes, their pelages—not gray only, as in the later time, but spice colored, like the trunk of a great upland pine, and black, blue, dun, yellow, brown, fawn, white, all beautiful. The foxes sat in the night and looked at Sakeema with shining eyes, and the wolves and the spotted wild dogs brought him meat, and the deer lay down by his side.

I was not the only one who followed him, though I was the first. There came to be many others, and whatever questions they asked him, he would try to answer. And tales were told throughout the demesne of the marvels he did and of his wisdom, until at last, warily, the very kings came to him for counsel, and he spoke long with them.

So another marvel came to be, that all six tribes learned to speak a common language: the Herders with their six-horned brown sheep, the salmon-eating Otter River Clan, the Red Hart, the Seal Kindred, the solitary Cragsmen, and the Fanged Horse Folk, fiercest warriors of us all. Even they followed peaceful ways during that time when folk called Sakeema "High King," though he claimed no such title.

One day in springtime—though in my vision it seemed always to be springtime—one day when the spotted lilies bloomed, a woman came and stood before Sakeema where he sat in a hemlock grove.

"Honor me," she told him with a smile. "I am your mother."

"I have no mother," Sakeema said.

The woman said, "I am your mother. Provide a home for me."

He got up slowly to stand and stare at her. "The All-Mother is my mother," he said in a roughened voice, and only in that way did he ever call himself a god. And only I stood by to hear.

"I am your mother," the woman said. "I gave you life." And he went to her and embraced her.

"Turn your back!" I reproached him. "If she speaks truth, she abandoned you, left you in a cave to chance's care!"

"She speaks truth," he said. "How can I turn my back? Life itself is the greatest gift."

In my vision it seemed as if he had built her a home at once, with the embrace, a great lodge of stone and timber standing in the midst of the demesne. The kings of the six tribes came there to hold council. Sakeema did not dwell within. He roamed under sky as always, and I with him.

The woman who called herself his mother—perhaps she was his mother, for she possessed something of power. For evil. Her hand could never clearly be seen, but always after the kings met in her house there were spiteful faces, skirmishes in distant places, a feeling as of thunder forming in the reaches of sky, and Sakeema walked long and far to quell it.

It was the female king of the Otter who made the accusation: that the mother of Sakeema was guilty of abomination, of loosely consorting with men pledged to others, and with boys so young they were yet nearly children, and even with young girls. It was whispered that she lay also with her own son. But that charge was not made. So on a day in springtime, on a day when the asphodel nodded yellow, the council of kings met and brought the charge of abomination, and they called on Sakeema for justice.

I knew whose blood they truly craved. His. For being what he was, far greater than they.

In my vision I cried out in despair to Sakeema, "All falls to ruin!"

"Say not so, son of earth." He was sitting by me amidst grass greenwild with spring, in a meadow where many deer grazed. Purple spires of amaranth swayed, the healing flower born of his own hands, loveliest of flowers, which after his passing withered and died. Except for me and the deer, all his friends had forsaken him. The beauty of the place where we sat only deepened my despair.

"There may be dreaming and doing, and wonders without number, yet it all falls down into ashes again, always! I am young, yet I have seen it too many times. Has it not always been so, since the beginning of the world?" A plea in my voice, for him to tell me No, I was wrong.

But instead he said, "Listen to me, son of earth." All his great heart in his voice, for he was trying to teach me and comfort me, as he had taught and comforted so many. Yet he would not tell me other than truth. "Yes, it has always been so, turnings upon turnings. But think also of the things you cannot see. When the All-Mother carved stone and made mountains, when she took many colors of wool and wove the coverings of earth, when she wept and set her shining tears in the sky, she wept for love. When she took clay and made humankind and set us free for the wandering of this place, she wept the oceans for love of us. But there is a love farther away, which we cannot see, and next to it the love of the All-Mother is as hatred."

He spoke of the All-Mother as if he knew her, as if he

had sat by her side and talked with her, as I now talked with him. But the rest of what he was saying was utterly new to me. "What love?" I whispered.

"A love greater than sky, a love without ending, which you can scarcely understand, in the heart of the god who broods half a hundred worlds under one great starry wing. He is too vast for us to see or name, and so also is his brother, whom he loves as much as he does us."

"Brother?"

"His half-witted brother. You have known such folk? They put all to awk and awry, meaning no evil, no more than a toddling child means evil. The god's half-witted brother often grows angry and jealous, as such folk do, and in his rages he sometimes destroys what the god wishes only to cherish."

"He should be punished," I muttered.

"But the one who will never cease to love us, should he then cease to love his own brother?"

I had no answer.

"Haply," Sakeema added with a warm smile, "the brother must sometimes sleep."

He could jest? With his mother's house looming in the distance, within which the council of kings waited?

"And the god," I said in a low voice. "Does he also sleep?"

Sakeema did not cease to smile, but he said softly, "This is a time, I think, when the god is sleeping."

The woman who called herself his mother, she also deserved punishment, to my way of thinking. The charges against her were just—I had seen enough to know that. Though charges might never have been brought had she not been meddlesome as well, or had certain power-craving kings not desired to strike down Sakeema through her. For Sakeema gazed on me in farewell, and I knew well enough that his was the blood that would be shed. He loved and honored his mother, and he would not stray from justice. In only one way could he serve both justice and love: by taking her punishment upon himself.

The penalty was death.

Still faintly smiling, Sakeema rose, and I sprang up to

stand before him, grasping at him in a panic. My sudden movement startled the deer, sending them bounding away into the forest beyond the lodge.

The den where death waited, sharp of tooth and claw.

"Do not go in there!" I begged, though I knew well enough that he must, and I did not take pause for him to say it. I swallowed instead, squared my shoulders, trying to still my own quaking. "I will come with you," I said.

He shook his head—not to forbid me, but because he knew, even then, that I could not. "Set yourself no such task, son of earth. You will fail."

"I would never fail you!"

"I ask nothing. It is yourself you would fail, saying so. Mortal courage has limits."

"You—you cannot face them alone!" For his mother had long since fled, westward, somewhere.

His face went bleak. He looked around him, taking in all the world with that look. I remember white wool of clouds in the sky, flicker of birdflight, somewhere the hoarse song of frogs. Mountains. Treetops. Somewhere there were small hiding creatures, and roots deep in earth. . . .

His gaze returned and was for me alone.

"Do not be so willing to give up life. The plenum of life, it is all I can give you. Life in beauty, in plenty—it is the only gift, but love, and it is love, the very gift of love. Son of earth, as you love me . . ."

"Yes," I whispered, though I could barely speak for sorrow.

"Cherish the deer. Cherish all creatures, all things that live, even the earthworms . . . and you will cherish me. I live—in all creatures. Be still sometimes and see the creatures and know that I am yet with you . . . if you feel so much as the flying of a midge in the night, I am yet with you."

Mutely I nodded. He looked at me, then bent and brought up loam with his fingers, offering it to me in cupped hands, as he had on the first day we met. "For you, my friend," he said softly. And it turned into a songbird as red as his blood, and flew away.

And he walked away after he had embraced me, toward his doom. Toward the doorway that opened on darkness.

I could not bear it. I let out a sound that was half shout, half sob, and ran after him. But he was right, of course. My courage failed me at that entry—I could go no farther. I stood outside and wept, and railed at myself.

Time jumped, as it will, in visions. Perhaps a quarterday had passed, and somehow I had shamed and threatened myself into moving, or in my despair I no longer cared about my own life. I went in, found the inner chamber where the council sat in a wide circle. They looked like six figures of dark clay, sitting there in the gloom. At the center of their circle stood Sakeema, naked except for a breechclout, hands tied to shame him. Blood on his back—he had been flogged. On his face, nothing yet but calm.

"This man has done nothing to deserve punishment!" My voice shook like my knees, yet I managed to say the words and make them be heard. "He is blameless, as innocent as a rainbow. What charge can you make against him?" And I strode into the circle to stand beside him.

Then truly my courage was gone. For the kings looked at me, and their faces showed that they saw only more meat for their killing. The giant Blue Akabu of the Cragsmen grinned like a skull. The Fanged Horse king smiled in his sooty-black beard, and even my own king of the Red Hart stirred like a hawk rousing to stoop on its prey. The young fools who ruled the Herders and the Seal Kindred lifted their chins, on their mettle. Only the female king of the Otter looked uneasy, for she had started this game, and it had gone far beyond what she had wanted or expected.

And Sakeema, gazing at me—his face did not move, but tears ran down it like freshets down the mountains in the springtime. Tears of love and joy, and not because I had saved him, forsooth. There was no way of saving him. Somehow, even with his hands bound, he had saved me.

I had intended to demand his right to lay his case before the people. Though likely, led by their jealous kings they would have condemned him as well. . . . It did not matter. Nothing mattered but that Sakeema spoke to me with glowing eyes.

"Go, live," he said, his voice so low it was a breath, a whisper, like woodland breeze. "Have many children. And because you have come to me . . . I give you this promise, that I will come to you when you need me worst."

Already his enemies, the six, had called for guards. I had to leave his side or die. So I sprang away, my heart breaking, and fled through the guards, and escaped.

They killed him by the cruel ways while I lay in hiding on the mountainside. And when they let his body be brought out at last, I went with the others to look on it, stood by the bier with the creatures, the foxes, the wolves and wild dogs, the deer, for few people dared to come there. And in my grief it seemed to me that I would never need him more than then. Like a madman I shouted his name aloud to the wind.

"Sakeema!"

There was no answer.

"Sakeema!"

Nothing but the sighing of the wind.

"Sakeema!"

Again and again I called for him, with sobs that roared in my chest. He was gone, gone, my god was gone and did not heed my cry. I felt bereft, betrayed, fit to die with sorrow, and I was lying on hard ground, weeping and shouting his name. . . .

Someone shaking me. I looked up, blinking. A man, bending over me, his face darkened and unseen against a white and shining scarrow-sky, his head banded in that glory . . . My heart leaped like a courting deer.

"Archer? Are you all right?"

I groaned and closed my eyes in disgust. It was only Kor.

Sakeema, Sakeema, Sakeema, he-whom-all-we-seek . . . The dream had been so bright, so true, and now it was leaving me. I had said . . . I had said I would search for him unto the end of the world. If he had not yet come back to me, I must find him. . . . But I could not remember his face!

Though I clenched my jaw and pressed my palms against

my eyes, I could not remember his face. With a whispered curse of fury I flung myself away from Kor and pounded the rocky ground with my fist.

"You were calling on Sakeema," Kor explained softly. "You sounded as if you were in agony. Archer, what did you see?"

Giving it up, beyond words, I opened my eyes to look at him again. Over his head, between him and sky, a speeding shadow passed. All the small birds in the seaside forest fell suddenly silent, cowering until the hawk was gone.

"Talu," I said suddenly, a word in the old language of my people, from the time before Sakeema. I felt weary but blessed. A name had come from my god, a name very fitting for the mare.

Kor made a wordless noise of inquiry. I caught hold of him and stiffly rose.

"Harrier," I explained. "Hellkite." A drab bird, ugly even, but swift and fierce.

"It suits her," Kor agreed.

I wobbled when I turned to salute the mare. "Talu," I told her, "good night." And she merely glanced at me, without striking.

Korridun had to support me as I walked. I went with him into his sea-carved home and ate what he gave me and slept in my chamber there. But my dreams were full of longing.

Chapter Four

Though I could not remember Sakeema's face, I remembered the dream, or at least broken shards of it, bright and strange. A sense of longing stayed with me, a restlessness, a yearning—folly. Only children yearned for the moon, and only a fool for Sakeema, the harsh old saying went. Yet there was a murmur of hope in me, for he had said he would return when I needed him most, or when his world needed him most. . . . It was folly, it sifted to the bottom of my mind. There were many other things to be thought of, things to be done. But the bright dreaming sense, longing and hope, murmured through my days, hidden, like snowmelt running beneath talus, almost beyond hearing, but constant, like the burden of a song.

There was the fanged mare to be attended to.

Three days later, when I asked him for the things I needed to run the mare, Korridun found me a long line of braided seal gut, such as the sea hunters made fast to their weapons when they speared the great fish, the cachalot, very strong. Also he brought me mitts of leather such as the fisherfolk of his tribe wore to protect their palms from the lines, and long withes of basket willow from which I plaited myself a stinging whip. In the morning, early, before there were many folk about to be trampled, I took the things and went out to the pen where the fanged mare was tearing at her fish.

"Hail the day, Talu," I greeted her. She kicked at me with her hind hooves, almost absently, never lifting her head from the ravening of her food.

I waited until she had finished, hoping she would be more sluggish on a full stomach. Then I climbed the corner and dropped a loop of my line over her head.

She shot up with a surge that stopped my heart and left me feeling as if I were trying to tame the surf. But at the same time her passion did something odd to me: deep, within an inward darkness, I felt a kindred rage move, washing up in waves that threatened to engulf me. I smothered it. Not the foremost danger—the mare nearly took the wall down, and me with it. I snubbed the rope around the topmost log and strained to keep it taut so that she would not tangle herself in slack and snap a leg, struggling. "Talu," I shouted at her, "calm down! I don't want to hurt you!"

She only fought me the harder. Korridun came walking up behind me, trying to look as if he had just happened by. The mare's breath was rasping and rattling in her throat. I eased the rope from around the log, but the loop that had tightened around her neck did not loosen. Squeaking, bound to self, it kept its deathgrip on her.

"She's strangling!" I exclaimed to the air or Korridun.

The mare's eyes rolled back so that the whites showed, and she went limp, crashing to the ground. Like a wantwit, knowing I could be killed, I jumped down into the pen with her.

There was no way out—

"Kor!" I shouted wildly. "Get that gate open!" But he was already at work, tearing off the poles that closed the entry. Whether he intended to come in after me, or what he intended, I am not sure. I kneeled by the mare's bony head—*aaaii*, those fangs. Sharp as a woodmaster's adz. Gingerly I loosened the loop from around her neck and, knowing I had maybe the span of three breaths to work in, I brought it up to her ears, passed leather through leather and made of it a sort of headstall with the trailing end coming down between her eyes, where her tearing teeth could not reach it. . . . Blue-brown eyes fluttered open. I sprang back.

"Kor! Get out of the way!"

I snatched up my willow whip, ready to lash the mare

across the soft flesh of her nose if she attacked me.
Though truly, there would not have been much chance for
me if she had been intent on killing me. I hoped she would
be more intent on her freedom, and, as luck would have it,
she was. With a shrilling neigh she leaped for the square
of light that had opened in the wall of her prison. Korridun
had most of the poles down, and she splintered the rest,
surging out at the gallop. I trailed along, stumbling, at the
end of the rope behind her.

That was my mistake, to let her get ahead of me. If I
had gone out before her and kept her head turned toward
me I would have had a hope of controlling her. As it was,
I was only a nuisance attached to her, and she commanded
the whole forward force of her body with which to throw
me off. She careered wildly across the mossy rock, kick-
ing her hind heels high into the air, bucking, throwing her
head, trying to snap the rope, and I was dragged after her,
staggering in a wild run on my feet at first and a moment
later down, dragged on my belly, my back—only the moss
saved me from being totally flayed.

"Archer, you fool, let go!" I heard Korridun shout.

"Not on your life," I muttered between clenched teeth.
My will was given over to the combat, my grip locked on
the rope.

The fanged mare reared up against her headstall, almost
snatching the lead out of my hands. Sprawling, I caught a
glimpse of her ungainly belly and her flailing forehooves
as she teetered on her hind legs—then another jolt hit the
rope. Korridun. I had not known he was so strong. He
flung himself against the taut line, planted his feet and
pulled. Taking her off balance as she was, he nearly pulled
the mare down! She came to all fours, and in half a
moment she leaped away again, but it had been respite
enough. I was on my feet, shortening up on the rope, and
her head was toward me.

"Kor," I panted, "thanks. Now get out of here before—"

Before he became tangled in the line. He saw the danger
as plainly as I did, dropped to the rock and flattened
himself as the rope passed over him, then sprinted for the
nearest vantage of safety, a twisted pine, and swung him-

self up. The mare circled and circled around me at the dead run, still pulling against me with her neck and heavy head while I braced my heels against the rock and pulled back, knowing that if she started away from me again I would lose her. Sometimes, trying to take advantage of me, she would suddenly switch about and change directions, snatching at the rope, trying to reach it with her fangs. But the advantage was all mine, for I shortened up on the line of seal gut each time and refused to give back what I had gained, no matter how she tugged. She was streaming with sweat, wet and foamy as the sea, and for my own part I could feel the salt trickle stinging my bloodied skin, bathing me, though the day was chill. This quiet, constant battle went on for half the day, Kor told me later. I had no thought for time. The circling movement of the mare blurred my sight, dizzying me, and I had long since passed from a screaming agony of my every muscle to a sort of trance. Nor had the mare slowed much in her running that I could tell—

Without warning of any sort she turned and hurtled toward me. The sudden slackening of the rope staggered me. I nearly fell, and before I knew what was happening she was on me, her head flung up and the muscles on the underside of her neck bulging, her fangs slicing down at me, and only then did she give forth her battle scream of fury.

I had forgotten about my futile whip. Moreover, there was no time for it. I dodged—I had just that much wit left—I let the force of her charge carry her past me, and as her shoulder hit me I grasped her mane at the withers and leaped, swinging myself up onto her back. You will think that I am boasting, but I am not. There was no bravado left in me. I merely leaped to the only half-safe place left to me, the place where her fangs could not reach me, her back—and it was all slippery with sweat.

I locked my heels around her barrel and hung on to her mane. I remember she spun like a dust devil, reared and came down stiff-legged. Then I do not remember much more, which is perhaps a mercy, for the ride is all a blur of jolting motion, confusion and pain. Talu's bony spine culminated in a withers hard, jutting, and agonizingly high, such a knife edge that I felt she would make a castrate of me, or kill me—the one fate seemed as bad as the other. There were cliffs all around, and they seemed not to concern her. She careered wildly down between the lodges toward the sheer drop to the sea—I came out of my daze of pain long enough to get hold of the trailing line, jerk her head around, kick her hard in the ribs with my boots. Up the headland again we went. I could hear some-one shouting something at me, some warning—it must have been Kor. But I could scarcely see for the sweat in my eyes, or exhaustion, whatever. Fearful of trampling someone, I pulled the mare's head around again. She slashed at my leg with her fangs, and I kicked at her nose. Angry, in pain, I no longer cared if she hurt me, and I kept her head pulled tight around, nearly to her shoulder—let her slice herself with those fangs if she liked. She blun-dered onward for a while, unable to see where she was going, and then she spun. Then—it is not clear to me whether she tangled herself in the trailing rope, or dizzied herself, or simply fell from exhaustion, but all in a mo-ment she was down, and I was off her. Kor seemed to think afterward that I had kicked myself free so as to save my leg from being crushed, but I think that was not true. I had been losing my seat when she spun, and I think I fell when she did.

All was oddly silent for a moment. Breath knocked out of both of us, the mare and me. Then I got up, lash of pride stung me up, for I would not have Kor helping me again, and I knew he would be at my side in a moment— and in fact he was by me as I stood. I said nothing, but went to the mare and took the loose end of the leather rope down her forehead, through her mouth and around the soft part of her nose. She was starting to stir.

"Talu," I told her, "up." And she scrambled to her feet. I felt a secret relief that she did not seem to be hurt. She squealed and slashed at me, and I pulled the rope tight around her nose. Narrowing her eyes with pain, she stood still. The fray was over.

For the first time I became aware that there were people

everywhere, watching from the lodges, from the mountain cliffs, from the safety of the trees. Korridun's people. For the first time also I became aware that the day was more than half spent. The sun was slipping toward the ocean, westward—or rather, the white spot in the haze that should have been the sun. I blinked to clear my eyes of weariness.

"I have sent someone back for a blanket for her," Korridun said.

"What?" I mumbled, trying to jest. "You sent? You did not run after it yourself?"

"I will put it on her myself," he said, "if you will hold her. Can you?"

I nodded groggily, hardly realizing at the time that he was risking his life for the sake of my private battle, thinking only, Folk of the Fanged Horse tribe do not blanket their horses, they think of them no more than they do of their slaves, but we of the Red Hart do not so lightly let our ponies die.

I said, "Take the water out of her pen also, or she will kill herself with drinking."

It was in a heavy wooden trough, and he heaved it over himself. Then Birc brought the blanket. Kor took it and laid it over the mare's back, tying the corners of it in front of her chest. I came to my senses enough to watch her narrowly. "Talu," I warned her, "don't move." She stood with her ears flattened to her neck and her teeth bared, but she stood still. Then I led her into the pen, borrowed Kor's knife, and cut the line, leaving the head-stall on her with a short end dangling. I backed away from her, holding my whip at the ready, but she was intent on working the loop loose from around her mouth and nose, and she did not attack me.

Kor set his men to work closing off the entry. They were doing a makeshift job of it, I noticed, but I was too tired to care. The mare was in no condition to break down the bars, I hoped.

"She's had exercise enough to calm her, I think," Kor said dryly, echoing my thoughts. He had got my cloak from somewhere, and he put it around my sweaty shoulders, and his arm over it, half leading me down the headland toward Seal Hold. "We must tend those wounds of yours."

I shook my head in vexation, throwing off his guiding hand. "Scratches!" And I went at once to my chamber, too weary to eat. He dressed the wounds anyway, blast him, but I did not know it at the time. I was deeply asleep, and I slept the day and the night away.

The next morning when I came to the room with the hearth, Istas spat at me. The others avoided me, though they did not flee. I scowled and told myself that I cared only for the food. Indeed I was ravenous, and I ate heartily.

Kor walked in with his willow basket, back from giving Talu her fish. "Is the mare lame this morning?" I asked him.

"No whit. She is in fine fettle, and far quieter than before." He sat beside me. "And you? Are you stiff?"

I only shrugged by way of answer, for we of the Red Hart were not much in the custom of cosseting ourselves. I had been stiff and sore, more or less, since I had come to him, from the smoky weather, the chill and dampness, and—though I would not think it—from whatever had happened—before, days I could not remember.

"Will you try the mare again today?"

"Later."

We talked for a while about Talu. Then he went off somewhere and I wandered outside. It was a fine morning, less wet than most. Tide was high. Half-grown children were fishing with dip nets made of nettle fiber. Korridun's twelve, his personal retinue of warriors, was assembling on the flat of the rock for some weaponswork. I had watched them during the days of my vigil, and I sat to watch them again. They were only nine instead of the traditional twelve, and they were all youths and men instead of being half women as was the Red Hart custom. But they fought well.

Stone knives drawn, they paired off for mock combat, leaving one standing by himself. Without much thinking about it, rather as if by instinct, I got up and went over to join them.

"I will stand the odd one a bout," I offered.

All came to a sudden standstill, though what I had said was not so extraordinary. They crouched and stared at me, silent and very taut, though not as if in fear, or not entirely, for they did not shrink away from me.

"Bout?" I proposed, speaking more slowly and simply, thinking that perhaps they had not understood me. "Your rules," I added. Indeed, if they were at all afraid there was no reason for it. Such practice was only for agility and skill, and no one needed to be hurt. I did not see much fear in them. Their faces were like masks. Though I thought I saw a trace of something I had not expected: contempt.

We stood tense and silent for too long a time. I could not think what to do. They were not going to meet me or even reply to me, and I could not with much honor walk away.

"I will stand you a bout, if you like," came a quiet voice from behind me.

I turned, knowing already who it was. Kor, of course. There he stood, straight-faced, swinging a bag coarsely woven of sea grass. Then he set it down and pulled out of it a couple of small leather shields, offering one to me.

I put it on without a word. It galled me to once again accept his help, but I had no choice. To refuse his friendly challenge would have been discourtesy.

"Do you use a skullcap?"

"No."

"No more do I." He reached into the bag again. "I have your weapon here."

A hubbub went up from the men standing by. I glanced round at them in surprise, and when I looked back to Korridun he faced me with an immense, shining knife laid across his open palms.

Shock like a spearhead went through me, and a peculiar pain. . . . No one had ever seen such a knife. Hilt and blade, the weapon was made of something that was neither flint nor blackstone, wood nor horn nor shell—my small hairs prickle yet at the memory of that moment and that blade. Very smooth, very sharp, nearly as long as my arm, thrice as long as any knife of flint or obsidian could ever be! And shining the color of the sun. Wondrous, like a weapon in a dream. In the pommel glimmered a stone, a round stone as darkly yellow as upland poppies, more polished than any river pebble could ever be, with depths that seemed to glow. . . . It was not the strange stone that frightened me, but the blade, the long and shining blade, frightened me so that I staggered at the sight of it. I was terribly afraid of it, more frightened than made sense, and, what was worse, something in it called to me as if it knew me. A dark call, that, an eerie recognition. Yet I had no mindful memory of the weapon.

"My king, you have gone mad!" one of the men blurted. It was Birc.

"I think not." Korridun came a step closer, offering me the great knife, and his eyes were intense, deep as the glowing stone. I felt my senses reeling, spinning away into blackness, and I blinked and shook my head to clear it.

"It is yours," Kor said, taking my gesture for refusal.

"I—how can that be? I have never seen—"

"It is yours, or at least you brought it here with you. Take it."

There was a hint of command in his voice, at once delighting and vexing me. I wished to defy him—but I needed worse to defy my own fear. I reached out, annoyed that my hand shook, and took the thing by its strange, smooth hilt. It would make a heavy, unwieldy weapon, I thought—and then I hefted it, and found to my terror that the balance was soaring, superb, the blade only aided by its own weight. I stood with the uncanny thing lifted toward the sky, and Korridun brought out of his bag a sham knife of similar length, a copy rudely hacked out of wood. So that was how he had spent some of his time, the days past.

"My king, you cannot!" It was Birc again, pleading, and other voices joined with his.

"Nonsense. I am in no danger. The rules of the match protect me."

He knew better, of course, but that was his courage.

Kor squared off against me, touching his sham blade lightly to mine, which was sharp and real.

We fought. I fought at first as if he were made of

eggshell, terrified of hurting him, feinting and parrying lightly with the great knife, feeling its deadly agility. Kor was hesitant at first with his wooden weapon, unaccustomed to the length of it. Then, with a glint of daring in his eyes, he deftly worked his way through my defenses and pricked me in the gut.

I struck his blade away angrily. Slighter than I though he was—and he was as strong as most men, and as tall—he was lithe, balanced, and controlled in a way that I never could be. His quick grace made me feel like an oaf. My only advantage lay in height, weight, and main strength, and almost in spite of myself I moved to use them, letting my blows be swift and heavy.

We were well matched. We circled, panting, seeking openings, parrying strokes, neither one able to force the other back. Around us the guardsmen, the twelve, formed the limits of an arena, and in a vague, questioning way I noticed how strained their faces were, how pale—

Korridun struck a skillful blow, sending me half a step backward. My curse on him, the king had the advantage of me—

The king.

Black, black, it was all black and drowning deep, and my enemy waited to kill me, and I surfaced gasping and shrieking with an eerie weapon in my hand, it broke his off at the hilt, he was helpless, mine to slay, sever his head, no, spill his innards, one slashing blow would fell him—

My—my enemy whom I loved—

I think I screamed, but I do not truly know, for I was out of my mind. Screams surged up inside me, for certain, and I faintly heard Kor shouting ''Archer!'' as if calling to me from a great distance, and then I came to myself somewhat, my face pressed against the rocky ground, gasping. Crumpled there, crouching like some hunted creature, and there was noise, clamor of voices, and Kor had his arm around my shoulders, trying to comfort or protect me—

''Archer, are you all right?''

I raised my head enough to look at him, to see—blood on his neck.

And I came up on my knees, hands to my head, and screamed—roared, rather, a cry that felt as if it would tear my throat out, and my heart with it. From a small distance came an answering shriek and the sound of splintering wood. Then the babbling crowd scattered as Talu came to get me.

Kor tried to hold me. But I flung him off, staggered to my feet and grasped the mare by the mane. I vaulted onto her back. A sickly trembling had overtaken me so that I scarcely had strength to ride. But ride I did, and at a dead run she took me up to the forest, through the dense spruce and along the mountain's flank, away from the headland.

Chapter Five

At some distance from the village of the Seal Kindred, Talu took me down a steep, shelving rock face to an expanse of sandy beach. She chose the path, not I. Ravaged by my own strange passions as I was, I had not even reached for the single rein of braided seal gut trailing from her headstall. The blanket that still covered the mare had wadded up underneath me, giving me a ride far more comfortable than the one the day before, but even if it had been otherwise I think I would not have noticed. I wanted only to run, hide, flee from—something I could only feel, not remember. Talu took me at an easy lope along the strand, running head up and nose thrust forward through the spray and shallow seawater that washed at the wet sand. I dare say it was beautiful, but an easy lope to cover the distance was not enough for me then. I wanted her wild, crazed gallop again. I kicked her in the ribs.

She threw me.

Limp oaf that I was that day, she threw me with a single hard buck. I fell off seaward, landed on my butt in salt water and wet sand, amazed to find myself looking up at her instead of on her. She gave a snort of scorn, spun on her hocks, and left me there.

Getting up, I set off down the strand again, stumbling even on the hard-packed sand, I was so distraught. I had no thought as to where I was going, or why. I could only walk. After a while I came to more rocks. High islets of gray-green stone towered out of the sea, some with grotesque twisted spruces clinging to them, weirdly beautiful.

Greenstones, I later learned they were called, or sea stacks.
.One mighty stone had an arch cut in it by the sea. Landward loomed more masses of rock, and as I came around
the knees of them, picking my way along the narrow
margin of the sea, I came upon many seals, seals by the
tens, seals spotted like winter apples with bubble-patterns
of white, gray and brown, males as large as I, bewhiskered
mothers, big-eyed half-grown pups. They lumbered away
from me and splashed into the water, but I could have
overtaken them easily, even at the walk. Carved by the sea
under the lee of the rock was a tunnel or cave. More seals
looked out of it, talking among themselves in yelps and
squeaks of consternation because I stood between them
and the water. Something about them, their ample flesh,
their softly rounded furry faces, looked immensely com-
forting. I did not care if they turned on me to slash at me
with their teeth—I walked right up to them and sank down
among them. Nor did I mind their smell as of a hundred
wet dogs, for I had slept in the same tent with hunting
hounds all my winters. We are not reared to be squeamish,
we of the Red Hart. . . . And smelling that reek, remembering a yellow-headed child tussling with the tan deer-
hound puppies on the dirt floor, I remembered something
more, and my face pulled taut with pain.

Like the infant Sakeema suckled by a cow seal I lay
against the warmth of the seals' dense fur, craving comfort, burrowing ever deeper into the darkness of the seaside cave, and they accepted me.

I do not know how long I lay there, an animal gone off
to lick its wounds in a dark, still place. I know I grew
somewhat calmer. My panting quieted, and I passed into a
merciful sort of numbness. Even when I heard footsteps I
did not look up.

"Archer."

It was Kor. He had trailed me there. "Go away," I
mumbled.

Instead he came in. The seals stolidly made way for him,
and he sat cross-legged near my head. I looked up. He was
only a featureless shape against the light of the entry at
first, but then I saw the cut I had given him, the dark line

of dried blood along his neck, the streaks where it had run down. I winced and closed my eyes, full of shame that I had hurt him, not knowing how much more I had hurt him ten days before.

"I've taken far worse," Kor said dryly, as if sensing my thoughts. "You dropped the great knife even before it touched me. Only the weight of the blade itself struck my neck, not the strength of your arm."

"So I am only half a madman," I muttered.

"Archer, listen. I want—"

"Dannoc," I told him.

"What?"

"My name is Dannoc." It meant "the arrow" in the language of my people, and arrow-sharp pain went through me for remembering even that much—and I did not know why.

"Dannoc." Korridun said the name softly, as if testing it, and he nodded. "Do you remember any more than that?"

"No."

"Dannoc, listen, please. I want to tell you something."

I laid my head against the soft flank of a gray cow seal and let him speak.

"Kela was my mother's name, as you have said, and my father's, Pavaton. I am their only living child—others died in the birthing, brothers and sisters I have never known. I am Kela's heir, for she was daughter of Kebek and king of the Seal Kindred, and my father was her consort. He was of the Otter River Clan.

"At the start of my tenth winter I was stung by an asp, up on the mountain slope, in the scree, where the whistling rockchucks live. My own stupidity—I thrust my hand right into the nest. By the time I walked back to the village, the poison was all through me. I became mortally ill, and I died."

Startled, quite startled, I looked up at him. He was gazing off toward the ocean, somber.

"I remember leaving my body. I saw myself lying on the sealskins, a small boy, far too thin. I saw my mother weeping and my father trying to comfort her, though he was weeping as well. I wanted to say Sakeema's blessing to them, but they could not hear me.

"Then I was out over the ocean—I was a sort of flying thing, part of the air. I struggled back to the land, for I did not wish to leave it, even though something seemed to tug me toward the ocean, and I circled the headland, saw my folk putting my body in the snow, for what reason I could not imagine. I did not like to see it there, in the cold, and I hovered near for what must have been many days—I had lost sense of time—and my folk also kept watch. But my mother was not there. And the pull was still on me to go to the sea, so that I surged back and forth like the tides, and finally I left my body and the land.

"Swimming in the salt water, flying in the air, it was all one to me. Soon I was in the greendeep. Mahela, the great devourer, glutton goddess, she holds her court at the far abyss of that ocean."

I listened intently.

Kor said, "I saw her, just for a moment. She sat raised high above everything around her, on a seat all shining with pearl and—and sunstuff, like your great knife, but even brighter. And carved into shapes more fanciful than those of driftwood, and her clothing was such as I had never seen, dress and overdress floating and flowing and edged with pearl and fringed like—like a scallop, as if she were a great sea aster. But her head and neck were the head and neck of a cormorant. And at her feet, lying as a dog might lie, was a badger."

"A badger?" I exclaimed. "In the sea?"

"Even so. And I think there were many creatures and people around her, but I remember only dimly, I saw it all too quickly. She was hearing petition, and the petitioner was my mother in her seal form."

I sat up, seals lying all around me, opening and closing my mouth as if I were a fish.

"I knew her by her slenderness and the pattern of her dapplings," he added.

"Kor," I protested, "If you are trying to divert my mind with marvels—"

"I am telling you only what is true. My mother was

Kela, daughter of Kebek, daughter of rulers of the Seal Kindred back to the time of our seal ancestor Sedna, a time before the coming of Sakeema. She had power to be a seal.''

"And do you have that power?" I challenged him.

"Not at this time. Perhaps someday it may come to me. I think—perhaps I am afraid. She lost her life—"

He was having difficulty, and yet he seemed compelled to tell the tale. I sat and let him continue.

"She lost her life through the usage of that power for my sake.''

He spoke so softly that I had to lean forward to hear him.

"I saw her only for a moment, saw her there at the feet of Mahela. I felt Mahela's eyes on me, a glance like a blow. Then I remember nothing for a while. When I awoke, I was back in my own bed at Seal Hold, and my father was with me, and I was getting better. But it was some few weeks later before my mother came back.

"I was nearly well when she arrived, and she embraced me, she seemed quite placid and happy. Then she began to make her preparations. She had bargained for a year's delay, it seemed. She explained nothing to me, and even my small knowledge was too much for a child to encompass, so I told myself—what I had seen—perhaps I had dreamed. Nor did my father understand what was happening, even as she gave away belongings and set the affairs of the Kindred in order. The seasons drifted around the cycle of four. And the very last night, as she made her way down to the sea, she awoke me from my sleep and told me what was happening, so that I would not feel that she had abandoned me. Then she kissed me and left, gone back to the realm of Mahela for good.''

"So she gave herself in trade for you," I murmured.

"She gave her life for mine.''

He paused, then finished the tale starkly.

"My father was wild with grief. She had charged him to care for the people and for me, but within a season he left both in the hands of a regent and went after her. He took a coracle, but no food or fresh water, and sailed westward. . . . I did not expect him to return, and he has not.''

He exhaled a long breath, blowing away the past as a fighter blows away the pain of a wound, and for a while we sat in silence.

"Is your mother yet alive, Ar—Dannoc?" Kor asked softly.

"No."

"How did she die?"

"I—" Suddenly I was deep in blackness again, I could remember nothing, and I was angry. "I don't know!" I shouted at him, making the seals raise their heads. "Kor, will you stop trying to trick me! When I remember, I will—" I sagged, my anger gone as suddenly as it had come. "I will tell you," I said wearily.

He was more distressed than I, then. "I was not trying to trick you into remembering," he told me. "Or not that time. I learned better, this morning."

"Enough," I mumbled.

"I am sorry. I will never—"

"Let it go, I say!" The thought of the eerie knife was harrowing me. "I never question the reasons of kings. Why have you told me this strange, long tale?"

The telling of the tale had cost him somewhat, I sensed, for he did not seem wont to talk about himself.

"Because—since that time, there has been a—an odd thing about me. Since the time I was dead. I feel—call it a power if you like. I feel what other people are feeling. Joy, sometimes, or love, but also pain. I felt—I felt my parents' grief the night I died, not only my own. I could tell the difference quite plainly. An adult's grief is a more echoing thing than a child's, a child's passions are cleaner. . . . I felt my mother's loving courage, a courage such as I had never known. And once I was back in the body, I felt the ambitions and petty angers of people all around me. My father's grief after my mother went away nearly destroyed me. I was glad to see him leave, and hated my own joy. . . ."

His voice trailed off into a whisper, and he stopped, not looking at me but staring into the great eyes of a young seal pup.

"You can tell what other people are thinking?" I demanded. What a power for a king.

"Not thinking. Feeling. In my own body. Heartache, heart's ease, the shiver of fear or the knot in the gut . . ."

"Everyone's feelings?"

"No, no, not everyone, Sakeema be thanked!" He raised his hands as if in defense, and I began to understand what an agony this power might be. "Only those whom I know well, until lately. And only their higher peaks or lower valleys. But you, Dannoc—when you came, your passion beat me down with the force of a four-day storm."

I stiffened, not wanting to hear about how I had come, not wanting to remember.

"Madman, they call you, my folk. But I was with you in the prison pit, and I know better. Dannoc, something terrible has been done to you, and it has driven you outside of self."

His left hand reached over to touch me on the shoulder, and I drew back with such a jolt that I startled the seals. I would have wept if he had touched me, and there was something in me that would not weep. A hard, heavy feeling—

"Like a stone," Kor said softly, "pressing down on your heart. Or a great, taut knot—"

"Go away!" I shouted at him, suddenly furious. "Let me alone!"

"Dannoc, if you could only—loosen the bonds—"

"Get out of here!" I screamed with a vehemence that set the seals in motion. They blundered out of the cave and plopped into the sea. Kor and I were left alone, I glaring and he pitying. Damn him with his gentle eyes, for all the world like a seal's soft stare, I wanted to hit him, but I knew guiltily that I had hurt him already. I lay flat on the damp cave floor.

"Remembering cannot be much worse than what you already suffer," Kor muttered.

"Kor," I panted, "get out of this cave before I lose what little sense is left to me."

"Well." He moved toward the entrance with a sigh,

giving up for the time. "We cannot stay here in any event. The tide is coming in."

"I don't care." I put my face down against the wet stone.

He crouched in the white winter light of the entry, looking at me. If he had commanded me to come out, I think I would have defied him and died for the sake of my spleen. I think also that he knew it, or felt it, and he studied me before he spoke.

"Get out of the cave, and I will leave you. Otherwise, I will come back in and badger you some more."

After a moment I crawled out. The sea was lapping at the lip of the cave, and we had to walk in the water, coming around the rocks. When we had reached the sand, I turned up the shore and sat atop the rocky pile. Kor nodded at me, unsmiling, then trudged down the strand toward his home, not speaking and not looking back. I watched him go—it was what I wanted, was it not, that he should go? Then I watched the tide come in and fill the cave. I watched the sun sink and darkness spread in the east. Finally I got stiffly down off my stony seat and walked back toward Seal Hold in my turn.

It was not that I had nowhere else to go. We of the Red Hart tribe knew the ways of survival, of hunting and foraging. Each of us, youth or maiden, was taken upon our coming of age to a distant mountain shoulder and left there for a month to find name and being. So I could have fended for myself in solitude well enough. But I never thought of it. I turned back toward the village of the Seal as if I had been born there. My being was with Korridun, for the time.

True dark came, but there was light enough to see by. The moon was bulging toward the full, shaped like a bowl heaped with millet. Even under the firs and spruces of the mountainside there was a faint gleam, and I thought I saw a gray owl—it looked white in the moonlight, but the white owls of Sakeema had not been seen since my great-grandfather's time. I came out on the headland near Talu's pen and looked at it wearily. One wall was broken wide open, but something moved within—it was the mare, bolting fish with an uncouth noise. She snorted loudly as I passed. "Same to you," I said sourly, and I went on down to the Hold, leaving her at her liberty, no longer caring how she came or went.

I was not hungry. But the way to my chamber ran through the room with the firepit, so I walked that way.

And as I approached I saw that the place was all alight with a glow of a hundred lamps, and full of the Seal Kindred. Sakeema, no, I could not bear to see them shrink from me again, not at that time. . . . I stopped in the shadows, staring. Korridun was there, seated by the hearth, somewhat above the rest, and for the first time I saw him in gear such as kings should wear. Around his brow was a headband that shone with polished beads of shell, and on his upper arms were similar bands over a fine tunic of the most delicate leather I had ever seen, leather made of the skins of seabirds. Picked out on it in tiny beads of many colors were outlines of seals and whales, pelicans and grebes and shorebirds. Korridun held his head straight and steady as he sat, and he looked a worthy king. The thought troubled me, for in fact he looked much as he ever had, level gaze and all.

From somewhere came a thin sound of plucked strings. Music! That was the occasion, then. It was not often that one heard music. Minstrels had come—Herders, probably, for they were peaceful folk, they excelled in claywork and music. Herders, but as was the way of minstrels, they would sing the songs of their host tribe, the songs their hearers loved. A man's high voice, along with the plucked strings—I moved forward half a step in my shadow, looking for the singer, and instead I found Istas's cold eye on me, hard with hate. I matched her stare for a while, but my heart was not in it, and I turned my eyes and my mind back to the music.

It was a story-song from the days before all the Seal Kindred lived together, about a poor tribesman who went out to kill a seal for the sake of its oil, to help his wife's aching-sickness. He carried his only prized possession, a well-made spear. And on the shore he found two seals and hurled his spear at the nearer of them, driving it deep into the beast's side. But the seals dove into the surf and swam away, spear and all. The man went home and mourned the loss of his spear and wondered how he would now make his livelihood. After nightfall there came tapping at his door a woman, a stranger, beautiful, far too beautiful for mortal sort, with long hair the color of the wrack, wearing a cloak of sealskin. "Come with me," she begged, "and save my husband from death. Only you can help him." He was a brave man, and kindhearted, so he went. She led him down the dark shore, and there in a sea cave he found a fine, comely black-haired man moaning with the pain of a great wound in his side. "Touch it," the weird woman said, and the tribesman did. Instantly the black-haired man was well and whole, and in another breathspan he and the woman were both seals, and away they lunged into the sea and away they swam. So the tribesman went home, feeling well enough off to be alive. But in the morning his spear was waiting for him on his doorstep.

Even more than we of the Red Hart cherished the deer, these folk of the Seal Kindred reverenced the seal, I sensed. We killed only as many deer as we needed, and wasted nothing. But Korridun's people ate mainly fish and took each year only a few seals, then fasted and purified themselves as if they had done something shameful. And it was forbidden to kill a nursing cow seal or a pup, even in greatest need.

One of the minstrels brought out of his tunic a small clay flute, the sort that hangs by a thong around the neck, and there was a coracle song. And then—

Then a stocky man, a Seal, a man no longer young, made his way out from the crowd, stood near the king, and, as far as I could tell, requested the use of the harp. And it was given over to him. His voice was not fine, but it was deep and strong and it carried to every part of the room.

This is the song that he sang:

The Shaming of the King

"Deep in a night of the dark of the moon,
    The young king kept his vigil,
    And in winter's sky the thunder boomed,

The very omen of evil.
And off to the west the lightning flamed,
And out of the east the rider came.
Sing shame! Shame! Put to shame
Was young Korridun the King.''

Startled, I shot a look at Kor. His face had not changed much—there was a hardness about it, but he had not moved. Then I felt the eyes of Istas on me again. Malice on her face, along with a peculiar pain.

''And in burst the rider to raid the place
Where the young king kept his vigil,
And in his hand a monstrous blade,
The very token of evil.
And pale as the lightning his long braids
    streamed
—as for his guardsmen the young king
    screamed. . . .
Sing shame! Shame—''

''Stop it!'' I shouted, striding forward into the midst of the chamber.

The uproar that followed would have been sufficient to put a halt to the mocking music. But no one fled, for the presence of their king held them, and when Korridun rose to his feet, all uproar fell to sudden silence.

''Pay no heed, Dannoc,'' Kor said to me across half the hearth hall, speaking to me as quietly and easily as if we were sitting together on a rock or log. ''It has been a long time since Olpash has wished me well.''

''But did I do that? Did I attack you?''

''You did more than that,'' the stocky man growled, still standing. ''There are more verses to my song.''

''Silence, Olpash,'' Kor commanded him, ''or your life will pay for your noise.''

The man staggered half a step backward, pale. Evidently Kor was not much in the custom of making such threats. Plainly, also, Olpash could tell that the threat was meant. Korridun the king spoke with grim force. What he would not do to succor himself, it seemed, he would do for me.

On his neck a dark wound showed.

"Did I attack you?" I demanded. "That first night?"

"Why, yes. You broke my knife with your first blow." On his face I saw a warm, quiet smile, and his eyes also were warm, looking at me. "What of it?"

"But—I have humiliated you in the eyes of your people—" It seemed monstrously unfair that such happenstance as an enormous knife made of something strange and sharp should have caused him dishonor. "Kor—I would never have done it—knowingly," I faltered.

"Of course not! I know that. There is no need for speeches."

No need? I could not meet his eyes. I turned abruptly away from him, facing the silent assemblage of his people.

"Listen to me, all of you!" I scolded them. "Korridun your king is worthy of your deepest loyalty. How often have you known anything but kindness from him? It is a shame on all of you that you let such mockeries be sung of him."

Something was wrong. No one replied, no faces moved, even, but I could feel it. They had closed their ears against me.

I tried again. "Listen!" More entreaty, this time, than scolding. "I am Dannoc, third and youngest son of Tyonoc, he who is king of the Red Hart people—"

"King, and a valiant warrior." It was Kor, who had come up beside me.

"We rear our kings for valor." I spoke to him, but I spoke also for his people to hear. "But I think, Kor, in your way you could match any of them."

He snorted like Talu. "Give it up, Dannoc, and go to bed. These folk think I have betrayed them for your sake." His voice grew softer. "And, I suppose, in a way I have."

Something in the quality of his calm voice touched me with despair. I could do nothing to help him—I could only make the case worse for him. He wanted me to leave the gathering, but what if they should start to cry shame at him again? With my eyes I found the stocky man, and I sat down where I was and stared steadily at him. He would not dare to speak again while I was present, not after his king's command.

"Give us a merry-go-sorry, you two," Kor said to the musicians.

They played, but there was not much more music, one or two more songs, and then the folk scattered. Everyone was very silent, and some of the Seal Kindred looked distraught. For my own part, I sensed that it would not be well for me to stay. One of his own people might want to speak to Kor privately—no, blast it, better truth was that I did not know what to say to him. So as soon as Olpash had gone out, I also left, found my chamber, and settled on my bed of skins.

I was very tired and I slept. But sometime past the mid of night, when the world was at its very darkest, I had a harrowing dream. Black, drowning black and deep—that was all I could remember when I awoke, but I was awash head to foot with sweat of fear, and I was shouting—well, screaming, if truth be told. When I stopped screaming I started to shake. Seal Hold rang full of echoing voices, for I had roused the whole place, and in a moment a light showed in my passage. Birc held a torch, standing cautiously back of the entry, and Kor strode in.

He was buck naked but for a loincloth, having put off his finery to sleep. I saw scars on his arms and shoulders and a couple of ugly scars on his chest and ribs—it was as he had said, he had at some time taken wounds far worse than the one I had given him. He came straight over to me, but he seemed to know that I would not welcome his touch, not then.

"Sorry," I muttered, meaning my noise or the cut or the shame, I am not sure which. Or all of them.

"Don't be. What was it?"

"Nothing."

He crouched down beside me. "A mightily fearsome nothing!"

I merely looked at him, and after a moment he nodded. "Very well, nothing it is," he remarked, and he got up and went away, taking Birc with him and leaving me in darkness.

I did not close my eyes again. I lay until dawn staring up into that darkness.

Chapter Six

The next night I muffled my mouth with the torn end of
Talu's blanket before I went to sleep. But I had no more
than dozed when I was jolted wide awake and rigid, choking back a shout, at the hint of a dream. After that I did
not even attempt to sleep, nights. Nor did I keep to my
dark and solitary chamber. I prowled the headland, the
strand, the seaside forest. The loneliness of vast ocean,
vast sky, towering mountain seemed cleaner than my loneliness inside Seal Hold.

I could catnap sometimes during the day. Never deeply
asleep, I could hold my own against the dreams. The rest
of the time I talked to Talu, mostly. Except for Korridun,
she was the only one who would abide me. It could no
longer be said that the Seal Kindred were afraid of me, for
they no longer fled at my approach, but they sullenly
avoided me, giving me no answer if I spoke to them.
Plainly, I was shunned. I did not in turn shun them, but I
knew that I was, in a sense, mad—for staying, for stom-
aching cold shoulder, snubs, rebuffs. I knew my name, my
father's name, he, Tyonoc the king, and of him I remembered only greatness and his warm regard. I remembered
my two brothers: Tyee, gentle and good, and Ytan, sour
but steady, as a strong horse is sometimes sour. And my
people, my wandering fair-haired people—I could have
found my way to their encampment. At any time I could
have left Korridun's village and gone back to them. Yet I
stayed.

Some of the Seal Kindred I already knew by name, just

61

from listening to them. Especially the maidens. There
were Lumai, "the hummingbird," and Lomasi, "sand
flower," and Winewa, "beautiful." I watched the maidens hungrily, very willing to love one of them. They were
fair, the maidens with their smooth shell-tan faces and
their long clouds of soft brown hair, which they twisted
with strands of beads. And their strong young bodies—
there was not much to be seen of their bodies under
sealskins and woolens, but I tried to imagine. I liked the
way they laughed, often but not foolishly. Korridun's
people were much to my liking, all of them, tough and
lively and often generous in their dealings with each other.
Certainly I did not shun them. It was only they who did
not like me.

I told myself it was their dislike that troubled my sleep.

On the fifth night after my name had come back to me,
lying stark awake as ever, I waited until all was silent and
then walked softly out into the wider silence of the night.
The day's clouds had rolled away toward the east, all
except high, thin mares' tails so airy I could see the stars
through them. And I could see the white wisps of the high
clouds themselves, washed in moonlight. Looking at the
sky, I felt some nameless comfort. Perhaps, after all, the
nameless god did warm me under his bright wing. . . . I
gazed for a while, then walked aimlessly down the headland toward the ocean. Being a Red Hart hunter as I was, I
kept to the shadows and moved silently, stalking past the
largest lodge—

And something hit me on the back and shoulders with a
force that featly knocked me breathless. A wildcat—no, a
man, enemy, legs against my ribs, riding me, arm locked
under my chin, throttling me, denying me the gasp of air I
needed to fight back. My hands came up to claw loose his
hold, but he was strong and, what matters more, deft in
the fighter's arts. A well-timed shift of his body weight
threw me over, and in half a breathspan I was lying
helpless with a stone knife pressed hard against my throat,
blinking and gasping and staring up into the full moon
against which loomed the dark head above me.

One of them, I was thinking. Olpash, or one of the

others. It hardly seemed fair. "I am not armed," I said hotly.

"Dannoc!" he exclaimed, snatching the knife away from my throat.

"Kor?"

"I am sorry!"

"You?" My voice rose high in my astonishment. I sat up, and then I could see him in the moonlight. He looked dismayed.

"I have hurt you! The knife bit through the skin."

"Truly?" I felt at my throat, brought away fingers wet with blood. A perverse joy welled up in me and I laughed aloud, laughed as I had not laughed since I had so strangely come to this place. Finally, it seemed, something was going right for me.

"Why, then, we are even!" I declared, laughing.

He seemed startled by my gaiety, but then he grinned. "Matching marks," he said. The cuts on our necks were very nearly the same.

This time I did not scorn the aid of his hand as he helped me up, and I looked at him in admiration.

"I have never been more handily felled! What were you doing, skulking about and jumping me from atop the lodge?"

"I might as fairly ask what were you doing, stalking about below?" he retorted. "On a night of the full moon?"

Understanding struck me. The strange testing required of Seal kings . . . "Of course," I blurted. "Your vigil."

I sobered at once, and for his own part, I could see that already he was uneasily glancing about him.

"I more than half expect a challenger," he muttered.

"I will keep watch with you," I told him.

"Sakeema, no! It is not permitted. Go back and get some sleep."

"I have not slept in days. Moreover," I pressed, "I am a free hunter of the Red Hart tribe and I go where I will. Who is here to prevent me?"

Bluff, jest, and he knew it. He was smiling as broadly as I.

"Well, as that is the case," Korridun acceded, "I suppose you had better stay. Let us get out into the open, someplace where we can see them coming.''

''Is that permitted?''

''No more than you are.'' He swung one fist with sudden violence. ''To Mahela with it. I am tired of playing this prickass game. Most of us can prove themselves when they find a name and then be done with it, but I must go on proving myself again and again and again.''

We moved to the highest rock overlooking the ocean, and settled ourselves there facing each other so that I could scan the approach that lay to his back. ''How long have you been doing this?'' I asked. ''Keeping vigil.''

''Ten years. Since I was twelve.''

I believe I gaped. It scarcely seemed possible. ''They— they sent challengers against you when you were twelve?''

''None when I was twelve. It was ordeal enough just to spend the night alone, in the darkness, wakeful, expecting them. The first challenger came when I was thirteen, and he very nearly killed me. Only a stroke of wit saved me. I had to become a clever fighter early, as I was still small and thin.''

My astonishment turned to anger. ''Who would attack such a boy?'' I demanded. ''And why did you have to withstand it alone? Why at all? Where was the regent?''

''The regent would have killed me before then.''

He looked out over the ocean and told me the tale.

''His name was Rhudd, the regent, and he was an older man, and a decent man when my father left. I was grieving, and he spared me any worry about the affairs of the people, taking all such decisions upon himself. That was a troubled time; I can see as much now that afterwit aids me. There was doubt among the people, muttering in the council. Guardsmen deserted. The true ruler had left, and the Fanged Horse Folk were threatening as they always did when it was a hard winter on the high steppes, and the mood of the people matched mine. Rhudd had to take firm hold of power and wield it, or all would have come to bloodshed. But it was not long before power itself began to take hold of him, passion for power began to rule him, and he became a threat. Yet no one knew it but me.''

"Why not?"

"His conduct did not change at first. It was all—inward."
Kor leaned toward me, explaining. "I have told you how I
can—feel things, since I visited Mahela's realm. I felt
Rhudd's passion for power as it grew, and I felt his
struggle. Truly he was a decent man. He struggled hard
within himself, more and more desperately. Then one day
there was no more struggling in him, only something stony
and settled, and I knew he had made up his mind to take
the kingship for himself. It was only a matter of time and
planning until he killed me."

I sat uneasily, finding the story oddly disturbing. Oddly
so, because there was no doubt as to the outcome: Kor yet
lived, and by the looks of things Rhudd did not. Why,
then, was I clenching my hands so tightly together?

"In the same way that I knew I could not trust Rhudd,"
Kor went on, "I knew two whom I could trust utterly. The
woman who took charge of all the household affairs, and
the eldest among my guardsmen. Istas, and her brother,
Rowalt."

I tried not to groan at the mention of Istas. As for
Rowalt, I did not think to wonder what had become of him
since. I supposed he was one among Kor's people whom I
did not yet know by name.

"I had to assume there were spies, so I went to them in
secrecy, at night, and woke them out of their sleep to tell
them what I feared and why. Rowalt was a big, slow,
good-humored man, and, while he would do whatever I
asked of him, I do not think he believed me. But Istas has
a sharp mind, and she had seen a few indications on her
own. She took the change in Rhudd as seriously as I
did—I could sense that in her. With her aid, I felt there
was a chance for me.

"We thought at first to find out how and when Rhudd
would act. Istas listened to all the talk of the servingfolk,
asked discreet questions to draw forth gossip, even listened
on the sly to Rhudd's private councils. But she learned
nothing. Plainly Rhudd intended to act alone, and there
was no telling where or when. For my own part, I never
strayed far from the most open parts of the headland, and I

was suspicious of anyone who invited me elsewhere. Even though Rowalt stayed with me at night, I was afraid to sleep, and I made myself nearly sick with dread.''

"I believe it," I muttered. A severe test for so small a boy.

"Istas was more of a strategist than I, at the time. She came to talk to me in the dead of night and convinced me that we could not wait for Rhudd to act. The problem was twofold: we had not only to preserve my life, but to expose Rhudd's scheming beyond any doubt. The Kindred was sufficiently quarrelsome and divided as it was, and we wanted it no more so. We chose out several members of unquestioned probity, people whom everyone would believe, and we laid our plans. I was to be the bait.

"The very next day, making sure Rhudd heard me, I said I would go bird netting, alone, and named a place. In due time I set out. Once out of sight of the village I ran, knowing Rhudd would soon be after me. I had to be sure I reached the place where Istas and Rowalt and the others were waiting.

"It was a narrow scar halfway up the first slope, a place where the pink doves often came to feed on gravel. At the upper end stand some big boulders—the Seven Sisters, we call them. I ran and made sure my allies were there, hidden in the birch bushes to either side. Then I settled on the largest rock. When Rhudd came I was sitting there mending a net.

"I did not bother to feign surprise. He walked up to me with ready knife, and I stared back at him levelly.

" 'So you know,' he said. 'You have come out here as the doomed winter's elk calf once came out of the herd to meet the wolves, drawn toward death.'

" 'What do you plan to tell the others?' I asked him.

" 'Nothing. Let them think a demon has taken you.'

"He raised the knife then, swiftly. But I threw the net in his face, and Rowalt charged him with a bellow like that of a bison bull, and that ordeal was over.''

Korridun fell silent, looking out at the midnight sea. "The small creatures in the waves," he murmured after a while, "they glow like fireflies."

"What did you do with Rhudd?"

"I had him hurled into the ocean," he answered in a hard voice, "from this very cliff."

The matter did not bear more talking. "And you truly, yourself, took hold on kingship? At that age?"

"Yes. Istas advised me when I asked her, and her counsel was most often sound. I had many advisors. But the final say on all matters was mine and mine alone. There were quarrels, threats from within the tribe and from outside, the Fanged Horse Folk raiding as always, even the Otter River Clan feeling for advantage like a ringtail feeling for a frog. . . . I had to learn wisdom quickly."

Wisdom I must have sensed even then, for I did not laugh at him.

"And you had to start keeping the king's vigil," I said.

"Yes."

We sat silent for some small time. I scanned the moonlit headland behind his back. No enemy was coming.

"Dan," he said after a while, "the human enemies are the least of it."

A bittersweet pang, for that was what my friends had called me, Dan. Surely I had friends, still, somewhere. . . .

"Human challengers I learned to deal with after a while. In most cases." He gave me a merry glance, yet the smile quickly faded. "But the devourers, the servants of Mahela—three times one has nearly destroyed me."

I stiffened where I sat, unwilling to speak, unwilling to believe him, eyes on his face. He spoke evenly enough, his eyes on the sea.

"None came for years, at first. My mother must have bargained for that respite. Or perhaps it was that—thoughts of women had small power over me at first. . . . Whatever reason, I knew nothing of the enemies from seaward, and I grew overweening. I knew by then when the challengers from landward were likely to appear. I could tell, I could sense their jealousy hardening into hatred as they readied themselves. Some nights, young fool that I was, I deemed it safe to sleep rather than keep vigil. I would lie down in the lodge yonder, on the floor in front of the hearth, and like an innocent I would close my eyes.

"One such night I had a dream. . . ." He aimed a wry glance at me, questioning. "You know the sort of dream? When the cock awakens and lifts his head . . ."

When the breath deepens and the hands move. Yes, I knew that sort of dream well, and I had wasted my seed on more than one such. I grinned.

"I was dreaming of—a maiden. She was naked and lying atop me, caressing me, her breasts at my face. I was kissing her breasts in blissful pleasure, but at the same time I felt as if they would stifle me, and suddenly I awoke. And it was no dream, but no woman either."

I had stopped grinning. "What?" I whispered.

"A sort of a—great cloak of flapping flesh, cold as a fish. It was all over me and curling around me, taking me in. The breasts were real, huge, and they were in my face. But they were cold, nipples like nubbins of ice. The—cleft in which my left hand lay was real." Kor laughed briefly, a low-pitched laugh, mocking himself. "It was cold and full of slime. But where I had dreamed of a beautiful face—there was no head. A single eye above the breasts, and between breasts and cleft a—a huge maw, a hollow ringed with teeth like those of a dogfish, and the thing was sucking me in.

"My knife lay close at hand—at least that much sense had been left in me. And my right hand lay at the breasts; I was able to free it. I snatched up the weapon and stabbed. But I might as well have been stabbing seawater for all the effect it had. I tried to wrestle the thing off, but I might as well have been fighting the surf."

He was making me half sick, speaking of it. "What did you do?" I asked.

"I lay very still, and there was a sort of—a defiance in me, a stubbornness, that I was I, myself, and I would not be devoured and become something else, food for its ghastly maw. I lay there, and the power of the thought filled my body and made me hard. The struggle was to keep hold of the thought, not giving in to horror. The devourer did not give up easily, either. It curled ever tighter around me, like a starfish on a clam. Until dawn

I lay under it, and then it loosened itself, lifted and flew away seaward.''

"Flew?"

"Flew—or swam through the gray air. Cloak of flesh out to either side like blunt wings, or maybe sails, with the wind sending ripples back along the length of them. It shone like a salmon—it was very nearly beautiful. Then from a height it plunged into the waves.''

"Great Sakeema," I muttered.

"Yes, I wished he were with me.''

So Kor knew that yearning, too! He was silent a moment before he spoke on.

"Twice since then such a devourer has come to attack me, but they have not found me asleep since then. Not that it makes much difference," Kor added dourly. "They can all the better wrap around me when I am standing. But it is less—less humiliating to meet them so.''

He laughed softly, with no mirth.

"When they found I would not let them make me part of them," he said almost as an afterthought, "they tried something different. They let go of me and folded back, leaving the mouth foremost, then bored, like leeches. They tried to become part of me.''

"Kor," I burst out, "that is horrible! It cannot be true, any of it!" But even as I spoke I remembered the scars on his chest.

He looked at me in some small surprise. "I do not often lie," he said mildly.

"There are no such creatures! Death is not a horror, it is a mercy, given to us by—the god whose name has been forgotten, older than the All-Mother, greater than Sakeema, so that we might know joy of birth and grief of parting, lo—love. . . .'' Odd, that I found it hard to say the name of love.

"Who has told you that there are no devourers?" Korridun asked me quietly.

"My father!" The words came out sounding hard, though I had not intended them so.

"Ah." He looked away from me as if I had answered many questions. "Well, say I have dreamed it all, then,

Dannoc," he told me quite softly. "Believe what you like. But now you know why I watch the sea."

"I thought it was because you reverence the sea, you Seal folk," I muttered.

"I do, I love the sea!" Even in the low light of the setting moon I could see how his eyes shone. "There are marvels in the sea, beauties we can only guess at. Empty shells thrown up on the shore are only echoes, whispers of it. Fish drawn to the surface grow dull and die in the air. If my seal form would come to me, I could more than dream and guess. . . ." His smile waned. "But I suppose I am secretly afraid of that, as of so many other things."

Secret. Fear.

"There are terrors, also," he said, "hidden in the sea."

Hidden. Under water. Black, black and drowning deep . . . I felt the weight, pressure, presence, by now familiar, rising up around me or within me, and I shook my head to drive it away. It was not to be sent away so easily—I could scarcely breathe or see. But I could feel Kor watching me.

"Enemy," I gasped.

"There is no one. I have looked." I felt his hand on my arm, warm and firm, and I did not resist that touch. After a moment the panic left me, I could see him again. Nor was the sight unpleasant. I no longer scorned his concern.

"What is it?" he asked.

"I don't know. What is the secret about me, Kor, that makes your people shun me? Tell me." I sagged wearily toward the stony ground.

"I would rather you remembered it yourself," he said, his voice low and taut.

"I am too much of a coward to remember."

"No more coward than I." He raised his head, glancing around. "Look, it is dawn."

"Kor," I demanded, "tell me!"

"Not now. Not tonight. Vigils are times of danger and ill omen. Ask me again in three days if you have not found your own way to truth before then." His face looked bleak, reluctant. "Go in, now, before someone sees you here with me."

I got up and stood looking at him.

"And try to sleep," he added.

"I cannot sleep," I murmured. The terror lay too near the surface of my sleep. But he was right, what he had said some days before: remembering could not be much worse than what was happening to me meanwhile.

I went and lay in my chamber, eyes open, and planned a means of finding my way to some truth while sparing him the telling of it to me.

Chapter Seven

It was from the children that I found out.

Not the tiny children, the ones who clutched at Kor's knees, too small to understand, nor yet the striplings, old enough to be clever. I chose the children just old enough to spend some time off on their own, but not old enough to lie very readily, and I sat by Talu's pen and watched them, aware of other watching eyes from the Hold—children sometimes unaccountably disappeared, seldom but often enough to chill the blood, and they were being guarded even when it seemed they were not.

The second day I chose my moment. It was low tide, and the lot of them swarmed down to one of the pools left behind in the rocks by the sea, down below the cliff. Their elders could not see them from the lodges or the open spaces of the headland, and no coracles floated very near. I lazed down over the side of the headland in a different direction, then came around the base of it to where they were playing, picking my way as if at random down through the mossy rocks and those thick with lichens to where the limpets and barnacles clung between bunches of sea lettuce, down to where the red wrack and the dark purple carrageen grew. The rock pool lay just above the lowest level of low tide, that of the tangleweed, and it was rich with mussels. I sat amidst wet wrack and watched as the children tried to prod a crab from under a rock.

They were, as I had said, no longer afraid of me, but they were not supposed to speak to me either. I hoped they would forget.

"Look," I remarked after a while, "a sea star."

They left the crab to pursue the starfish, then remembered they were supposed to shun me and stopped. To keep them near, I came over and clumsily started to gather mussels and the great sea snails called winkles. Sea asters shrank closed as my shadow fell on them.

"In the summer, are there prawns in this pool?"

The youngsters would not answer me, though they stood clustered around me, watching what I was doing. I sighed.

"Why is it that you will not talk with me? What have I done?"

They glanced sidelong at each other but stood silent. I spoke as if half to myself.

"I dare say you do not even know why it is that you are not to speak to me."

"We do so know!" It was a small girl, shouting out with a proud lift of her chin.

"Alu, be quiet!" someone warned, perhaps an older brother or sister.

"Why should I? He thinks we don't know, and we all know how he killed Rowalt."

The shock nearly toppled me. I dropped the mussels and clutched at the rocks, then slowly stood up, hearing a vast silence, more than the silence of the children, and then an odd buzzing in my ears, as if of poisonous insects. If they had said "You killed a man" it would have been bad enough, for I killed nothing lightly. But that it should have been Rowalt—

Now I knew what it was that Istas had called me. *Hrauth.* Murderer.

The children were suddenly afraid of me again, though I had not moved from the place where I stood. They ran, scattering like young quail. In a moment I also ran, plunging up the rocks toward Seal Hold.

I knew the chamber where Kor spent portions of the days in council with those who helped him rule. I ran to it and in straightway, not caring what I interrupted. They were all there in their places on wooden seats in a circle, Kor and Olpash and Istas and some others, and I leaped to the space at their center, facing Korridun, plunging to my knees in front of him so that the level of my head would not be above his.

"Kor—"

There was a commotion of indignation all around me, and before I could speak further Olpash's voice rose above the others. "Show some respect, madman! Address the king by his full name and title."

"I am the more highly honored," Kor said quietly, "that Dannoc names me as a friend."

"A friend!" Istas shrilled, her voice rising so high it cracked. In her hatred I heard heartbreak.

"He who ought to be your worst enemy!" Olpash boomed.

"You dare speak to me of enemies?" Korridun's words were low, but at his tone all his counselors fell to stricken silence. He rose to his feet, spear-straight and shaking with a bitter passion. "You, who have come at night to kill me with a mask on your face? Not man enough to face me plainly—you think I do not know, but I know you well enough. You, and all you others." His glance raked the circle. There was not a sound. "My mercy gives you life this day. So do not begrudge me mercy." He stared them all down a moment more, then took a deep breath and sat down with a sigh, letting go of wrath.

"Of all my assailants, Dan," he said to me with whimsical calm, "you are the only one who has bested me, and the only one with honor."

"Kor," I blurted out, "they say I killed Rowalt."

Silence for the space of ten breaths. "Who has said this to you?" Kor asked in a low voice at last.

"The little ones. Please do not blame them. I asked."

"But you do not remember."

"If you tell me, I will know it is true."

"Tell him, my king. Tell him how he slew my brother and two others." It was Istas, sharp, poignant, cruel.

Two others! "Is it true?" I demanded of Kor—I hope I did not beg.

Pain in his sea-dark eyes, and he could not or would not speak. He merely nodded. My head spun, and I pressed my cold hands to my temples to clear it.

"*How* did I kill them?" I whispered.

"Tell him, King." It was Istas again, malevolent.

"Silence," he told her. But he could not threaten her to enforce it, and she knew it. She had lost a brother, and she had never come against Korridun in the night.

"How," I pleaded, plainly begging now. Kor could no longer deny me.

"One, you sliced off his hand, and he bled to death soon afterward. One, you beheaded. Rowalt"—he had to force himself to speak on—"you disemboweled."

It was a hideous thing to have done, an ugly thing, of all ways the last way that Dannoc, son of Tyonoc, would have chosen to slay an enemy. I hid my face in shame. "Mahela must have hold of my soul," I breathed.

"You were out of your mind with grief," Kor said.

"It doesn't matter." I raised my face, and, though they burned as if on fire, my eyes were dry. "What is the penalty?"

"It does matter! You were not in self. You cannot remember doing these things. In a sense, it was not you who did—"

"The penalty, Kor."

Something in my tone defeated him. Or perhaps he knew, even then, in what way healing must come to me. It seemed that I chose hard ways, always. . . . He was silent for some time, and when he spoke his voice was very low.

"The younger two, Voss and Taditu, were fosterlings with no kin to seek revenge for them except me, their foster sire, and I waive revenge. As for Rowalt: the bloodright belongs to Istas."

Before him I had knelt to face him as a petitioner—though in fact I found that I fronted him levelly, as a friend. To face her I stood, a prisoner, and I met her gaze steadily, though it was a hard thing to do—her black eyes glittered with hatred.

"And with my own hand I will take it," she said softly, far too softly, "and at my sweet leisure."

It did not comfort me any that a woman would have the killing of me. In my tribe, as in the Otter, women ride to war alongside the men, and I knew how women, though not as strongly thewed as men, could be relentless when men gave in.

Istas pulled out the thong that laced her sealskin boots, came to me and tied my hands behind me, pulling the knots hard and tight. This was to dishonor me, saying, in effect, that I was a coward who would run away were I given the chance. Spiteful old woman. She slit my boots with her stone knife and stripped me of them and my clothing, then and there—she, flinty old beldam, there was no modesty left in her. Then she herself elbowed me up the headland, with half the Kindred trailing along to watch, and sent me crashing down into the prison pit.

There I stayed the rest of the day and the night, and not even Kor was allowed to bring food to me.

Or perhaps he could not bear to come.

No one came near me. The waiting was to make me miserable, I knew, and to give Istas time to smack her lips and make her plans. Strangely, I was not as miserable as she would have liked. Though the night was cold and I had no covering, though my arms ached and Istas's thongs bit into my wrists until my hands were numb, still I slept deeply and soundly, without a dream. It was quite settled that I was going to die, so of what use was dreaming?

Therefore, I was strong and steadfast when she came for me in the morning, and I had made up my mind not to speak to her lest folk should construe it as pleading, but to go out with honor.

There was a problem for Istas and her followers—I found it very nearly laughable. I could not climb the notched pole with my hands tied behind me, so they had no way of getting me out of the pit without approaching me, and they were afraid. Also, there must have been some shame in them, for they would not send for Kor. They sent for Birc, finally, and he climbed down the pole, came over to me and cut the thongs. My wrists were so swollen by then that he sliced my skin in doing it, and I noticed that he would not meet my eyes. I centered myself and climbed up the ladder on my own. Istas did not attempt to bind me again—they were all afraid to touch me. So of my own accord I followed her to the great lodge, and no one afterward could deny it.

Most of the tribe was there, pressed back against the walls, leaving a sort of clearing, an arena, under the reed-thatched roof. But I saw no children there, and I was glad of it. These were at their centers a gentle folk. I hoped Kor would not be there either, but he was, awaiting us at a place before the hearth that was marked with red ocher spilled on the ground. After a moment I understood. It was the place where Rowalt had fallen. I had been brought there for my doom.

Like a puppy, I thought. Taken back to have my nose rubbed in my misdeed. Nothing seemed very real, and the thought made me smile. Kor saw the smile, but I think he could not bring himself to answer it. He looked ashen, as if he himself were to undergo a slow execution, and I could tell nothing from his eyes when I stopped before him.

"Dan," he said to me, but loudly enough so that the others could hear, "I tell you again, there is no need for this."

I did not answer. Madman and murderer though I might be, I yet had my pride, and if I had done wrong I would pay with my own blood. I met his gaze and did not speak. For the sake of my honor I had decided to be a mute, so that I would not cry out. Though more willful, it ought to be no harder than forgetting my own name. . . .

Korridun sighed and stepped back, yielding me up to Istas. There was a breath and a murmur from the waiting crowd, then utter silence.

Istas advanced on me with a knife of jagged blackstone. How droll it was, truly—she was a stumpy little woman with a hump on her back, she stood fully a head and a half shorter than I, and I was going to let her kill me. Droll—but her face was so full of malice, it frightened me. She held the knife up a finger's span before my face. I refused to blink. Swiftly she moved it—

And cut off the long yellow-brown braid of my hair, tugging hard at it as she did so, trying to bring water to my eyes, notching the rim of my ear with the knife. Then she

took off the other. I should have felt relieved, perhaps, but
it was not so. I was stricken, chilled with fear. It had not
occurred to me, somehow, that she would know me so
well, that she would take my hair. She took away my self,
my manhood, when she did that—she might as well have
cut off my cock and had it done with! Perhaps that would
be next. . . . She threw my braids down in the dirt of the
floor and stamped and spat on them. Then, to humiliate
me, she flogged me.

It was not so bad, merely a willow whip. I had taken
worse from the Fanged Horse Folk in combat—they fight
with deadly long heavy whips made of bisonhide, and they
can flick out an eye with the end—but that was fighting,
and this was punishment, and therefore harder to bear. It
was Istas's malice that made the difference. I hardened my
will against her, standing still, making no outcry.

Nor, I noted, did the people shout out to goad Istas on
as she gifted me with the shirt of red laces. They stood as
still and soundless as I. They were not bloodthirsty,
Korridun's folk.

When she had flogged me enough so that the blood ran,
Istas took up her knife again and stood before me, leering
up at me.

"Now," she said, "listen well, for I am going to tell
you exactly what I intend to do to you."

It would have been easier, of course, not knowing, and
that was why she told me, in detail. She fairly ground out
the words of the telling, as if she were grinding out millet
meal, food of her hatred. The substance of her plan was
that she would disembowel me, as I had done to Rowalt.
But before that, she told me, there were many ways of
inflicting pain. There was my cock to be attended to. And
my eyes. And many members more . . . She sickened me,
I admit it. She was cruel, hateful, keen and cruel. I wanted
to look at Kor for comfort, did not dare for fear that he had
no comfort to give me. I stared over the old woman's head
at a silent crowd instead and squared my shoulders,
straightening myself to receive the blandishments of Istas's
esteem.

It must have enraged her, my stance. She broke off her recitation and stamped hard with her booted foot on mine that was bare. I felt the small bones break, even heard them snap, so deep was the silence in that place, and my muteness deserted me all in a moment. I gave a croak of pain, and pain brought me to my knees—I could not stand on the broken foot. Not knowing what I was doing, like a falling child I clutched at her skirt for support. She flung away my hand. Her sharp blackstone knife was at my gut. Odd, she had forgotten her lengthy plan, she was going to open me there and then—

Her face loomed within a handspan of my own, the look on it all at once wild, crazed, grieved, frightened—that anguished look shook me as her hatred had not. I felt her knife shaking, sawing into me, just below my ribs. Then with a terrible cry she sliced it downward, cutting through the skin clear to my crotch, but only the skin. . . . She flung the knife away to one side and hid her creased old face in her hands.

From somewhere close at hand Kor came over—but not to me. He bent over Istas, placing his touch on her shoulders, which rose and fell with her sobbing breaths. For a moment she lowered her hands to face him, and I saw in her look a terrible sorrow. I no longer cared to stare at her.

"It is as you said," she cried to Kor. "The hating has made of me a thing more fell than Mahela."

I felt someone take hold of me. It was Birc, of all people, helping me up, slinging my left arm across his shoulders. I leaned on him, and I was not ashamed that I was trembling. Another one of the twelve came and supported me on the right.

"Are you satisfied of your bloodright against Dannoc?" Kor asked Istas, quietly, but clearly enough for the assembled Seal Kindred to hear.

"I am satisfied. I am sickened."

I do not remember how I went back to Seal Hold. They told me later that I hobbled there, but I think that once in my chamber I fainted.

When I awoke some time later, I found myself slippery

with seal grease and swaddled in lambswool bandaging
from my neck to my thighs, and my foot was tightly
wrapped. Birc was sitting by me, unarmed and, by the
looks of him, uncomfortable.

"Hungry?" he asked me abruptly, the first time he had
spoken to me. He, or any of the others except Kor, Istas,
Olpash, and the little girl Alu.

His gruffness was not because he disliked me, I decided, but because he was shy. He was a boyish youth
with an awkward look about him, eyes often downcast,
brown hair out of control over his forehead.

In fact, I was not hungry. I felt sick and weak. But food
might help, I decided, and I nodded.

Birc went out for a moment and spoke with someone.
Shortly afterward there was a stir in the passageway and
half a dozen women and maidens crowded into the chamber, each bearing a portion of a feast: bread, heavy pottery
bowls of food, the basin, towel, and ewer for washing
with.

"Great Sakeema," I protested, "I am not hungry enough
for all this."

Then, as they laid a cloth and set the things on the
uneven floor, I saw what was in the bowls.

"Red meat!" I exclaimed.

The maidens smiled and laughed, and one of the women
nodded. "Istas thought it would please you and give you
strength. She sent out everyone she could spare with spears
and arrows and snares."

Istas!

"She is troubled, but more like herself now," the woman
added, "and we are glad of it."

The three maidens whose names I knew, Lumai, Lomasi
and Winewa, came and helped me sit up, settling themselves behind me to support me. Out of the corner of my
eye I saw Birc backed up against the far wall, eyeing them
and grinning sheepishly.

I made up my mind that I was going to eat every morsel
of the meat, even though it was only tough old winter
rabbit. The soup was good, and shaky though I was I
spilled only a little. The women nodded and smiled at

every bite I took. I gorged myself to please them. It was hard work, being an invalid—no sooner had they left than Birc had to help me to my cuckpot, both of us swearing softly with embarrassment. Then no sooner had I slept a small while than the maidens were back, the three of them, with water, tallow soap, and several of the long clam shells, sharper than knives, such as their men used to scrape the beard from their faces.

"What, more torments?" I jested. "I don't need to be shaved." Men of my tribe grew very little beard, less even than the Seal did. The Fanged Horse men, on the other hand, were bearded worse than mountain antelope—

"Istas wants us to do something about your hair," Lomasi said.

I felt my smile fade, and I raised one hand to feel the hacked stubble of my hair where the braids had hung. An odd lightness about my head, as if I were now unrooted, a leaf in the wind, a drifting thing. Perhaps I knew even then that in a sense I would never be a Red Hart again. A fell stroke, what Istás had done to me—my face grew so somber that the maidens knelt beside me.

"She wants us to cut it like that of a clanfellow, Dannoc," Lumai said softly.

An honor I could scarcely refuse. And though I scarcely knew it, I bade farewell to a Red Hart's selfhood that day. I let the young women take me in hand, and they washed my head and trimmed what was left of my hair fur-fashion, so that I resembled a Seal tribesman. Their soft touch cheered me, and I talked with them as they worked. One of the maidens in particular, Winewa, had wise, sleepy eyes, and I think she knew what I was thinking. Though I was in no condition.

The next day, when I felt stronger, Istas came with the women who brought the food.

I grew grave when I saw her, not because I bore a grudge or was afraid of her, but because I did not know what to say to her. She herself brought the bowl to me, full of good dark stew. Her eyes, as the women had said, were troubled.

"You will walk again on that foot," she said curtly, "or I will give you mine. I bound it up myself."

Her tone so astonished me that I smiled. "Am I under your orders, then, to get better?"

"Yes, you young fool. You wanted to die!" I heard anger, accusation, but as much grief as anger. "You were willing to stand there and let me torture you, mutilate you—"

"You have not mutilated me!" I hoped not.

"Your ears."

I reached up and felt at the notched rims, then shrugged. "The hair will grow over them."

"Bah." She grimaced, more annoyed now than passionate. "So you would have let me kill you. All for the sake of a crime you cannot recall . . . It is not natural."

"Dannoc is very brave," one of the other women interposed gently.

"It was more than courage. It was despair." Istas faced me quietly, her anger spent for the time. "My lad Rad Korridun was right. Something terrible has happened to you, and it has made a madman of you."

I looked away from her. "Sakeema help me if I ever remember what it was," I muttered.

"Remember, go ahead and remember! I remember everything, and it is not so fearsome. And in my way I was as mad as you."

What a woman. Blunt and hard as the seaside stones.

"If a storm wind had toppled Rowalt into the sea," she mused, "or if a wave had come up and taken him, would I then had hated the sea, taken a knife to it, hurled myself against it? That would have been madness, and it was just as mad to hate you. When you slew Rowalt you no more knew what you were doing than storm, sea, or wildfire."

I shivered for a moment. The thought of such storm troubled me. If ever it came on me again, might I not hurt someone I—cared for . . . ?

"I am not mad now," I muttered, fighting down fear.

"Are you not? If you still wish to die, you are."

The barking words, the dour face of her! Suddenly happy and more than a little perverse, I grinned. "No, I no longer want to die, Istas," I retorted. "I got over such nonsense the moment you pressed your knife to my gut."

She did not cringe at the words. "So I cured us both at a stroke," she said dryly.

"Yes. And as I heal, so must you, Istas."

"I am tending to it," she snapped. And she sat by me sternly to see that I ate what she had brought me.

That night as I lay drowsing, not quite asleep, as if by some signal Birc left me and Winewa came in to me. That was her courtesy, I knew, and no one else's. Women of the tribes bedded as they saw fit until they chose a lifelove. I felt both ardent and honored, though I did not think I was able—but she was deft and tender, keeping away from the wounds and delighting the rest of me very much. Talu had not hurt me after all, nor had Istas, for my cock raised his head happily, and presently Winewa eased on top of me—I did not have to move. Her breasts were small and firm, the nipples brown, her buttocks round and firm, just as I had imagined them. And ah, she took me expertly. Bliss . . . I had never been bedded so softly, lying as still as if in a dream, first my mouth to her breasts and later my hands— her breasts were warm, and I remembered the warmth of them when I awoke in the morning.

Chapter Eight

So taken up was I with the many who came to see me, with relief at being no longer shunned, with delight in Winewa, with dreaming of her, that it was not until the third day that I started to feel uneasy about Korridun. Though I had been wondering for two.

"Why has Kor not been to see me?" I asked Birc.

His thoughtful look told me that he had been wondering the same. "Perhaps it is that—there are others to care for you now. . . ."

"Would you tell him I asked, when you see him?"

He told him at the noon meal. But the rest of that day went by and I saw nothing of Kor. When the following day was half spent in like wise, I asked Birc to find me a stick.

"It is time I was up and about, anyway."

"If you hurt that foot," he warned, "Istas will have your head."

"She wanted parts of me badly enough before, and refrained. Can you find me something to walk with?"

He returned some time later with a piece of spearpine by way of a staff, and he helped me wrap on my lappet and leggings. No harm in that, for most of the wounds were on the upper part of me, and they had scabbed up so nicely that we had taken off the bandaging the day before, the maidens and I. It did not occur to me to cover the ugliness of the wounds with a tunic. I had gone bare-chested since I was born. I pulled a boot onto my right foot, and Birc helped me up and watched me crutch my way out, my left foot held well up off the floor.

"Kor is in the hearth hall, last I knew," he remarked.

He was there yet, sitting idly by the blackening fire, though the place was dim and empty. His glance flickered up when he heard me, then down again when he saw who I was, and I knew at once that my surmise was right, that he had been avoiding me. I was amazed.

"Why?" I exclaimed out loud.

"Why what?" He met my eyes finally, but his were hard.

"Why are you angry at me?"

"Angry? You tell me. Why should I be angry?" There was no heat in his voice, but something like irony or bitterness, and I noticed he did not motion me to sit down, though I stood leaning on my staff only a few paces away.

"I don't know!" I spoke with heat enough for two. "Unless you are only now waxing wroth at me for what happened more than half a month ago, and that seems unlike you. What have I done to you since? I have tried to act with honor—"

"Honor!" The word brought him to his feet, his eyes flashing. "You and your bloody honor! If I had thought only of honor, you would have been dead the day you came here!"

"And that might have been better," I shot back, knowing at once that the words were untrue—my heart had fainted for joy the moment I knew Istas would not kill me.

"You proud ass. You and your fool's honor be damned." Coming from him the words stunned me, widened my eyes, for I had never known anything but kindness and mercy from him, had scarcely ever heard him raise his voice. But he was shouting now. "Do you suppose it was easy, standing by and letting you and Istas play out your vicious, hellish game? Do you really think that, just because the blows fell on your great hulk of a body, they hurt me any the less? I knew Istas would come to herself, she had to, but I never thought it would take her so long, so cursed long—and you, you damned cock-proud jackass, you would not cry out, and no more could I. . . ." He was shaking with passion, and though his voice fell to a whisper, the words came out no less intensely. "By great

Sakeema's blood, I would far, far rather have taken that suffering, yours and hers, on my own body than to stand by so helplessly.''

It was true. Why should that stagger me, I who had never heard less than truth from him? But it was true, fire-true and not just a manner of speaking, all that he had said. He had felt my pain, redoubled with hers, redoubled with—his own. . . .

I could not speak. I could only grip hard at my staff for support and stare into his furious eyes, myself now helpless—the look in those eyes had struck me to the heart. In a moment he turned stormily away from me and strode out.

I wanted to sit down, I felt weak. But not there. I needed air, out, outside. . . . Half desperate—or I would not have found the strength—I hitched and plunged my way out and up the headland. Talu whinnied when she saw me, but I did not greet her. I crawled to the edge of the forest, collapsed under the wind-beaten spruces and closed my eyes, listening to the wailing of the gulls.

When Kor found me, half a day later, I was numbly watching a red squirrel nibbling at the early spring buds.

Kor sat silently beside me. I knew without looking who it was. He watched the squirrel with me.

"In the time of Sakeema," he said softly after a while, "my elders have told me, there were gliding squirrels, fawn-colored and with great eyes and very beautiful."

"Time of Sakeema be damned," I muttered peevishly, though I had not known until then that I was sulking. I had believed that I was drawing solace and strength from the wild things in the manner of my people.

"Well," Kor said wryly, "we've damned a lot today, between the two of us."

I rolled over to face him, at that. "I didn't know," I blurted, getting the words out quickly, for this was not easy. "You told me, but I—I didn't understand, Sakeema forgive me. I never meant to burden you with my pain."

"Stop it," he said.

I sat up so that I could face him more levelly. "If you feel all that I do," I told him, not quite steadily, "then I had better go away, for there is a plenitude of hurting in me.''

"Dan," he said in gentle exasperation, "don't be an ass. You can barely walk."

"I can ride. Talu will take me."

"She threw you off!"

"Only because I tried to master her. I can sit on her and let her take me where she will. Or, what am I saying, she is yours. Where is my own pony, the one they said I rode here?" With my mind whirling as it was, I thought perhaps he had hidden it along with my great uncouth weapon.

He sighed, not wanting to reply. "It died shortly after you came," he said finally.

"How so?" Some strange seaside disease, I thought.

"You had ridden it to exhaustion, Dan." Very softly, very gently. He knew me.

For a moment I could not believe him. I, Dannoc son of Tyonoc, ride to death one of our tough little blue-eyed, curly-haired ponies, the tribe's pride? I would as soon have ridden one of my brothers—*ai*, Mahela's hell. Despairing, I dropped my head to my knees.

"I suppose you want to know the penalty for that, now," Kor muttered. He was trying to jest, but the words jarred me. My head snapped up.

"I have told you, I will go away! My troubles will not trouble you much longer."

"Dan, you sound like a child! Run away, don't care where, poor thing. Plenitude of hurting, bah."

"I am trying to spare you!" I flared at him. "I see no end to this."

"Well, I do." Kor stretched out on the mossy ground and surprised me by grinning up at me. "Istas is almost herself again, my people are singing with happiness that they need no longer shun you and quarrel with me, you are dreaming of Winewa—don't look so aghast, Birc told me. And I have at last vented my spleen after twenty-some long, long days."

I stared hard at him. "It was more than just venting spleen," I said slowly.

"Not much more. Great Sakeema, can't a person do

some shouting once in a lifetime without having poor invalids riding off on wild mares?''

I had to smile. "Well," I admitted, "your spleen is perhaps an improvement on my early days here. You were so—so sweet, half the time I wanted to hit you.''

He sat up and laughed aloud, a joyous laugh. It warmed me to hear it. But then he sobered suddenly.

"Dan," he requested, meeting my eyes, "don't think of leaving yet awhile. Please.''

"But why? I have caused you nothing but trouble.''

"Yes," he agreed lightly, "and having gotten thus far with you, don't you think I want to see trouble through? Stay awhile. Truly, you cannot go off with that foot unhealed, even on a horse.''

It was true enough, and I nodded. There were better reasons, but he was not speaking them, and I was too tired to seek any longer for reasons. It was sundown, though the sunset was only a yellow blur in the foggy white of the western sky over the ocean. Kor looked that way a moment, then stood up and reached down to me, helping me rise. With his arm under one hand and the staff in the other I hobbled back toward the Hold.

There was a distant flash in the yellow-white of the sky, a flash or glint as bright as that great, strange, fearsome knife of mine. Kor stopped where he stood and squinted toward it, frowning.

"No bird shines so," he said.

Very true. It shone like a fish, but large. Perhaps a sea hawk had caught a great salmon. No, no hawk—

I could see it flying with a rippling motion and drawing swiftly closer. I could not help gripping Kor's arm. It was—Sakeema help us, it was the thing he had told me about, the soul-swallowing, life-sucking, destroying thing, bluntly broad at the front and then tapering, taller than I from head to tail—no, there was no head, only a single eye staring whitely and a mouth, a maw, like that of a starfish, leading directly into the belly of the thing's bulk—it was altogether eerie, silent as an owl in flight, and it was coming straight at us.

"A devourer," said Kor in a voice gone dead.

"Your knife!" I urged him. I had worn none since I had been a madman.

He stood still. "Knives do no good," he said in the same way.

I saw the breasts—large, comely even, but gray, and sickening on that strange cloaklike body of cold flesh. I saw a sort of clamshell-shaped organ farther back, under the tail, which looked strong, like a thick, flattened snake. . . . I had once seen eels slithering across the grass by a river on a moonlit night, but I had never seen anything that made me shiver as did the sight of that devourer.

It shot over our heads and veered off inland, rising until it had disappeared over the snowpeaks. Kor and I stood rigid in the darkening day, looking after it, and only when it had been gone ten breathspans did we speak.

"I like that no whit," Kor said, grim. "I have never seen a devourer in daylight before. Never at all, except on my vigil nights."

"It is dusk," I said. "Perhaps the thing has an errand to another king, somewhere." My own words chilled me, though I had intended them as jest—no other kings but the Seal kings kept vigils, to my knowledge. Suddenly I could not still my own shaking.

"Perhaps. Sakeema help him or her if it does."

"Was that the same devourer you have seen before?"

Kor turned and stared at me.

"I mean, can you tell any difference—"

"Dan, I was too stupid to think that there might be only the one! You mad dreamwit, you are trembling. Sit down." He lowered me to the ground, sat beside me. The look on his face had lightened somewhat.

"Perhaps it is Mahela herself in one of her many forms," I said.

"What a comfort you are." Irony, now. "I had thought that the things were her minions, and that there were many. But I have not seen more than one at a time. How would one tell any difference, in the dark?"

"The size of the breasts, maybe," I said promptly. "Or the shape of them, the feel—"

I spoke in all seriousness, but he started laughing.

"Dannoc, I am not such an adept with breasts as you seem to be!" He laughed without much mirth, and he sobered suddenly. "Dan, how is it that the women take to you so easily? Winewa is not the only one willing to bed you. Half the maidens in the tribe look with warmth at you, and they would have let you know it long since if it were not for Istas and her grudge."

"Truly? Confound that interfering old woman—"

He would not be diverted. "*Dan,*" he insisted.

I looked at him. Darkness was gathering quickly, and I could scarcely see his face, but I could see the tense line of his shoulders.

"Do you mean to say—they do not come to you?" I could scarcely believe it. He was comely enough, and king, and a worthy king.

"No." Flatly.

"But why?"

"I am asking you, Dan," he reminded me, half amused, half annoyed.

"Well . . ." I floundered for a reason. "I do not understand these women of your tribe," I admitted at last. "They hold themselves apart from men, aloof, as if there were a mystery to their affairs. Yet the men stand in scorn of the women because they do not go out in the coracles."

Kor shrugged. "I have thought perhaps it is because I am king. But you are a king's son in your tribe. Did you have lovers among your own people?"

"Yes." Memories came back to me in a sudden rush, making me feel warm and easy, so that my shaking left me. Sakeema, yes, there had been lovers, Olathe and Naibi and Leotie—"white fawn," that meant. Leotie was a beauty. Every buck in the tribe had wanted her. She had favored me for a while, and I was so happy I could scarcely walk for dancing. Then she had left me. A sweet pain, remembering, for it had been a tender leave-taking.

Then a harsher pain, and I frowned. There had been some reason why she had left me—but I could not remember what it was.

Kor sat watching me.

"Never mind, Dan," he said abruptly. "I must be an idiot, keeping you out here in the dark and chill." He got up, helped me up, and gave me my stick and his arm to lean on. "And I know you have not eaten, for I drove you out."

"Poor invalid, I."

"Make the most of it."

Never mind, he had said. Even so, that night when Winewa came into my chamber and gently woke me, I was not entirely willing that she should play with me in her usual manner.

"Do you like me, Winewa?" I asked her.

"To be sure, I do," she retorted promptly. She was nothing if not prompt and ready, my Winewa. "I am not much in the habit of bedding with men I do not like! Would you think that of me?"

"No, no. But how is it that you like me?"

"For yourself! You are different, and I will never forget you. But I do not love you," she added in her frank, forthcoming way, "if that is what you mean."

I smiled, having known full well the limits of dalliance. Questions, though, were easier to ask in numbers. "You, your friends, the other maidens, Lumai, Lomasi," I went on, "do none of you ever go to Kor?"

"King Korridun." Her candid voice grew softer than I had ever heard it. "We would give life and breath for him, make no mistake, Dannoc. But no, we do not lie with him."

"Why not?" I felt my smile fade.

"He is too—too fearsome."

"How so?" I let her hear my astonishment. "It can hardly be said that you lack for boldness, Winewa."

She smacked me lightly in reproof. "He is an oddling," she said defiantly. "His father was of the Otter. He is different from the rest of us."

"Winewa!" I protested. No one could have been more different from her than I, with my hair the color of bleached seregrass, my blue eyes. She raised her hands in a gesture of surrender.

"I—I don't know, then, why he is an oddling. But we all feel it, don't you? Something—fated—about him."

My skin prickled, and I kept silence, I who had seen his eyes blaze earlier that day. After a moment, in the same very low voice, she went on.

"Something—so old about him, though he is yet so young. As if a god lives in him. I—if I were to go to him, it would be like—like going to death. I could not come back. I could never leave him, not after even the one night."

A long silence before I stirred and spoke. "As you will leave me," I muttered finally.

"As you will freely let me leave you, Dannoc, you rogue. You know as well as I what we are."

"Sparring partners?"

Then I quelled her retort with a kiss. I liked her, indeed I liked her very much, brash and honest as she was. That night I did not lie still and await her, but it was I who made love to her. And when she took her customary place atop me, I thought briefly and uncomfortably of the devourer I had seen, the devourer of which Kor and I had told no one, grim thing. . . . Winewa's breasts were far smaller, far sweeter. Still, I rolled her over into my furs so that I straddled her. It pained my foot only a little.

Chapter Nine

Those were good days, and they went quickly. Birc found me an aspen with a broad fork—he tramped for miles, I learned later, in search of it—and he cut it to the right height, burned the end hard, and padded the top of it with fleece to make a comfortable crutch for me. I hobbled about merrily with it, flirting with Winewa and the other young women until they or Istas drove me away, then going out to flirt with Talu. As I generally brought her meat from the hearth, she seemed always to welcome me. She seldom strayed far from her pen, and Kor, trailed by a band of children, would bring her fish offal by the basketful. He found me a scrub cloth woven of tough sea grass, and I bound together a brush of the same stuff, and over the course of the days I managed to clean up the mare somewhat. She shied from the handling at first, but she did not maim me—perhaps she thought my crutch was a club to beat her with. As for the grooming, she grew used to it little by little over the days. Talu was shedding her heavy winter fur, and she itched. I rubbed the itch for her. Within the week I had the worst of the dirt and dead hair off, and I could see that she had gained some weight: she looked veritably sleek. Ugly, but sleek.

It was spring. The aspens were coming into pale green leaf, and there were bright yellow-green tips on the spruce boughs. More than half the time it rained, but the smell of the air was glorious, and when, as sometimes happened, the sun shone, then the misty air filled with rainbow upon rainbow. In the mountain valleys of the lower slopes Kor's folk were sowing oats. I could not help them, but Birc had brought me yew for a bow, ash for arrows, and I was working at the shaping of them. By the time I was well I would be able to bring in meat.

Winewa came to me nearly every night. It was spring, the season of love, and for a wonder she seemed to be in no hurry to leave me for someone else. In fact she exhausted me, and I always went to sleep soundlessly and dreamlessly after she had left me. But there was a night, a mere ten nights plus one after I had taken my wounds, that I did not sleep after she left me, but groaned and got up, struggled into breechclout and leggings, and crutched my way outside. By my reckoning, it was the night of Kor's vigil, and I had made up my mind that never again while I was with him would he keep that vigil alone.

It was very dark, the night of the new moon, even that thin crescent hidden in cloud, as were the stars. Only the greenish gimmer of the sea gave light. I felt my way warily, accustoming my eyes to the darkness, but even by the time I drew near the lodge I could see only a little.

"Kor, it is Dannoc," I said in a low voice so that he would not come pouncing down on me again.

There was no answer. Night crouched like a cat, utterly silent.

I made my way around to the door. "Kor?"

Still no answer nor any stirring. I went in, feeling my way along the wall, still calling out from time to time, not very loudly but a bit more loudly each time, beginning to be afraid—I did not wish to think it, but perhaps he was lying wounded! Perhaps even dead, all because I had dallied with Winewa, like a wantwit fool—though in truth, the night was not yet at its mid.

At the far end of the lodge I found the hearth. A few coals glowed. I stirred them into small flame and laid on dry kindling—a pile of wood stood at the ready, for this lodge had been the main hearth and hall of the Seal Kindred until lately, and the firepit inside the Hold only a sort of foul-weather cookplace. I crouched, intent on fanning and blowing the fire into a blaze, knowing that before I could be of any use I needed light. At last I had it, and I took a flaming pine splinter by way of torch, then went in search.

Within three steps I saw him standing like a monolith at the center of the hall. Man-high and man-shaped, it had to be Kor, but it did not look like him. I saw a strange and swaddled thing, like a gray cocoon—

A devourer had him!

I dropped my torch to the dirt and hobbled forward, nearly falling in my haste. He stood completely hidden in the chill folds, even his face and head, how could he breathe? I got hold of the top of the fishy thing and struggled to wrestle it off and downward, feeling its snake-like strength as it resisted, glimpsing the angry flash as it rolled its single eye at me. Desperate—then I could see Kor's eyes, closed, his face, very calm and pale, so quiet that I could not tell if he was breathing. In a moment the devourer slithered out of my grip and its horrible breasts closed over him again.

Frantic, for the second time I forced it down and off his head. Great Sakeema, how I longed for my full strength, for two strong legs to brace with, the use of two arms! I wedged my right elbow against what should have been the thing's chest between the breasts, braced my right hand against Kor's collarbone, hoped my crutch would hold steady and reached with the other hand around his back to peel loose the folds there. Kor's body was cold, and I did not dare to feel for a pulse—

He stirred slightly under my touch, turning his head a little, taking a breath. "No use," he murmured.

"Kor," I bellowed in his ear, "come back!"

His eyes snapped open. At the same moment the devourer, clever demon that it was, let loose its hold on him, throwing me off balance. I swayed on my crutch and lost my grip on the slithery thing, and it made for me. Kor's eyes widened.

"Dan, 'ware! No, curse it, you monster, you cannot have him!" He had moved nearly as quickly as the devourer, catching hold of it by one flange as the other closed around me. He hung on doggedly, and I hitched backward, unwinding myself, gagging, nearly retching—

the slimy breasts had touched my face. In a moment the
thing moved to change its line of attack again, but I
grasped it with both hands by the other wing.

"Kor! We have it!" I was exultant, though the devourer
still fought us with all the force of a three-day storm,
buffeting us and dragging us about the floor. "Hang on,
get it down on the ground and we'll sit on it! In the
morning we'll cut it apart and see what it's made of."

"Sorry, Dan," Kor panted, though he did indeed hang
on. "You keep forgetting these creatures don't mind
knives."

"Fire, then! I'd lay my life it doesn't like fire. Let us
see if we can drag it back toward the hearth."

Forthwith it was no longer trying to attack us, but
hurling itself away from us to escape. The sudden change
of direction unbalanced us. My weight came down on my
injured foot, I yelped, and my hands let go. The thing tore
loose from Kor's grasp—I gulped in fear, but it shot
straight away from us, seaward, toward the door. Like the
sea, it gave off its own greenish light. We watched as it
swooped out the doorway—I had once widened that entry,
by the looks of things, and it stood open to the weather,
yet unrepaired. Just outside, the devourer collided with
something. We saw it shudder in its flight. There was a
fishy, smacking sound and the shriek of a man in utter
terror. Then a stocky fellow in a doomster's mask got up
and ran speedily back toward Seal Hold, giving forth a line
of small screams, like beads on a string, all the way.

"Olpash!" Kor exclaimed, and he laughed so hard he
sagged against me. The devourer soared upward, disappeared in the darkness over the ocean. A strange catch
came into Korridun's laughter, and with a shock I realized
he was crying.

"Kor!" I put my arms around him. "What is it?" He
was weeping against my bare shoulder. He scarcely knew,
I think, what he was doing, and in a moment he stiffened
and stepped back, head bowed, pressing his hands to his
face as if to force down the sobs.

"Sorry," he muttered.

"No need!" I reached out and touched him on the arm,

felt him quivering. "Has the devourer hurt you?" I demanded, frightened.

"Not much."

"Sit by the hearth, let me see." I urged him to the king's place by the fire, stumbled to one knee at his side and tried to open his shirt. He gently pushed my hands away.

"Truly, it is nothing." He lifted his tunic himself to show me the red marks. No blood had been drawn. "Clothing can be of good use, Dan," he teased me. But scarcely had he spoken than he sobered. "The thing has never before come so early in the night. I had scarcely entered the lodge before it was on me. And I—I am not sure I could have lasted until daylight."

"Is that what is wrong?"

"Wrong? But wrong doesn't make me weep. Something is right for a change." Kor wiped his face with his sleeve, wiping away tears and the faint reek of the devourer. Looking down at me where I kneeled, he gifted me with a small, grave smile. "Ten years, ten hellish years have I kept this vigil, and no one has ever helped me—except on that one uncanny night when I screamed for my twelve—"

I winced and turned away. He reached down and caught me under the chin by three fingers of his right hand, directing my gaze back to his. His eyes—I have never been able to tell truly what color were his eyes, as green-brown-gray as the sea, but they were as dark and deep as that ocean.

"It means much to me that you are here, Dan," he said.

"I would walk through fire for you," I told him softly.

Sakeema knows why I said that, except that it was true, but it stunned him. His eyes widened, his hand dropped limply to his side.

"I would," I told him more firmly. "I would beard Mahela herself, in her own den, if it could help you. Kor, make me your guardsman, so that I may serve you."

"Dan—"

I interrupted his protest. "Your guardsman and your fosterling. So that I may swear allegiance to you. Please."

"Dan, no! I have retainers enough. I need—far worse than warriors I need—a friend."

Kneeling there at his feet, ready to swear to him my loyalty, I heard that word and it touched me to the center of my heart. Kor, for his own part, had straightened where he sat and spoke to me fiercely.

"Do you really think, if you were my guardsman, you would have come here tonight? Could have? Guardsmen must obey commands. Do you think there is anyone in my Holding, any clansfellow of mine, whom I can talk with as I talk with you? Anyone whom I can tell the secrets I have told you? Anyone here who calls me—who calls me Kor?"

A pang of shame. "I meant it for mockery at first."

"I know it. But I loved it, even then. Dan, you great-hearted dolt." He spoke more softly, but even more intensely. "Did you really think I would have let Istas slay you? If it had come to that, I would have stopped her, even if it had meant leaving the kingship and my tribe. Do you still think you have meant nothing but trouble to me, Dan?"

I could not answer. I could not speak. After looking at me a moment Kor reached over and gave me a quick, hard hug, then pulled me up to sit by the hearth beside him. Recklessly he piled more wood on the fire, until the whole lodge danced with light. Apparently he cared no longer for the censure of his people. For some time he and I sat side by side, saying nothing, letting fire settle into warmth. Vigil night though it was, it seemed no longer perilous as we sat there together, but full of comfort and friendship. When Kor spoke, his voice was quiet, easy.

"Anyway, you cannot be my fosterling, Dan. You have a father."

Very true. And following the thought there flowed a tide of memories of my father, all bright and warm, as if the warmth of the night had drawn them forth, the warmth of Kor's regard. Odd that I had thought so seldom of Tyonoc since I had been with the Seal Kindred.

"And he is king of the Red Hart tribe."

"Yes," I said promptly, "and he was a valiant king."

"So I have heard. Tell me about him, Dan."

There were too many things to tell, all in a jumble. How his braids were the color of tufted grass in winter and came down nearly to his waist, with the blue-gray feathers of the mountain peregrine tied in them, feathers of a bird not seen since the time of Sakeema, emblems of a kingship passed down since that distant peacetime. How he often carried a gray falcon on his ungloved hand. How his face was browned with weather, though his eyes were a brighter blue than the skies of mountain summers. How he had once turned a running herd of many forest bison away from the meadow where the children played by charging at the huge beasts on his barebacked, unbridled pony. I had been one of the children, and I had seen, and remembered.

The pony. "He taught me to ride," I said, speaking, for some reason, with difficulty. "He sat me on the horse with him before I was old enough to walk, and when I was ready to learn to ride on my own he taught me." The talking grew easier as I went on. After a moment words came in plenty. "He put me on the oldest pony, and for days he stood by and taught me with never a harsh word, only many reminders. But the old, safe pony was balky and galloped with a thudding effort, and I had dreamed of racing the wind across the meadows, but it seemed that riding was nothing but rules and reminders after all. I hated the rules, the old pony, the riding itself. And my father saw the hatred in me, though of course I did not speak it, and he did something brave and great of heart. He brought his war pony, helped me on and placed the reins in my hands. Then he went away."

I paused, smiling at the memory, and Kor was grinning broadly. With his people, I had noted, his face was most often sober, and I felt blessed by the smiles he sometimes gave me.

"Was it as wild a ride as the first one Talu gave you?" he asked.

"Very nearly! I was so scared I soiled myself, and ecstatic. And I raced the wind, and did not break my foolish neck.

"After that I rode every horse in his herd. He owned many ponies, more of them or less as he traded or gifted or as they foaled, but the ones he kept or gave to his honored guests were always the best ones in the tribe, their manes and tails falling in long curling locks, the hair of their flanks thick and curling but as fine as spiderweb. I helped him train the fillies and colts. He trained his ponies as he trained his children, by patience, and I never knew him to punish a horse by beating it, and seldom even by scolding. We boys spent much time with him and the ponies. When we were old enough and had undergone our name vigils, we each chose one of our own."

"What was yours?"

"A sorrel, mane and tail the color of the snowpeaks at sunrise on a fine day. Her name was Nolcha, 'the sun child—' " I turned to Korridun in sudden alarm. "Tell me not that it was she I rode here!"

"No," he said briefly.

"I am glad of it. She was a good pony, swift but kind. Swift and fierce when we rode to war. I rode her the night the Fanged Horse Folk raided us, and she was one of the few steeds that gave scars rather than got. My father lost a horse that night. . . ." I paused, thinking.

"How long ago was that?"

"Some few years. He was a great war leader, my father. When he led, warriors followed unquestioning, for he led rightly. He rode forth only to drive back attack."

"Or to drive the Herders from your hunting lands," Kor said quietly. I looked at him blankly.

"He would not have done that! Some warriors and counselors of my tribe wanted to, but he always maintained that there was room enough for all. Even those uncouth Cragsmen he left in peace, for the most part. And they would sometimes throw stones down on us, or frighten the deer as we stalked them."

"Times must have grown hard of late."

"But why do you say that? Deer are plentiful since there are fewer wildcats and hardly any wolves. At least that is what my people say. Though at night around the cooking fires we tell tales of what it was like to have seen the great cats, to have heard the song of the wolves."

"How many were there around your fire?"

"Five. My father, and he would tell us all the old tales and sometimes teach us the chants. My mother, Wyonet—'magic dancer,' the name means. She could ride as fast as he, but by the fire she would stitch tunics of white doeskin for herself, or stroke the throat feathers of a hooded hawk. My eldest brother, Tyee—he was a good heart, but always standing in my father's shadow as the high plains stand in the shadow of the mountains and receive no rain. My elder brother, Ytan—he was sometimes as ill-tempered as a wild boar, but I never knew him to do dishonor. And I."

"No sisters?"

"My parents were not blessed with many children. I do not know why. It was not a thing one asked."

"I suppose not." Kor stirred absently. "What else do you remember about your father?"

A bittersweet memory. "There was a time, once, when I caused a pony to take colic and die through my carelessness, and he felt he had to beat me because it was not his pony, but a tribefellow's. Moreover, I had been very stupid and caused it great pain. And I was old enough to know better—I was nearly of an age to take a name. So he took a leather lash and led me out to a secluded place. I stood sullenly, and he struck me three times and then threw the lash away in an odd sort of rage, pulled me into his arms and we both wept." My eyes moistened even to speak of it. "I grew a handspan that day."

"Were you his favorite, do you think?" Kor asked. Something taut in his voice, but thinking of my father, I noticed and paid no heed.

"I was the one who gave him the most trouble, I dare say!" I laughed, thinking of the times I had strayed while hunting and he had left his own trail to find me, the times I had disgraced him by speaking out before the tribe, the times I had acted against his counsel. "For the most part he let me run as wild as the colts, finding out in my own blundering way the things I had to know. I would not always listen to him. I was stubborn."

"Truly?" said Kor in tones sweet with irony. I struck him lightly on the shoulder before I went on.

"My brothers and I, when we fought, he made us settle

it among ourselves. We gave each other far more blows than we ever received from him.''

"He had the raising of you, mostly? You were young when your mother died?"

"Not so very young, I think," I said slowly. "Kor, I still cannot remember—how she died, or when, or of what cause."

"But the things you have told me—they all happened while she was still alive."

I thought back on what I had said. "Yes," I admitted, wary. I smelled black water.

"You say it was that way, it was this way, years ago. Is there not something that you remember of your father since? Something within the last turn of the seasons?"

A simple enough task, that I should remember back a year, but the request filled me with terror and anger. "No!" I shouted, jumping up before I remembered my hurt foot. I sank back with a groan, and Kor gripped me by the arm.

"Dan, forgive me and have patience with me. Just one more question. Please."

I owed him more than my life—I could bear with one question more. Facing him, I nodded.

"When you speak of your father, you say, he was valiant, he had many horses, he was a great war leader. As if he no longer lives." Korridun's sea-dark gaze held me as did his hand on my arm. "Why is that?"

Again I was terrified, but this time I leashed the terror. For the most part. "I don't know," I whispered.

"Is he dead?"

"Would you not have heard," I cried out, "if he were dead?"

"One would think so," Kor agreed, letting go of me.

I snatched up my crutch and struggled to my feet, very angry. "Are you saying I killed him?" I shouted.

"No," said Kor so flatly that all my anger ran away like mountain rain. He got up to stand beside me. "I am thinking that perhaps you should have," he added very softly, as if to himself.

"But why?" I protested, shocked. "He was—is—my

father. Tyonoc of the Red Hart, a true and worthy king.
He was—is—"

Puzzled, I stood with my mouth going silently like that
of a sea bass, for I could not say "good to me."

"Would you walk through fire for him?" Kor asked
with some small edge in his voice. The question smote me
like a Cragsman's cudgel. Years before, I knew, I would
have answered without hesitation "Yes." But since—
something had happened—black water all around me, and
I think I whimpered. I could not see, but I felt Kor
tightly holding me. In a moment my vision cleared and I
could look into his face. It was full of shame.

"Dan, I am sorry, truly sorry. I have no right—"

"Hush," I muttered at him, breathing deeply.

"I who call myself wise, I am no better than a jealous
child." He stepped back and sank down by the hearth,
despairing.

"Kor, you ass, let it go! I do not need coddling. I
hope." I shook myself like a pony coming out of water,
sending splinters of fear away. "You have every right," I
added after a moment. "I killed your guardsman and
lifelong friend. You are the king, and you have the right to
do what you will with me."

"In that case," he remarked, "you have just called the
king an ass."

The thought amused me. I grinned at him.

"I'm no king to you, Dan, Sakeema be praised, and you
know it." He still looked distraught. "And friends should
not hurt their friends."

"Kor, my friend, I think you have helped me far more
than hurt me." I said it to comfort him, but in the same
moment I knew that it was true. I spoke half to myself in a
sort of wonder. "I am no longer very much afraid."

"Perhaps your long night is nearly over, then." He
came and stood beside me, laying a hand on my shoulder.
"Courage, Dannoc. The dawn cannot be far away."

Chapter Ten

Spring came on apace. Catkins grew on the birches. There were two terrible storms, roar of thunder and surf and the ocean lashing at the headland clear to the top of the cliffs—the fury of that ocean terrified me. No one else seemed perturbed, though most of those who lived in the lodges came into the Hold for a few nights, and it was crowded. For the first time I shared my chamber with folk other than Winewa. Then, when the weather had calmed, the lodge-dwellers went back out to the lodges, and some of those who lived through the winter in the Hold went as well, to stay in the lodges during the milder weather of summer.

Kor passed two more vigils, and I kept vigil with him. No challengers came, though he was frankly uneasy, expecting some. My foot healed enough so that I could rest some weight on it, and I put away my crutch and took up my stick again. I took to roaming the mountain slopes behind the headland, and I ventured out farther and longer each day. A strange wanderlust was growing in me, and a thought, half-formed, perhaps drawn out of me by the storms, that I had to—do something, face something, turn and retrace my tracks and find out the name of the thing that was chasing me, turn and stare down my shadow. More of me than my foot had to heal. Courage, Kor had said. There was growing in me a will to be strong and well.

In a way I was very content among the Seal Kindred. I busied myself, found things to do, or others found them for me. The first quiet day some of the men offered to take me out in a coracle on the sweetly bobbing sea, and I went. But even that slight tossing of the waves sickened me, and the sight of so much water, so dark and deep, filled me with fear. I had always been afraid of drowning, ever since I was small and had bad dreams and cried in the night—they were always nightmares of drowning. Since then, until I had come to Kor, I had known no waters larger and deeper than beaver ponds, and I had ventured into no waters except the shallow mountain streams that came down over rocks with a singing sound, fell off cliffs in cascades. Or none that I could remember. . . . I had never envied the Seal tribe their fishing life, and I envied it even less after I had cowered in a coracle amid the vastness of the sea.

Daily I sat on the headland and worked at shaping my bow and arrows, to keep up my spirits in thoughts of hunting again, of stalking the highmountain meadows. And I thought often of my father as I worked, he who had taught me the stable stance of an archer and the way of smoothly drawing the bow, he whose presence had given me the strength and heart to master all hard tasks—I who had not remembered him, I was now full of warm thoughts of him. Seldom was I lonesome, thinking of him, for in my mind I drew him there beside me, as he had so often been beside me when I was a stripling. But sometimes, when it rained, I would go into a lodge while I worked, for warmth and for the company of other folk.

When I tired of working I would go to talk with Talu, or with Kor, or with Winewa and her friends, or with Istas. She had given over her shame on seeing me, Istas had, and I mine on seeing her. Shame had worn us down, and there was no use in it. She was a tough, busy old woman, and I liked being with her.

One day as I lazed near her in the deep cave where she kept the grain a shout went up, and in a moment a boy came hurrying in.

"A runner, Grandmother, from the Otter River Clan!"

She was not his grandmother in truth, for she had borne no children, nor had she been pledged. But all the youngsters called her Grandmother. She frightened them not a whit, for all that she could be so stern.

"Shall we bring him in to you?" The lad was dancing with excitement.

"Slime of Mahela, no!" she snapped. "Don't let him in here. I'll come out." She strode off after the boy, puffing and grumbling, and I limped along behind her.

The runner was entirely naked except for a sort of pouch on a thong to cradle his cock, and all his long, flat muscles glistened with sweat. Being of the Otter River tribe, he was somewhat darker of brown hair than the Seal, and slanting of eye, and there was a bony sharpness about his face while theirs were more gently rounded. But he wore his hair cut fur-fashion like theirs.

"Old Woman of the Seal Kindred, greetings," he told Istas. "Old Woman" was a title of honor, for the rulers of the Otter River Clan were women, and the older the better. "I come by order of my lady liege Izu to request your aid."

"So the salmon are less again," Istas grumped.

"The salmon are less than ever before. Every year they have been less. We hunt, we plant, we gather, but our Riverland is small, hemmed in by the Red Hart Demesne, the Seal Holding, the Cragsmen—"

"All these things I know," said Istas curtly. "What I do not know is how it is expected that I should feed the world. Rad Korridun!"

He ambled out as if he had just happened by at that moment, though in fact I am sure he had been listening and watching.

"What am I to do? They want fish again."

"Is there enough?" he asked her gravely.

"Well, if the season favors—and if the planting gets done in good time, so we can send the men out in the coracles—and if we eat lightly—and if that accursed fanged monstrosity finds her own meat, forsooth, or if a certain outlander shoots it for her—" Sour old eyes blazed at me, but then suddenly Istas gave up her spleen and flung her hands skyward. "Yes, blast it, I dare say we can spare a little."

"Have Izu send pack beasts," Kor told the messenger. "Will you eat cod and jannock, and sleep a night in my Hold?" I sensed that this petition had been granted many times before.

"Many thanks, but I must go back at once," the runner said. "And there are no pack beasts, Korridun King. We ate them over the winter."

Kor frowned. This was new. "How will you take the food, then?" he asked quietly after a moment.

"In dugouts, perhaps. We will paddle it over to the mouth of the river, portage it upstream. But the canoes are heavy and narrow. If you can loan us your coracles, which hold more, all will go faster."

"There are no boats to spare!" Istas protested.

Kor was thinking. "You send folk," he said finally, "and we will help you make boats."

"But then those who are sent will be gone the longer from the work to be done against next winter. Less will be gathered and laid by." The man spoke softly, his look worried.

"We need our coracles for fishing," said Kor, not harshly but firmly. "The fish sustain us and sometimes you. I do not know what other offer to make you or your ruler."

"Izu will decide. Perhaps we can somehow bargain pack beasts from the Herders, should any of their traders pass our way." The messenger bowed. "You are very generous. The matter is pressing, and I must go in all haste."

"Stay for the noon meal, at least."

"I cannot, Korridun King. But if you will give me what food I can carry in my hand, I will be glad of it."

Istas sent for bread from the hearth and dried fish from the stores stacked deep in the Hold. The runner loped off to drink lightly from the spring, and the moment the packet of food was in his hand he was on his way again, southward along the mountain flanks, the sweat not yet dry on his body. We all stood and watched him go. He carried not even a blanket for sleeping under.

"He could not spare even a day," Kor murmured. "Things must be hard with them."

"We will be hearing from Pajlat," Istas said in dour tones.

"I do not doubt it." Kor gave her a crooked smile, which seemed to vex her. She sniffed and marched away.

"What will you give Pajlat?" I asked Kor.

"Oats."

"Do you always give him what he wants?"

"Not all that he wants—we would be long since starved and dead if I gave him all that he wants! But I always give him something. Better so than that he should come and take what he wants perforce."

Undeniably better. I had faced the Fanged Horse Folk in battle, and I had no desire ever to do so again. They fought with shriveled human heads hanging from their bearskin riding pelts. Nor was their joy entirely in killing. Sometimes they took captives who were later "set free," sent stumbling across the rocky steppes "in red boots," with all the skin flayed from their feet up to their ankles. Alone of all the tribes they kept slaves, and they were so proud, it was said, that sometimes they killed the slaves for no better reason than to boast of their wealth to each other, showing that they did not mind the loss of a slave or two. Sometimes they even killed their horses in like wise, when their warriors vied with each other for honor.

I shook myself, shaking off thoughts of Pajlat, turning my thoughts to Talu. "Give me a leg up?" I asked Kor. "My foot is well enough, and I would like to try riding that mare again."

He eyed me doubtfully. "What if she throws you and you land on it?"

"She will not throw me. If she acts as if she might, I will swing down by her neck. Come on, Kor."

He complied. Talu was in among the aspens, hunting for mice and voles in the ferns. She had found a rabbit's nest and was busily munching up the hairless morsels therein, so she let us approach without being coy as horses so often are. I threw my cloak over her back and Kor locked his hands to receive my knee, hoisting me up onto her. Talu's head came up with a snort, and I passed a leather thong around her neck, mostly to hold on to—I did not have much hope of guiding Talu.

"Are you sure—"

I never heard the rest of what Kor said. We were off, the mare and I, plunging away from him and down the side of the headland. But for all her snorting and leaping it was a glorious ride. She soon settled into a steady lope along the mountainside, and the jarring of her gait pained my foot only a little. And oh, the spring-green cool smell of the blue pines, the smell and the sound of the freshwater torrents up on the slopes, the call of a falcon carrying far on the air . . . Up on the high peaks the snowmelt would be starting, the deer sleek-red for spring, the harts in velvet antler, and I longed to be there to see them. It was only after hours, reluctantly, that I coaxed Talu to a stop and turned her back again toward Seal Hold.

After that, though I did not speak of it, I felt an ache other than that of my healing foot, and again I grew restless at night, though in a gentle way. After Winewa had gone off to her sleep I would get up and wander into the forest, the thick, wet, salt-swept coastal forest, spruce and birch all dark green with moss, trunks and dead lower branches dripping with it, dead ancestor logs plumed with ferns and glowing eerie orange with fungi. Sometimes young trees grew out of the bodies of their parents. It was a very different place from the open mountaintop forests I remembered. It troubled me that I did not know the names and customs of half the plants, the flowers. I felt very much the stranger there. Still, forest was forest, and when I was wakeful I went to forest for comfort.

There were tiny white flowers growing amid the rubble under the trees, welcome-spring flowers, and in the darkness they seemed to shine with their own small light, like constellations and scatterings of stars. Perhaps it was moonlight made it seem so, for the moon was nearing the full. Though moonlight scarcely reached into that dense gloom beneath the evergreens.

On the night of the full moon I made excuses to Winewa and went out to keep watch with Kor.

He was openly waiting for me on the sea cliff, amused and defiant. "There are three who might come," he reported. "Olpash not among them. He is more likely to poison my soup than face me, after blundering into the devourer as he did. But there are others. I have faced them before, and I am tired of it. Let us go someplace where we can talk in peace."

"Where?" To the forest, I hoped.

"Down over the cliffs, with the seals." Then he laughed at me, I suppose seeing the look on my face, or perhaps not needing to see it. "No, I am only half serious, Dan. We would not be able to hear there, not with the surf running high. Let us go where you and Talu rode."

We skirted the great lodge and walked up through the dark forest until we were entirely away from the headland. Like a boy shirking work, Kor was in high spirits. Even the midnight forest, full of the rustlings of owls and martens and the screams of dying mice, seemed friendlier to him than the place he was supposed to be. As for me, I felt yearning grip at my heart again, and I pretended that the crashing of the sea was the sound of wind around the great yellow pines that grow beyond the snowpeaks.

"There is no need for you to stay here forever, Dan," said Kor quietly and suddenly out of the darkness. "When you are well, you should go. I have seen you looking away toward the mountains."

I stopped in my tracks, at the same time overjoyed and stricken. "But—how can I go?" I protested, full of shame. "Only a few weeks ago I offered you my lifelong allegiance—"

"And I told you I was no king to you, but a friend. And friends help each other, as I recall."

Even in the darkness I could feel the pull of the snowpeaks, I knew when my face turned toward them. As most often it did. Nevertheless, if it were only that longing . . .

"I would not leave you for so slender a reason," I said. "If it were only to roam on the mountains."

"But . . ." Kor prodded.

"But the thought is in me that I must go back to my

tribe. To my father and my brothers. Tell them I am alive, and try to find out what mystery has darkened my mind.''

''Ah,'' Kor breathed.

''I ought to, I must, if I am to be something more than a madman.'' I was half afraid, even of the words, and my voice faltered. The next thought, though, burst from me. ''But how am I to leave you here with your precious Olpash and those thrice-accursed devourers and this blasted vigil?''

''For the matter of that,'' said Korridun, ''if you will let me, I will come with you.''

''What? How? You can't!''

''I can and, Dan willing, I will. Stop yelping and listen.'' We had reached a slope of scree, gray-white in the moonlight, and Kor settled himself on one of the larger rocks. ''Sit down. In the first place, I have been thinking for some time that I would like to confer with your father.''

''What for?''

He did not answer me at once, but turned and looked up the rock field that tumbled behind him. ''Because the whole world is falling to bits, Dannoc,'' he said finally.

''Kor—''

''I am serious. See this mighty pile of talus? Each of these stones was once part of the peak, but they have fallen away as if chipped off by a great hammer. All the world is being chipped away like that, bit by bit. I am yet young, but I can see it happening, the salmon less each year, and the doves, and—everything, the white weasels, not once seen since three years ago, and the singing heron, six. There were gannet nesting on the rocks along the coast when I was a boy, and gair fowl, they darkened the cliffs with their numbers. None since. Where have all the wolves gone, and the mountain lions, and the great blue bears? If one of them came right now and stood before me, I would not care if it rent me. I would die happy to have seen any one of them, just in that one dying moment of my life.''

His words filled me with longing, the more so since I remembered a certain dream.

I said, ''I have often thought the same, and so has every

hunter of our tribe, I dare say. But what can my father tell you of these things that you do not already know?''

"Perhaps nothing.'' Korridun's voice grew more grim—it was the king who sat and talked with me, now. "But if it goes on—as I can only believe it will go on—then within a few years there will not be enough fish for the Otter River people or enough forage for the Fanged Horse Folk, and perhaps not enough deer for you. But my people fish the endless sea and live in one place and grow oats. And there will be many others who will want the fish and the oats. But my Holding is small, a toehold between the mountains and the sea. . . .''

He wanted to make my father his ally, then. A fitting business for a king.

"Perhaps you could talk to Ayol of the Herders, also,'' I suggested.

"Perhaps.''

"But can you leave your tribe for so long?''

Kor stretched himself contentedly and grinned. "Not only can I, but it will be by far the best thing for me to do. My counselors are a sullen lot of late. I forced them into open enmity when I revealed that I knew who my masked challengers were. And I am weary unto death of these vigils. And I am—'' He lowered his voice. "I am none too willing to face another devourer.''

"It is a wonder you have not found excuse to go wandering before.''

"I have often thought of it! But there was no one to leave behind as regent, no one I could truly trust, until lately.''

I blinked at him. "What has happened lately?''

"What has happened! Dannoc—'' He seemed about to mock me, gave a low laugh and let it go. "Istas has learned the meaning of mercy,'' he said.

"Mercy,'' I murmured, remembering myself as a sullen boy, remembering a father who threw away the lash, wondering why the memory hurt me.

"Yes, mercy. I love my folk, Dan. Sakeema be praised that I learned mercy early, or half of them would be dead, for they are a fractious lot at times.''

The wry affection in his voice made me smile. "When did you learn?"

"When I had Rhudd thrown off the cliff."

My smile faded, for I heard sorrow. "But what else could you have done?" I protested. "He had planned to kill you. He was a traitor, and a danger to you!"

"What else could I have done? I could have let him live, of course, and perhaps he would have come back into being the decent man he once was. Failing that, I could at least have had the courage to slay him with my own hands." Kor's voice was shaking and so low I could scarcely hear him. "Mahela knows I wanted to. I dreamed of tortures, I was eaten up with hatred of him for what he had put me through, poor little me! Even then I knew that it was wrong to hate so, and I thought I would have mercy and forgo the tortures. I would merely have him quickly killed. So I sullied the hands of other men with blood that should have been on my own." His voice grew softer yet. "Olpash was one of those who sent Rhudd to his doom."

"You think—" Dimly I saw the line of his reasoning, and I was doubtful and amazed.

"Yes, I do think." He got up to pace. "I know it hardened him. A man who has once killed in cold blood, however justly, will not hesitate so long to kill again. A lawful challenge, a lawful killing, very much like an execution within the law . . . Perhaps Olpash knows what I have made of him, and hates me for it. My hatred has begotten his. Hatred begets hatred, and blood—"

"Kor," I interrupted, standing in my turn, "you were young, in danger, nearly helpless. It would have been folly to let an enemy live."

"Was it folly to let you live?" he retorted.

The words shook me. I hoped not, by all the powers of Sakeema I hoped not, but if ever the madness should come over me again and I should turn on him . . . For his sake as much as my own I had to find my way back to the beginning of it.

"Your folk thought so," I whispered.

He came over and laid his hands on my shoulders. "They were wrong, and they know it now," he said gently. "And I have told you what you have meant to me, Dan."

So his mercy had given me life. No more than I already knew. No need for tears . . . At random I walked away from them, and Kor walked beside me. Moonlight on starflowers at our feet. I could walk strongly that night, without much aid of the stick, even on the slopes.

"You understand well enough, for all your protesting," Kor said quietly after a while. "But Istas never understood. It seemed to her only simple justice to punish where there was wrong. She is the most deft of managers and she is masterly at reaching agreement in the council. She knows the ways of the tribe and she settles quarrels. Everyone loves and respects her. Olpash and the others would be ashamed to contest for power against such a venerable old woman. Also, she knows how to deal with trouble that comes from outside. . . . But if I had given her power over the tribe even as recently as a few months ago, I would have feared for my people. She did not yet know the meaning of mercy."

"And now she does," I remarked.

"Thanks to your good services."

He spoke in jest, to tease me into a lighter mood. And he meant only that she had tested her mercy upon my back. But my mind shot at once beyond, back to—

Rowalt, and that first night in the lightning, the surge of storm. Crazed horse between my knees, lunging and floundering and glistening with sweat. Kor's staring face before me as he dodged out of the way, and the sweep of the great knife, and the feeling—nothing in the memory frightened me as much as that feeling, and I could not yet put a name to it. And the scream, Kor shouting for his twelve. And they were dragging me from my horse at the same time as it fell, but they could not hold me, for I was as powerful as the storm. A head flew off, a hand, and then—*ai*, so pity me Sakeema, I remembered the face of the man as I sliced open his gut—

An honest, homely face.

I gasped for breath, doubled over with shock and pain, clinging to something hard for support, sick unto death, as if I had taken the knife in my own gut. So that was Rowalt, and that was what I had done to him. The memory was clear enough, but the feeling about it all dreamlike, untoward, as if out of otherness, as if I had been some-one else.

I came to myself in a moment to find myself clutching the resinous trunk of a pine, my face in the moss, holding onto the tree so hard that I shook, and Kor standing by me, watchful.

"My—my horse," I stammered. "It was a roan."

"Yes." He reached over and started to peel my locked fingers loose from the tree. "Dan, ease up."

I could not manage more than the single word, to ex-plain to him. "Rowalt," I said.

"You remember?"

I nodded, letting my forehead sag against the pine, my arms loosen. Tears would have been a relief, then, and I would not have swallowed them any longer, not for pride's sake, not with Kor. I closed my eyes, they burned so. But there was something in me that was too heavy and knotted to let me weep.

"It will come," Kor said quietly.

"How am I going to face Istas?" I muttered.

"I think it might be better to say nothing to Istas. Anything you could tell her would only distress her. And my news will distract her from the look on your face."

His mercy was perhaps more for me than for Istas, but I did not argue. I straightened, let go of the tree, picked up my stick. We walked on again.

"Better?" Kor asked after a while.

"Not too poorly. It would have been worse a month ago."

"You grow stronger every day. The memories come back as you are able to bear them."

"May the worst of them come soon," I told him. "The sooner the better, for both of us."

"We will see to it," he said.

Chapter Eleven

Kor had intended that he and I should go off by ourselves. He hated to take folk away from the tribe—everyone was needed. But Istas would not hear of the scheme unless he took with him at least half a dozen guardsmen. And, as Istas was at the center of the venture, her will prevailed. Kor chose Birc, among others, to go with us.

Ten days went by in preparation. There was business to be settled. It could have taken far longer, but Kor was determined to be on his way before the time came for another vigil.

"Will Istas stand the vigils?" I asked him privately.

"Not on your life!" He grinned with delight.

"Leave my life out of it," I told him, "where Istas is concerned."

"What?" He pretended shock, knowing quite well that I was joking. "Why, Dan, bite your tongue. She adores you."

Winewa happened by just as he spoke. "Who?" she asked suspiciously, and we both teased her and refused to tell her until we were laughing giddily, like striplings.

I was often dizzy with excitement and joy, those days. Soon I would be seeing my father again! I thought of him as I finished my arrows and bow, as I cut a thick deerskin sleeping pelt into a riding pelt, padded it between layers with moss, fitted it with tie-thongs for bags and bedroll and with a surcingle measured to span Talu's girth. My foot was not yet sufficiently healed for walking the distance of our journey, though I walked strongly about Seal

Hold and had given away my stick. Of necessity, I would ride the mare.

"Good riddance," grumbled Istas—she grumbled often those days, even more so than usual. "Get the monstrosity away from here. One less greedy mouth for me to feed."

But there was a problem, to my way of thinking. There were no other steeds, for the Seal kept none, and I hated to ride while Kor walked. When I mentioned my unease to him, he told me cheerily not to be an ass. We would be keeping to a foot pace in any event, what with all the blasted retainers, and he had walked with his men all his life. Privately I hoped Talu would carry him along with me, at least part of the time. But it would be slow going. A pox on Istas and the blasted guardsmen. A pox on people who kept no horses.

The Otter River folk came for their dried fish. But they had no beasts, we knew that already.

There was a great bustle of provisioning that seemed endless. Sometimes I dreamed of my father, sometimes of showing Kor the mountains. Sometimes I paced and fumed, for I could have made ready for myself in a quarter the time. But I could not be always ill-tempered. There were gifts for me. From Winewa, a leather case for my arrows. Warm woolen blankets smelling of the cedar in which they had been kept, a bride's blankets never used, from Istas.

On the eve of the journey Kor and I sat high on the headland by Talu's empty pen to watch the sunset.

It had merely happened so, that sunset had found us there. We had walked out to talk of routes, the mountain passes—there were three main trails across the mountains, not counting the White Eagle Way, which ran along the Otter River. There was the Blackstone Path, southerly, leading to the land of my people, and the Traders' Trail and the Raiders' Trail, farther north. The Raiders' Trail led only to the steppes, where Pajlat and his people roamed. Our problem was in choosing between the Traders' Trail and the Blackstone Path. The latter was rough, harsh, longwinding over the high Blue Bear Pass. It took its source in the midst of the Red Hart Demesne. The Traders' Trail ran through the Shappa Pass, a low pass that

would be less arduous for Kor and his followers, lowland-
ers all, not accustomed to the thin highmountain air—though
to him I said only that the pass was the one better suited to
a horseback rider. He took pause that the Traders' Trail
gave onto the southern fringes of the Fanged Horse shadowlands. Very true, but my father's warriors should have
pressed Pajlat's raiders back from those fringes. Just southward lay my people's hunting grounds where the red deer
roamed.

We came to no agreement and did not care, and did not
speak long of it. Instead we reveled in the day. It was a
glorious day, one of the rare fine days of that misty coastal
holding. A worthy wind had sprung up from somewhere
and polished the sky so that the air was as clear as mountain springwater, and at last I could truly see the vast
ocean, the blazing sheen of it and the changing colors,
green-brown-blue out to a clean distant line nearly the
color of the alpine violets that grow in the snowmelt when
spring finally comes to the highmountain meadows. The
sun set in glory over that sea, turning sky the color of
aspen leaves in autumn, growing ever more splendid, like
a fire butterfly spreading from the cocoon, but vast—I had
never seen such vastness of sky, even from the ever-
winter crags.

In silence Kor and I sat and watched the great bloom of
color in the sky, the sun like a bright prairie poppy at the
center of it, dipping lower over the endless water. The sea
lay very calm, and the sun sank into it with great calm and
sweet-scented peace, a floating flower. Sky darkened from
yellow into orange and lavender, all the colors of a wood
duck's wing.

"Time was," Korridun said wistfully, "when the sea-
faring otters would have been sporting yonder, in the kelp,
and when the white whales swam past this coast. One
could see them from this headland, my mother told me."

Time was Sakeema's time. He-whom-all-we-seek. A
remnant of dream turned like a honeyed knife in my heart.
Sun sinking, a poppy the color of blood . . .

And just as the last petal of it disappeared—it was a
vision, an omen, I can only describe it so. A flash went up

from the lost sun of the most impossible color, too red to
be called violet, yet utterly unlike the blood-red of the sun
that had just been, unlike any earthly color I had ever
seen, all light and shine, so pure and lovely I ached at the
sight of it, I felt my eyes sting with unshed tears, *ai*,
Sakeema—it was the clearshining red-purple color of the
amaranth, the lost flower of the god, if I remembered my
vision aright. Like a shimmering bubble of amaranthine
light it came up and burst and was as quickly gone all in
an instant, and Kor and I turned and looked at each other,
stunned.

"The blessing of Sakeema!" Kor exclaimed. "That
bodes well for our journey!"

"Have you ever seen it before?"

"Never! Few folk have. Istas did, once, when she was
young. She will be comforted—"

When he told her, he meant to say, but he fell silent and
stared. A solitary rider was approaching the headland,
walking his mount along the hard sand of the strand.

We looked at each other again, then got up and strode
down toward the great lodge to meet him.

Already the shout had gone up, and nearly everyone in
the village turned out to gawk. A visitor was not a common event. But it was the horse that held my eye as the
stranger rode up. I had never seen such a horse, neither
fanged and ugly like the steeds of Pajlat's tribe, nor small
and nimble and curly of hair like the ponies of the Red
Hart. This horse was as large as Talu but entirely different,
small of head with a fine eye both dark and large, small of
hoof but surefooted, flat-legged, deep-chested, well-sprung,
sleek of skin, with a neck deeply curved like that of a
brant—no, a neck such as a wild swan must have had,
days gone by—and flanks well filled out, every part of the
steed as pleasing to look at as a handsome woman. And its
color, unheard-of in horses, pure shining black, but white
surged up its legs and splashed its belly and its long, full
tail. And the mane lay on its arched neck like snow on a
willow.

"Peace," said the stranger. It was not a plea, so firmly
spoken, but a greeting.

"Peace go with you wherever you travel," Kor replied with the courtesy that cannot be learned, the comity born in him. "Welcome, and will you eat with us?"

"Gladly." The visitor slid down to the ground, and I noted with a small shock that his riding pelt was a wolfskin of shining gray. Not so very strange, for there were wolfskins yet to be found in the belongings of kings, but it was a boasting thing to ride on one, as the Fanged Horse warriors rode on the pelts of bears long dead. . . . What sort of man might this stranger be?

Then I looked at him instead of at the horse and saw that he was scarcely more than a boy. A beardless youth, comely of face, slender but so cocksure of bearing that I did not note his slenderness until later. He wore his hair falling loose in long, tangled locks like the wild tails of my people's ponies, and I gazed doubtfully at him, for his eyes were dark, his hair too light for him to be of the Otter River Clan or the Seal Kindred. Nor did he have the look of those tribes, and much less did he look like one of the hulking men of Pajlat's folk. He wore a tunic of soft, fringed doeskin—the Herders did not dress so, or ride anything but burros. As for the Cragsmen, their skins were stone red or granite gray or slate blue.

And he stood staring at me, straight at me and no other, as foolishly as we were all gawking at him, and though his fine face scarcely moved he seemed somehow shaken, his cocksure air lost, until he regained it with a proud lift of his head, his eyes still intently on me.

I had not thought how peculiar a thing it must have seemed, a single tall Red Hart oaf standing crop-headed amidst all the Seal Kindred, and I felt heat touch my face as I knew myself for the oddling that I was.

"Of what tribe are you?" asked Istas sharply, and for a startled moment I thought she spoke to me. But she was glaring at the stranger.

The newcomer blinked and seemed to take a moment to come back to self. "No tribe," he said after a pause.

This was a statement nearly impossible to deal with. A babble of voices started up at his words. "And what is

your name?'' Kor put in far more courteously, before the
uproar could take over. Folk fell to silence to hear.

"Tassida." The name meant simply, "horseback rider."
Coolly, almost haughtily, the stranger regarded Kor, look-
ing him up and down as if he were an adversary. "You are
Korridun, the king here."

"Yes."

"If you pay me," Tassida said abruptly, "I will be one
of your followers for a while, and fight for you."

The uproar redoubled. To fight, not out of loyalty, but
for payment! Istas looked ready to take back the hospitality
Kor had offered, but I had another thought.

"Kor," I told him eagerly, "see if you can buy the
horse."

The newcomer heard me. "No," he said at once, with a
hint of edge, "the horse stays with me." He was looking
at me once again in a closed way, so that I could not tell if
he was puzzled, or hostile, or afraid.

"If you stay with me," Kor asked, "might I have the
use of the steed? For the sake of Dan's compunction?"

"Korridun!" Istas stood aghåst. Kor, Tassida, and I all
ignored her. Kor was giving me a slight, teasing smile,
and the stranger was regarding him, appraising again, and
what he saw must not have entirely displeased him.

"If you will accept my guidance concerning the riding
of him, perhaps yes," Tassida said slowly. "I will not let
him be abused."

Him? But the steed did not have the swelling neck of a
stallion. Istas stooped in her forthright way for a look
underneath the horse. "A gelding!" she shrieked.

It was another shock. No proper warrior would ride
anything but a fierce mare, or, failing that, a stallion.
Gelding was a shameful thing, fit only for beasts of burden. At Istas's news, the noise from the Seal tribesfolk
reached new heights of outcry. Parents gathered their children and retreated a few steps, as if to protect them from
something unwholesome, but stayed, held by their desire
to see what happened next. Guardsmen shoved forward,
strutting.

"His name is Calimir," Tassida said, speaking of the horse to Kor, as if nothing had happened.

Kor stepped forward and laid his hand against the horse's nose. The steed generously yielded to him. The name meant "peace." Hardly a warrior's steed, however comely, but Kor seemed quite satisfied.

"We are going on a journey," he told Tassida. "Will you come with us, then? I am not sure how I will be able to pay you when all is done."

"I will come," said the stranger, but his reply was drowned by a shout from Istas.

"Rad Korridun, son of Kela, you have lost your senses entirely! This settles it—I will have nothing more to do with your mad scheme! Let you stay here where you belong! I'll be blasted by Mahela if—"

"*Istas,*" Kor cut in. The firm tone of his voice silenced her for the time, but there was amusement in him as well. "All can not be too far wrong. We have seen the blessing of Sakeema in the sunset, Dan and I."

That gave her pause. She stood with her mouth open and a wide-eyed, almost girlish look on her face. But others had not heard. Guardsmen were crowding up, looking belligerent.

"This stranger has only *said* he can fight!" Birc challenged. He was within his rights, and showed no disrespect to Korridun by so doing. The twelve always tested their new comrades. They needed to be sure of one who might sometime stand beside them in battle.

Tassida pulled a blackstone knife from its bisonhide case by his belt, tossed it up in the air—a circle quickly widened around him, even Kor stepped back—deftly caught it by the hilt across a finger and twirled it, then let it slip as of its own accord into his palm. He crouched and feinted at Birc, who could have been killed featly enough if it had been a fight and not just a practice match—he was standing stupidly, dazzled by the spinning of the knife like a deer dazzled by a fluttering lure. Half a moment too late he came to himself and parried. Then he and the stranger scuffled and circled and pricked at each other. It was a quiet, constrained bout, sufficient to show that the new-comer was not unskilled.

"That reminds me," Kor said to me absently, standing at my side and watching the mock fight. "Your knife."

I groaned in wordless complaint. It was true, I would need a knife, but I did not like the thought of the one of which he spoke.

"I have made you a sheath for it. Carry it. We are likely to need it if the Fanged Horse Folk sight us."

"It will be the Shappa, then?" I had favored the Trad-ers' Trail, the Shappa Pass, but suddenly I favored it no longer, not if I had to carry my fearsome weapon upon it. "There would be little risk of either robbers or raiders along the Blackstone Path," I said.

"Dan, have you not told me again and again that the Blackstone is rough and treacherous, hard going for a horseback rider?" Kor peered at me in puzzled annoyance. "And do you not want me to ride? You know I am no horsemaster."

I could not tell whether he was outsmarting me or taking me at my word, but either way I was defeated, and fully by my own doing. I nodded. "The Shappa, then," I muttered.

Tassida and Birc had concluded their bout, and Tassida was talking with him and the other guardsmen. No longer annoyed, Kor watched, and nodded with satisfaction.

"I am well pleased," he said. "Now one more of my own folk may stay at home, if I have my way with Istas."

It took him until long after dark to convince her, but he had set his mind to the task, and he was king, after all. And so it was that we set out the morrow dawn, with two steeds and six retainers, including the stranger, Tassida.

It was a quiet leave-taking. Winewa kissed me with affection but no fuss—we both knew she would be bed-ding with another before I was many nights gone. Istas was not inclined to kiss anyone, but she surprised me with a long, appraising stare. "There is something that you are not telling me," she said. "A sadness when you look at me."

I decided she deserved to know. "Rowalt," I told her simply. "I remember."

"Ah," she breathed.

"His face takes its revenge on me from time to time in my dreams. But still, I think, it is better to remember."

"Ah," she said in a more settled tone, and she narrowed her bright black eyes at me. "Do you yet remember what sent you here?"

I shook my head.

She surprised me anew. "Sakeema's peace come to you soon, outlander," she said, and she grasped my hand—such strength in her old, gnarled grip! As soon as she released me we started on our journey, I on Talu and Kor on the sleek gelding Calimir and the six afterlings at our heels. But Istas stood and watched us a long way up the mountainside. Looking back from time to time, we could see her, a stumpy shape on the headland, until the mist of low-lying clouds hid her from our sight.

"Out of earshot," Kor whispered, and then without warning he let out an uncouth, unconstrained shout of joy, such a shout that it sent Talu skipping and dancing along the ledges. His men gave him sidelong looks, but I saw Tassida grin.

Chapter Twelve

Those were the days of joy, as we followed the zigzag folds of the great peaks ever higher and farther—farther inland from the sea. With every dawn Kor's delight and amazement redoubled. Up on those slopes the blue pines grew tall and straight, so tall that it dizzied us to study the tops of them. Nor were they furred with moss, but grew clean, with not much except a thick covering of tan needles on the ground between them. A wanderer could see and breathe in this forest. Each breath was piercingly chill and sweet.

"The air!" Kor exclaimed some few days after we had left his village. "Different."

"No salt," I told him, and he blinked, for he had never been out of the scent-reach of the ocean. But the mountain air seemed Sakeema-blessed even to me. All the freshwater wet, thrusting green smells of spring and snowmelt were in it.

And the mountainside meadows, where the snow still lay under the spruces and the violets grew by the streams and the small yellow lilies bloomed everywhere amid the grass, curling their petals back so avidly that they spread their delicate innards like a sunburst . . . I felt as besotted with delight as Kor. And the purple bellflowers, their stalks curving and stirring like Calimir's graceful neck, and the deer grazing in the meadows even at mid of day—I put my bow to use. We did not lack for meat.

Once gone a day or two we traveled easily, not pressing

the pace of those afoot, feeling no urgency. I think neither Kor nor I wanted that journey ever to end.

I felt like a child for gladness, being back in my mountains. More than once, turning to gaze around me, I caught Tassida staring at me as he had stared the first time he had seen me, and so great was my happiness that I did not care how much he gawked or what he was thinking. Only after several days did I begin to wonder what ailed him.

At night the stars seemed to cluster like daisies just above the treetops, so clear was the air, and I would lie back and look at them. . . . But one such night, some days after the start of the journey, when Tassida got up and left our cooking fire to go off by himself for some reason, I got up also and followed.

I was silent—Red Hart born, I was always silent when I walked, though I was not stalking after him, or did not think I was. After we were well away from camp, just as he stopped to make water or whatever he may have been about, I called softly to him, "Tass!" giving him a friend's name, as we all did, for we all liked him. I liked him even though he stared at me.

He must not have heard me walking after him, for he jumped when I hailed him, badly startled, and crouched for a moment in the fighter's stance, a black shape in the dim starlit forest, before straightening as I came up to him.

"What do you want?" he greeted me sharply through the darkness, and if there was fear behind the edge in his voice I laid it to my having taken him unawares.

"I am sorry," I told him. "I did not mean to startle you."

"No harm," he said, though the bite of the words said otherwise. "You wish to speak with me?"

"Yes. I want to know why it is that you look at me." Though if he had questioned me I would have been hard put to describe the look, whether there was dislike in it, or dismay. There was much that was hidden in him, in Tassida.

But he did not question, or deny, or pretend not to understand. He stood silent, and when he spoke again, some few moments later, all the edge was gone from his voice and he spoke to me as quietly as I had spoken to him.

"Sometimes I think that I recognize you. That we have met before. Other times I am not sure."

I heard truth in the words and smiled, comprehending the doubtful look I had seen on him. "Have you visited my people, perhaps," I asked eagerly, "and seen me with them? But no, that cannot be. I would remember you." Oddity that he was.

"No. It has never been my honor to travel with the Red Hart Tribe."

"Where do you think you have seen me, then? When?"

"On these very mountains," he said with something secreted in his soft voice. "Last winter."

The trunks of pines in starlight appear black against air of misty dark gray. I noted it anew, turning my head away and staring off among the trunks of a hundred hundred such trees.

"The men tell me you do not remember," Tassida said.

"They speak truth. Though I would have sworn till now that if ever I had seen you, I would know it."

"It might not have been you. Are there many others such as you in your tribe?"

"One yellow-headed oaf is scarcely to be told from another, you mean?" Unfair of me to speak so harshly to him, for he was trying to be kind, but there was something very bitter in me. "Blood of Sakeema, it had to be me, the madman! No one in my tribe goes to the high peaks in the wintertime. What did I do?"

"What do you mean?" asked Tassida, too evenly.

"Some misdeed; I have done some untoward thing. I heard it in your voice. What was it?"

"Nothing," said Tass in a tone that warned me off. Whether for my sake or for his, he would not tell, and though he seemed scarcely more than a boy, his voice as high as a boy's voice, I heard such strong will in him that I knew I could never argue it out of him. So I did not try, but stood facing the night as if it were a barrier, wishing I could see his face, for he was like the pines in the night, a black shape, a blank, telling me nothing.

"I am not at all sure it was you," he added.

"Who else?" I muttered sourly, but he went on as if he had not heard me.

"No matter what you say, I am not sure. The looks were the same, but—you are so different, Dannoc, I—"

"Cold comfort," I cut in, "if it is in me to be so different."

"Think what you like, then." He was suddenly annoyed, the sharp edge back in his voice, as if to say, Go away with your complaining and let me cuck in peace. The matter is not worth being overly kind about. His vexation released me so that I grinned and left him to his business, making my way back through the dark pines, guided by the light of the fire where Kor waited. Nor did Kor ask me, then or later, what my errand with Tass had been, though he had seen me follow the boy into the darkness. He was youthful and wise, Kor.

So also was Tassida, wise beyond his years in his dealings with me. I sometimes regarded him curiously during the days that followed, wondering what he was, this youthful, homeless, tribeless wanderer, and I felt strangely drawn to him, liking him in spite of whatever secret lay between us. For his own part, he gave me a faint smile whenever he looked at me, and if he watched me, he also watched Kor, and all the others, with dark eyes that saw everything.

We climbed higher on the mountain slopes daily, until we reached heights where the clear mountain air was colder than cold had ever been in Seal Hold all winter long—and Shappa was the easy pass, lower than the rest. But my followers from Seal Hold shivered, for freezing cold seldom came to their home by the sea; they were not accustomed to it. In the starry nights we would have a blazing fire and gather around it with our pelts for sitting on and the thick blankets of good wool around our shoulders—even I would wrap myself in the blankets Istas had given me, so as not to be unlike the others, though under them my chest was as unclad as ever. And we would tell tales. And Tassida was our best storyteller, as it turned out, though among my people I was known as an ardent storyteller as well. But Tass knew tales I had never heard of. None of us had.

"You two remind me of Chal and Vallart," he remarked to Kor and me after watching us for a few days. The quiet glance of his eyes as he said it told us that it was meant as a good saying. He was giving us his friendship and trust. But we knew nothing of Chal and Vallart.

"Who?"

He blinked, seeming surprised that we did not know the names. "Legendary friends. Two heroes from the time when warriors wore the great metal swords."

"Wore what?"

"Swords." He spoke slowly now, as if uncertain whether he should have mentioned these strange things, whatever they were. "Great knives of bright metal, the glowing bronze, orichalc. There was a time, as long before Sakeema's time as Sakeema's time is long before ours, when warriors wore such swords, and robes of velvet cloth, and there were many other wonders, great fortresses of rock called castles, and large boats called ships that could carry many men across the ocean, far beyond the horizon, and return . . ." His voice trailed off as he saw the disbelief in our faces. "I thought you knew, Dannoc," he said to me. "You wear such a sword."

I brought it out, though the sight of it still harrowed me, and held it in both my hands, and it flashed flame-bright in the firelight, the yellow stone in the hilt glowing like a coal. "This comes to us from the time before Sakeema?" Kor demanded.

"Many generations of men before."

We could not dispute it with him, for I held the uncanny blade in my hands, but our minds were in a mighty uproar that stirred all our faces.

"Who are you, Tass?" It was Birc, at once shy and brash as ever, asking what Kor and I would not. "Or what are you, that you can tell us such things? Where are you from?"

The strange youth lowered his gaze to the ground. "Ask me anything but that," he mumbled.

"But—are there other tribes than the ones we know?" It

was one of the older guardsmen this time, a fellow named
Tohr, leaning almost into the fire with the force of his
query.

Tassida's eyes came up. "No," he said levelly. "There
are none. In all this vast land—and it is vast beyond
believing—there are only you six tribes left for Mahela's
maw."

Something in the ring of his voice spread silence over us
all, a silence that echoed with questions we could not
voice. We sat like a shaman's dolls of clay around the
fire, or like pebbles, like stones. Finally Kor stirred and
spoke.

"What of Chal and Vallart?" he asked mildly, taking
the talk back to the former matter.

"The legendary friends . . . There is a song that has
come down to us. Chal is the prince, and Vallart, the
comrade."

Tassida closed his eyes for a moment. The firelight
flickered on his still face. As if I had never seen him
before, I noticed how strange he was and how beautiful,
strong brows and a firm chin and a mouth recurved like an
antler-bow, strong features but so fine and even, unscarred,
that I wondered how young he was, perhaps no more than
a boy in spite of his cocksure air. Yet the seeming knowledge in him . . . Where could he have sprung from, his
hair light brown and gently curling in spiral locks, his eyes
startling and dark? Then he opened those eyes again, and
they were both young and as deep as time itself.

" 'Troth' is the name of it," he said.

And in a boy's high, strong voice he began to sing a
song that echoed out of the depths of time, the intervals
ranged in a mode so old I had never heard it.

> "Let me tell you a merry-go-sorry,
> Let me tell you a bittersweet tale
> Of a royal youth and his loyal companion
> Who pledged his friend his service and hand.
> 'My lord,' he said, 'you are made of legend.
> I will follow you to the ends of the land.'

'I have a quest to the Mountains of Doom,'
Said the prince, 'that lie beyond the dark tide.
Will you follow me there?' The other smiled.
'You doubt it, Liege? How can that be?'
'The way is long and the crossing strange.'
'I will follow you if you walk into that sea.

> What is a friend?
> Troth without end.
> A light in the eyes,
> A touch of the hand—
> I would follow you even to death's cold strand.'

So they rode afar to the kingdom's sea-reaches
And came in the end to the sundering strait,
And by that dim shore swam a ghost-gray ship
Low in the water but nothing within
Except shivering scent of fear insubstantial
And mournful voices of folk unseen.

'There is our vessel,' the prince said soft,
And toward it he strode. Then the follower blanched
And his breath came tight and his knees would not
    hold him,
He could not go on. Then, 'Liege—help me,'
He begged as he knelt on that far cold strand.
'I am not of the stuff of legends,' said he.

> A touch of the hand.
> 'I understand.
> For all friends fail,
> All loyalties end
> When they reach the end of the living land.

I will go alone. Now get you up,
Go home, be happy, live long and die merry.'
He kissed him, the kiss of forgiveness and love.
Then he boarded the death-ship. The vessel set sail,
The comrade stood still and watched it go.
In his ears rang a single living farewell.

For the prince yet lived where he stood inside.
And the gray ship sailed on the cold dark tide
Toward Mountains of Doom, harsh Mountains of
    Doom,
Heavy and slow on the dim washing water,
Then gone like a gray mist—how could that be?
The comrade stood on the land looking after.
Then he followed his prince—and walked into that
    sea.

> *What is a friend?*
> *Troth without end.*
> *A light in the eyes,*
> *A touch of the hand—*
> *I would follow you even to death's cold strand.*
> *To death's—cold—strand."*

None of us stirred or spoke when the song had ended. I sat deeply moved but afraid to meet Kor's eyes. That Tassida had compared us to these comrades was daunting. Still—I had said I would walk through fire for Kor. Was it so much worse to walk into the sea?

To me it was. Deep water, drowning deep . . .

I lifted my head at last and looked up to find him huddled next to me with a bemusement on his face that might have matched my own. He glanced at me with a look of terror and laughter.

"It is all very well that we're heartbound together, Dan," he said in most serious jest. "But if we are like Chal and Vallart, what is it to mean?"

"Well enough for you, still," I retorted in like wise. "The prince at least took the ship to his doom."

"Why do you say that? Which of us is the prince and which the follower?"

I had thought quite surely that he was the king and I, the afterling. Yet it was my quest we journeyed on, his look told me, at least in part, and I who led the way. The thought struck me to silence—I could no longer jest.

"They sank the dark mountains beneath the sea," said Tass after a small while, "somehow, and came back to the

land of the living. They were great kings. And they brought
back with them some sort of secret, some magic, so that
they kept living, they refused to stop. The story has it that
somewhere they are living yet. Chal was killed. . . .''

Tassida paused, thinking, and I knew the look on his
face because I had so often seen it on my father's face
beside an evening campfire when I was a child. He was
remembering another tale.

"It was when they were battling the warriors from the
east. Those who might well be the rootstock of our own
dear Fanged Horse Folk." Tassida quirked a wry smile at
the fire, and we all grinned. "The enemy warriors had no
swords, but they were many. Chal and Vallart and their
people were few, but with their swords they fought mightily.

"Indeed, their swords all but doubled their numbers, for
each one was centered as if it were alive. Each had been
shaped by its wielder and master and named while still
infant, in the making, with a gift of the maker's blood, so
that a bond was between the swords and their heroes like
the bond between blood brothers. And a sword so named
and so bonded could never be turned by an enemy against
someone the swordmaster loved, but would cleave to his
hand, come to his hand from afar if need be, and follow
the promptings of his heart.

"Vallart surged a bit to the fore in the battle, and many
enemy warriors faced him, pressing him on three sides, so
that he was hard beset and in mortal danger, and he began
to stagger. And when Chal saw his peril, though he was
paces away from him, his heart went out to Vallart in fear
for him, and where his heart went his sword went also, to
Vallart's defense. And the sword of its own accord, flying
more swiftly than any warrior hand could wield it, beat
back the foes that harried Vallart. Therefore, when the
battle had ended, Vallart was standing, his forces victori-
ous. But Chal, who had been left weaponless, lay dead of
many wounds.

"Then Vallart saw, and sank down by the side of his
slain friend." Tassida stared into the darkness above the
horizon as he spoke, seeming almost to see the legendary
friends of whom he told. "He took Chal's bloody and

lifeless body into his arms, and he wept, and could not be comforted. All the night he stayed that way, weeping, and no one could console him or persuade him to come away.

"And with the next day's dawning, Chal stirred and breathed, and at daybreak he was whole, and at sunrise he opened his eyes, sat up, and smiled. And he spoke, and got up and walked, and ate, and lived for many years more. Perhaps he yet lives somewhere. But no one knows how Vallart wrought the sorcery that gave Chal life after he was dead, or if he brought it back with him somehow from the Mountains of Doom."

Chapter Thirteen

All those days on the Traders' Trail we met scarcely any traders, and were too foolish to wonder why, but told ourselves it was because of the time of the year, spring just beginning in these uplands, the nights yet chill.

Up near the timberline, where the trees began to grow short and twisted, where snow still lay in the shadows of rocks and stunted spruces, we encountered our first Cragsman.

He was sitting on a ledge that overlooked our path, a great, bald-headed, slate-green lump of a man, naked, of course—they went naked always, even in the eversnow. We bare-chested Red Harts were mollycoddles compared to them. Their hair, when they grew any, resembled lichens, and their skin was of stone colors, gray, slate blue or green, dull red, and seemed as hard as the peaks. Folk said they were sprung from the stones, as indeed they might have been, for there were no women or children among them. Cragsmen were troublesome. Not evil, exactly, not as I later learned to know evil, but—feckless. As distant as sky. They did not care about those who dwelt below them, and they did not always act in ways we could expect, even of an enemy.

There he sat, in any event, by the way we had to pass, and there was no telling what greeting he held in store for us. I motioned the others to stop and sent Talu forward to meet him, as I had sometimes spoken with Cragsmen before.

"And what sort of traveler are you," he challenged me,

"who comes with the look of a Red Hart tribesman and the cropped head of those who call themselves cousins to seals and riding the steed of a Fanged Horse robber?"

I grinned, for I knew the Cragsmen could sometimes be amused. "And would you love me any the better if you knew what sort of traveler I was?" I retorted. I had no desire to tell him my name. We of the Red Hart had not always been on good terms with the Cragsmen.

He grunted, shifting his position slightly so that I had a glimpse of the huge blackwood club he carried. "What is your business in the Shappa Pass?" he demanded. The name of the pass meant "red thunder," and the names of the peaks on either side were Shadzu and Coru, "red cougar" and "antelope." So many places were named after the animals that no longer lived there, names that wrenched the heart. . . . What did he think I wanted in Shappa, to call up ghosts? Or slay them?

"Only to cross," I told him, treading as finely as I could the line of courtesy between arrogance and fear.

He grunted again, but seemed somehow mollified. "You know that you will pay the toll in order to pass here," he said.

Kor had come up beside me. "And what is the toll?" he asked.

"How should I know?" The Cragsman shrugged his giant gray-green shoulders at us. "But surely you will pay." With a lazy gesture he waved us onward.

By the next day we had made our way to the steep alps above the tree line. These high meadows have always seemed to me places of wonder, different from any other, full of small flowers of which I did not know the names, many sorts, very numerous, very beautiful, and strange mosses and herbs, they and the flowers all growing in low hummocks. Far above loomed the great slopes of sheer rock where the bearded mountain antelope had once lived, and the wild sheep yet did—we saw them sometimes, standing on the steepest cliffs, on tiny ledges of the steepest cliffs, as if they were on level ground. Above lay the eversnow, where even they did not venture. And above

again lay sky that made Kor gasp, of such a deep, pure
blue as he had never seen.

"The highmountain sky where the black eagles fly," I
chanted, remembering a snatch of an old song. Then I
frowned. "Where are they?" There were black butterflies
encircling the low masses of flowers along with others of
yellow and sable brown and blue, but there were no black
eagles encircling the peaks. Nor did I see any in the days
that followed.

We traversed those high meadows slowly, very slowly,
for the thin air made us all pant and strain with every
uphill step. Kor and I got down off our horses and walked
with the others, for the horses were puffing as well. But
we all laid most of our gear on the beasts. A day passed
this way. We slept huddled in every covering we had
brought with us, even the horses' riding pelts, and still
shivered in the chill.

"Deer!" Kor exclaimed as we set out in the morning.
"Above the tree line?"

Yes, I had known deer came to the highmountain meadows in the early summer to feed on the herbs. They were
only ordinary red deer such as I had always known, hinds
with fawns—calves, we called them, and we called the
deer "Sakeema's cattle." And harts in velvet—but mist
was steaming up from the meadows in the low morning
light, the sunlight very white and slanting at that height,
and in the mist and the brilliant light the deer looked like
wraiths out of the eversnow. We all stood watching them.

As we watched, one of them left the herd and trotted
toward us.

A shapely hind, very beautiful, white—I blinked. Yes,
the hind truly was of a creamy white, the color of snow in
a winter's clear sunset, not merely whitened by mist and
sheen. It trotted directly up to us as if to greet us or confer
with us, the most comely of hinds, delicate head held high
and its eyes steady upon us with no sign of fear—I felt my
own sharp intake of breath. The eyes, herb green, looked
very human, unlike any eyes of deer that I had ever seen.

" 'Ware! The thing's not natural. Stay away!" I warned,
and without looking away from it I reached out to make

sure Kor was beside me—he was. Tass stood still. I heard
the older men mutter darkly. But Birc, in that headlong
boyish way of his, had already moved even as I spoke.
Delighted, he had stepped forward, hand extended, and as
I shouted his name he touched the hind, caressed it on its
head, neck, and milky chest—

It was as if mist swirled before our eyes, and more
quickly than I can tell it the creature changed shape. A
comely maiden stood there, a woman with a mane of hair
the color of a red deer in sunlight, with delicate brows and
softly curving lips, every feature very fair, but her purple-
green eyes somehow no less strange in that human face.
She was naked, and all over her well-formed body grew
fine, pale fur like that of a fawn. And Birc was standing
with his hand on her breast.

"Birc," I cried at him, "back!"

The look on his face was rapt, smitten. He did not move
except to place his other hand around her waist.

I strode forward and snatched him away bodily—he
struggled against me. With a whizzing noise someone
hurled a knife—it was Tohr. The blow would have killed
the deer maiden in her human shape. But on the instant she
was a hind again, and she took the knife in the thick,
meaty swelling of her neck. She bounded away, leaving
splatters of blood bright on the herb leaves, and the knife
went with her, stuck to the hilt in her flesh.

"No!" Birc cried wildly, fighting to throw off my grip.
"No, let her be, let me go! She is—mine, my lifelove, my
destiny—"

I tried to reason with him. "How can you say that? You
have only just the once seen her."

"The thing's a demon," Tohr growled.

"Let me go!" Birc started to sob. "Sakeema, she is
running away, how will I find her again!"

"Tie him up," said Kor softly, reluctantly, "and sling
him over one of the horses."

We did so, putting him on gentle Calimir, and Birc
protested through the day, shouting, sobbing, and cursing
us by turns, and refused to eat or drink. It was a wretched
day. Even being among my own beloved peaks again did

not much cheer me. Not far beyond the pass, just south of
the shortgrass steppes, lay the high valley, the Demesne of
my people. It did not matter. Nothing seemed to matter
much while Birc lay crying. I had not realized how much I
liked him.

Kor walked by his head and tried to talk to him. It made
no difference. After a while I remembered that the look on
Kor's face, a taut, pale look, was not merely the sem-
blance of my own discomfort. Whatever anguish Birc was
feeling, likely Kor felt as well. My heart sank, but I could
not go to him to comfort him, not before the others, for
they did not know his secret.

By nightfall Birc had exhausted himself, and though he
would not eat, we hoped he would sleep. Tohr spoke up
for the first turn at guard, and the rest of us welcomed the
mercy of slumber. We all slept numbly, deeply.

In the morning, when we awoke, Tohr lay dead, his
own knife sheathed to the hilt in his chest, and Birc was
gone.

The six of us who remained stared at each other for a
time. I privately thought of the Cragsman's words concerning a toll and hoped that this was the total of it. It was
not a thought to be spoken. Kor finally broke silence.

"Well," he said heavily, "I cannot just let him go. Can
you track him, Dan?"

I circled our camp. The only trail, leading back the way
we had come, was that of a deer. The pointed marks of the
hooves were deeply pressed.

"He rode her," I murmured in wonder.

The trail was plain enough to follow, and after we had
raised a cairn over Tohr we spent the better part of the day
tracing it back. Birc's mount was swift. If they had kept
going we would never have caught up to them, afoot. But
they had stopped and undertaken mounting of a different
sort, in human form. When we found them they lay pressed
together and deeply asleep in a mossy dell between rocks.
My heart misgave me to see them so, naked, like two
innocents, at our mercy. Kor and I crept up and laid hands
on Birc as gently as we could without losing him, and the
deer maiden sprang up, took her hind form and fled. No

one offered to harm her this time. A crust of blood stood brown on her neck, and I flinched at the sight of it.

Birc wept, but he no longer cursed us. Indeed, he seemed to have lost the power of speech. Hands bound behind him, he walked with us through what was left of the day, silent except for his sobbing, no matter how gently Kor spoke to him. That night, though we had bound Birc hand and foot, we all kept vigil, forming a circle around him, and all night Birc bleated out soft troating cries, like the cries of a rutting hart. Those cries pierced my heart. Next to me I felt Kor trembling, and from time to time I would reach over and touch his shoulder, trying to comfort him.

At the first light of dawn we could see the hind standing at a small distance, very fair, very white and spiritlike in the dim break of day. Birc saw her as well and sat up, sending to her his bleating call.

"Kor," I said, "look."

I went to Birc and parted his forelock, showing Kor what I had seen. Just at the hairline above either eye stood a bony knob, and growing from each one, the beginnings of an antler in velvet.

All the men gathered around and saw, and their faces turned bleak. Birc gave his troating call. From out of the dawn the hind bleated in answer, stepping delicately closer.

Kor loosened Birc's bindings, slipping them off his arms and legs. Birc stood up eagerly, but Kor detained him yet a moment longer, embracing him and giving him the kiss of a king.

"Farewell," he muttered, releasing him, and Birc bounded away.

With a single vaulting leap he was on the hind's back, his feet hanging down over her shoulders. Then with a high, joyous, springing stride she carried him off, not fleeing but rather, I thought, delighting in his weight. Up the slope to the beginning of the naked rock they went, and as the hind paused for a moment there, looking behind her, the sun reached over the shoulder of the mountain and touched her. I have always remembered that sheen of light on her, on Birc, like fire of passion. . . . Kor lifted his hand, and the hind raised her head, but Birc made no gesture of salute, sitting entranced on her back. Then around the angle of the rock they went, and we lost sight of them against the blaze of the eversnow.

We who remained went on with our journey, and for the full day no one spoke.

We crossed the high pass, then descended nearly to the tree line, and our breathing grew easier. The next day we put away our sorrow and started talking to each other again. The trees comforted us, though they were not spruce and fir but the great yellow pines that grew on arid slopes—for we were on the shadowland side of the mountains now. They were spaced far apart, making glades and parks where deer might graze. That night, once again amidst trees and mountainside meadows, we made ourselves a blazing fire of deadwood pine.

"Do not think too badly of the deer people," I told the company. "We of the Red Hart call them blessed. Perilous, yes, but very beautiful, and blessed. There is a tale of the deer people and Sakeema."

"Tell it," Kor said.

It was only a small tale.

"When Sakeema lay dying, all the creatures of forest and meadow came to him and pleaded with him to live, but he had given up all the life that was in him. He died. Then, as he lay dead, the creatures stayed by him and mourned him, among them the deer he had cherished, the red deer and also the great elk and the spotted deer, the yellow deer with spreading antlers, the blue deer of Sakeema's making, and all the many other kinds now gone. They kept vigil as women washed the body and prepared it for burial. Then the deer wept. Real tears welled out of their eyes and crept down the fine fur of their cheeks, and the people, the few people who were brave enough to be there, saw this and gave way, and the deer gathered close around Sakeema as he lay dead. And as the tears fell on his still body Sakeema started to breathe, and his body grew warm. Then the deer wept anew for joy. But no one could awaken Sakeema as he lay still and slept. So some of the deer took human form and placed Sakeema

on the backs of some others, and the deer bore him away
to the mountain cave where he had been born. He sleeps
there yet, and some time when we need him worst, it is
said, he will awaken and come back to us in a way we
least expect. . . . But ever since they wept over Sakeema
the deer take human form from time to time, my people
say, though they never speak to us.''

"If they could speak to us," someone remarked, "they
could tell us where Sakeema lies."

"Yes," I said heavily, "but they cannot." Yearning for
Sakeema burned hot in me, for I was remembering remnants of a vision.

"The Herders tell a tale of the mother of Sakeema,"
said Tassida.

"Mother of Sakeema!" It was one of the guardsmen.
"What tale can be told of her, the bitch?"

"Bitch, indeed, but also the goddess. It was the All-
Mother, they say, the old goddess whose name has been
forgotten, she who spun out the wool of which the world is
made and dyed it in colors too many to name and wove out
the world on her loom of sky, she who gave the Herders
their sheep as brown as earth with the six horns to signify
the six tribes, her children. She who gave the Herders clay
to form and red stone to carve and burros gray as mountains. This goddess looked down where the world spread
out like a great blanket to meet the sky, saw the greens and
browns and grays and yellows of it, saw men moving on
the surface of it and knew that all was not entirely right.
There were some angry things she had done and some
things of wonder she had not made, and thus men had
forgotten her name. So she sat down on the plains far
beyond the thunder cones—for only the grassy plains were
vast enough to hold her—and she conceived Sakeema from
white of cloud and blue of sky, and she gave birth. And
she gave the babe over to the keeping of a she-wolf, one of
the red she-wolves of the prairie, and she, the All-Mother,
went away again and left the righting of the world to
Sakeema. So it was that Sakeema loved creatures always,
and when his powers came to him he created creatures not

in the blanket colors only but also in blues and whites, as of cloud and sky.''

We all glanced at each other, thinking of the blue bears of Sakeema, the blue deer, the white sea eagles. The tale rang true, but because it came from the Herders some of us wished to fault it.

"These men with the great knives, the swords, of whom you once spoke,'' someone asked, "were they also the get of this goddess?''

"Ah,'' said Tassida, "that is another matter.'' And he leaned back, looked up at the sky above the treetops and told us tale after tale of the wonders of the time long before Sakeema. In that time, he said, all people wore glorious robes, all woven, not of wool only but of a shining substance called silk, and of a plant fiber called linen. And their tools and weapons were made of metal, a substance unknown to us, and those who remembered these people said they were full of magic and constantly performed marvels. They hewed the solid stone and raised great dwellings of it, all towers and walls, castles, and they built cairns like small mountains over their dead. He himself had seen on the plains the ruins of such dwellings and monuments, Tassida told us.

"Were these people like you?'' Kor asked him. "Light of hair and dark of eyes?''

"They were of many sorts of coloring, for there were as many sorts of people as there were many tribes: colorings and kinds of people you have never heard of. And the tribes were not tribes as you know them, Korridun King. The people of one small tribe might number a hundred villages or more. Such a king as you are would be reckoned only a petty chieftain of one small village by the kings of that time.''

"You mean—'' Kor struggled with this. "You mean the people of a king were so numerous that they could not all live in one village?''

"Even so.''

"But then how could he or she know them, to rule them properly?''

"These kings ruled by law, not by knowing. And there were no women among them."

Kor shook his head in speechless bewilderment. "But how many tribes of this sort were there?" one of the guardsmen asked.

"Many. Enough so that there were few places in all the vast land that did not have people to hunt them or till them or fish them."

"But these diverse people must have been as many as the stars of the sky," I protested.

"They were more numerous than the stars of the sky," said Tass.

None of us believed much of this, except perhaps Tassida, but it made a good tale and a way to beguile the evening.

"They made great boats of wood, boats great enough to carry a village," Tass went on, "and they put tall trees on them to take great sails, and they sailed them on the ocean. They sailed to distant islands, places we can no longer name or find, and they returned with strange creatures and marvelous fruits. And they grew the fruits in warm places inside their great stone houses, in courtyards covered with a roof clear as air, so that the sun could shine in and they could have fruits in the wintertime."

"A roof of air," someone mocked.

"Yes," said Tass fiercely. "Clear as air, but hard, and not letting in the cold. And they had boxes of stone, hot from the hearth, to cook their bread in. And they played music on great harps so large they sat on legs on the floor. Their homes were full of music. And they covered their floors and their walls with pictures made out of colored stones. I know this to be true, for I have seen the ruins of them. Other stones they wrought into shining shapes called jewels. Not the soft red stones such as the Herders carve, but hard, shining stones fit to cut with, such bright stones as the one in your knife hilt, Dannoc. And they had a stuff the color of the sun and nearly as shining: gold, they called it, and it was the most precious of all things to them. They made headbands of it called crowns, headbands with jewels set in, and their kings wore them with their shining clothing. And armbands and rings, finely wrought things

of all sorts they made out of it. They raised tame song-
birds, kept them in cages of the sunstuff called gold, and
they fashioned gardens meant only for beauty, where flowers grew and swans swam.''

''And I suppose they raised beautiful horses,'' said Kor
quite softly.

Tass gave him a startled glance and half opened his
mouth as if to speak, but did not.

''What has become of these wondrous folk, Tassida?''
asked Kor, his voice no louder than a breath of wind.
''They who tamed stone and sea, even the birds of the
air?''

''They dwindled, as all has dwindled,'' answered Tassida
just as softly, ''and their stone dwellings fell to ruin, and
their horses ran wild, and their great boats bleached into
firewood on the shore. They are gone. Gone. I have
searched and searched for them and I have found only their
empty houses, open to wind and rain.''

''And a certain horse,'' Kor mused. ''And now a sword.''

Tassida gathered a pelt around himself as if he were
cold, and did not answer. Kor sat staring at the boy's fair,
strange face.

We did not question him any further, for we were weary
of mysteries. We sat long by the fire that night, talked
much—though not of Birc—and grew warm and merry,
for who or what was there to hurt us anymore? On the
morrow, after we had passed the final rocky ridge, we
would be at the reaches of the high plateau, the steppes,
and just southward lay the fringes of the hunting lands, the
Demesne, of my people.

Chapter Fourteen

In the morning Kor took the lead. Talu was in heat and, bitch of a fanged mare that she was, she kicked at the gelding when he walked behind her, though Calimir was as gentle and courteous as he was beautiful. So the mare and I brought up the rear. A hot wind was blowing down from the mountains, as hot as the mare's temper, and I knew it could go on for days, sapping our strength. Witch winds, we hunters called such hot and relentless winds out of the west, and they were enough to make lifelong friends come to blows—the Herders said they made the sheep abort their lambs. But I did not tell the others this, letting them hope that it would quickly abate. Soon enough, in a day or two, they would be downhearted.

As it turned out, sooner than I knew.

We came to the last ridge, lower than the true peaks, and climbed to a rocky pass. Up on the alps we had been most of the time above cloud, but from this lower nagsback we could see the world spread out before us like a cloak trailing from the shoulders of the mountains, and the cloak was sand-brown and pebble-gray and patched with the dull green of blunderbrush—we hunters called it that because woe to the one who blundered into it, he would be bloody from brown thorns. Nearly everything was brown or yellow-brown on the steppes, even the grass—but there was more sand and rock than grass, which grew sparse and short. The yellow pines ended at the ridge, but a few twisted junipers grew beyond, looking no larger than brush balls in the great distances of the expanse that lay before us. The reaches of the sere plateau looked oddly pale against the darker blue sky.

"Drink sparingly of your water," I told the others, for although the rippling line of the greener hills to southward did not look far, perhaps a day's journey, I knew it might be much farther. Where there were no trees, there was no telling.

Still gazing, more in shock than in wonder, Kor felt for the goatskin full of water that hung at his knee. "But what has happened!" he exclaimed. "A day ago all was verdant."

"We have left the snowfields, where the snowmelt feeds the meadows," I told him. "And here little rain falls. These are the lands that lie in the shadow of the tall peaks. Water falls to the seaward side of the mountains and does not carry inland."

"But the upland valleys of your people—" He pointed east and southward, where he judged the place lay. "—they also lie on the landward side of the peaks."

I shrugged. "We bear Sakeema's blessing, and the rain finds its way to us."

Near my shoulder, Tassida snorted. "The line of the mountains curves away from the sea," he said rather too curtly for courtesy, "and the passes channel the clouds to you."

"Is that not Sakeema's blessing?" I retorted. "It is as well for us," I added before he could speak, "that we roam there and the Fanged Horse Folk here on the shadowlands."

"And the Herders," said Kor.

"Sometimes. But much farther eastward." I pointed, though I could see nothing but a low rise looming yellow-gray against the blue sky. "For the most part they stay near the thunder cones." The oddly shaped mountains that sometimes rumbled and vomited fire, that wore skirts of blackstone around their feet. "Sometimes they venture to the edges of the great plain that lies beyond. But that is a vast flatness even more arid than this. There no one goes."

"Am I no one?" asked Tass bitterly.

"Tell us the tale in the evening," said Kor. "For now, spare talking to spare water." He squared his shoulders and led us down from the ridge, between the last of the yellow pines.

Downward, into the open—

The Fanged Horse warriors struck out of the woods with a rush like storm, galloping at us from three sides, and Pajlat himself rode at their head, his black hair streaming like oily smoke and all his teeth bared in a killer's smile.

"Ho! Korridun, little king!" he greeted, his heavy whip of bisonhide already upraised.

"Calimir!" Tass shouted to the horse. "Fight!"

The gelding reared, striking out with his forehooves at Pajlat's vicious fanged mare, and Kor took the whip on his shoulder instead of his face, where it had been aimed. I saw how he was shaken by the force of the blow, but he kept his seat, clinging to Calimir's mane. Pajlat's warriors went at the men on foot, intent on trophies—the heads of victims dangled by the hair from their bearskin riding pelts. Kor had his knife out, but such a small blade would avail him little against the long reach of Pajlat's weapon, even less against the stone-headed clubs and spears of the others. And he knew nothing of how to use his horse in battle, for the Seal were not horseback riders. Calimir whirled and darted, keeping foes to the fore, but the fangs of the enemy steeds were coming at him, the mares roaring like their masters, deadly as so many horned bison—

And under me Talu was roaring as well, and springing forward, and slashing with her fangs, opening a path to take me to Kor's side, and the great knife, the sword, was ablaze in my hand.

I felt odd, very odd, as if there were two of me. It was the only way I could manage to do what I had to do, I was so deeply afraid. Terrified—not of death and battle, but of my own weapon, the great knife, the strange sword, and of the murderer it might awaken in me, and of memory. But for Kor's sake . . . And so it was that I saw the battle as if I sat aside and watched, and all the while my arm, my sword, and my steed did destruction.

But there were too many of them in the way, the raiding scum, too many between me and Pajlat's filthy face. There must have been a dozen or more of them against our six!

They trampled down the men on foot as if they were so much grass. And I could not soon enough get to Korridun's side, and I could have cried out as I saw Pajlat's sickening whip curl around his back. So far Calimir had kept the lash away from Kor's face, but if Kor weakened under those blows he would fall—

Astonished, I saw Tassida sidestep an attacker's charge, turn and seize Calimir's tail, vaulting over the gelding's rump to sit behind Kor. Saving his own life? Perhaps, but it was well thought of. With his heels and his shouts the boy directed the horse to greater advantage, and his back protected the king's. And there were now two knives instead of one—

And at last I was there, sinking my sword deep into the side of an attacker—the man's face took on a surprised look as he died. And Kor caught up his great club as it fell.

After that no one could come near him. He was strong, and roused, and as skilled a fighter as I had ever met, and his steed swifter and lighter of foot than any heavy-headed mare the high plains had ever fed. Tassida defended his back with a knife in either hand, urging Calimir on with a high, chilling yell. As for me, I struck down the Fanged Horse raiders one after another as coldly as if I were cutting down targets of straw. Pajlat kept away from me. He was afraid of the strange weapon, the sword, and so were his men, but they were afraid of their king's lash and his wrath as well, so they fought more bravely than he. No one knew I was the most terrified of anyone there. I had gone into a trance of killing, thinking only to clear this enemy out of the way, but all the while I stood aside and watched myself and cowered in fright.

Kor told me afterward that my coolness was terrifying. They stood against us so long, he thought, only because they were ashamed to leave us triumphant, the mere three of us against all of them.

But when I had hacked and whittled them down to five plus one, the one being Pajlat, they fled.

I could not comprehend it at first. Talu wanted to pursue

them, and we did so for a short while, but then I pulled her to a halt and blinked. Kor! Where was Kor?

He was not badly hurt. He had walked Calimir aside from the heap of bodies strewn amidst the blunderbrush and the short grass. He had dropped his club. But he still sat the gelding, and his face looked stricken.

"Help me with Tass!" he shouted at me.

The youth sat slumped against Kor's back—dead? There was blood everywhere, drenching the boy's clothing. I leaped down off of Talu, stumbling in my haste, surprised to find that my legs were shaking under me, and as gently as I could I got Tassida down from behind Kor. I laid him on the stony ground. At once Kor was beside me, kneeling and reaching over to feel at the pulse of the throat.

"He's breathing," I said.

"Yes, he lives. . . . Is he wounded? So much blood, he must be!" Frantically the two of us tore open his tunic, searching for the wound. For some reason Tassida wore a strip of binding around his chest. Kor yanked it away—

"Dan," he whispered in a small, stunned voice.

I saw in the same moment. Round, perfect breasts, pink-tipped, uninjured. Tassida was a maiden.

He—she might yet be hurt. Kor knelt by her as if frozen, useless. Clenching my teeth, I tore away her trousers, found no wound, pulled her up against my chest to look at her back. Three ugly whip weals, but they had not drawn blood. No, she was not wounded, or not badly, and as I moved her she groaned and pulled away from me. I laid her down, took off my cloak and put it over her. Within the moment she opened her eyes and stared up at us.

"Did you kill Pajlat?" she demanded of me.

I moved my mouth to reply, discovered I was speech-less, and shook my head.

"Blast." Tassida muttered a curse of pain as she sat up, then looked down at herself and burst into louder profanity. "Bowels of Sakeema! Was it necessary to strip me?"

"We thought you were half killed," Kor whispered. He seemed quite shaken. "There was so much blood. . . ."

"I was hit on the head, that was all. It must have

been someone else's blood, horse blood—Calimir! How is Calimir?''

I got up and went to look at the gelding, for I was glad enough of the excuse to get up and move around, clear my mind. Calimir bore many slashes from the fangs of the enemy steeds, and he had bled much, but a horse can bleed a puddle's worth and take no harm from it. None of the wounds looked deep. As for Talu, there was not a scratch on her.

"Flesh wounds," I called back over my shoulder to Tass. "He carries his head high enough."

Kor finally stirred where he knelt by her side. "Bring her some clothes, Dan," he called to me. His voice sounded strained.

Birc's pack had been loaded on Talu. I untied it and took it to Tassida, then touched Kor on the shoulder. Dazedly he looked up at me, then came with me to see to the bodies. They were all killed and already growing cold, the other three who had been with us. So also were all of Pajlat's men dead, and most of them beheaded. The sight made me uneasy, and hastily I went to the place where I had laid down my weapon, wiped the blood from it and sheathed it in the leather scabbard Kor had made me.

After a short while Tassida walked up to us, clothed in Birc's spare tunic and leggings, to all appearances a boy again, except that she had not bound her breasts. They made a small, soft showing under the fine wool of her tunic, and I tried not to stare. She handed my cloak back to me with a nod.

"Your head?" Kor asked hoarsely. He had not spoken to me at all—he seemed stupid with shock or fatigue.

"Hurts," Tassida said briefly. "It was a glancing blow, or I would be dead."

"You saved my life," Kor said. She looked at him in surprise.

"And my own."

All was awkwardness, for there was a matter that had to be broached. "Tass," I asked her, "why did you not tell us you were a maiden?"

She shrugged. "I always travel as a youth. It is more comfortable than sleeping with a knife in hand."

"My men are honorable," Kor said, too hotly.

"Were honorable. But all men are not so." Something passed across her face, some memory's shadow, quickly hidden. She faced Kor, appearing sure of herself to the point of arrogance. "And would you have taken me with you, Korridun King, if you had known I was a woman?"

He made no reply—I had never seen him so floundering. "We of the Red Hart welcome maidens as our fellow warriors," I blurted, just for something to say. Tass looked me full in the face and grinned.

"I understand you welcome maidens at all times and in all places, Dannoc," she mocked. "You nearly caught me with my trousers down, that night in the blue pine forest. Must I take a knife to my bed, now that you have had them off me?"

"Of course not!" Kor flared at her. Such vehemence was not needed, or usual in him—what was the matter with him? Quickly I spoke to Tassida again.

"Will you tell us your real name, now?"

"You know my name," she said. "What name I have."

"And where you are from, of what tribe—will you tell us that, now that we know your secret?"

"I cannot."

"Will not, you mean," I retorted, though not harshly, for I felt no anger at her.

"Not so. Dannoc, I cannot tell you what I do not know myself."

"What?" I stared at her, flirting with an unlikely thought. "You mean you cannot remember?"

"That is your problem, Dannoc, is it not?" She shot a crooked smile at me. "No, I remember well enough. I have traveled most of my life, far beyond the thunder cones, beyond the vast plains, even, seeking my tribe. I have found the ruins of ancient dwellings, but I have never found a people like me, or any people except those meager six with their stone knives. So I have no tribe, to my knowledge."

"But where were you born?" I insisted. "Of what mother?"

She turned away from me, and that was all the satisfaction we had from her.

We took what we could use from the bodies, and especially we searched out all the water they bore. The bodies of Pajlat's raiders we left for the kites, but we took the bodies of our comrades to a place apart and piled the loose stones over them to shelter them—it was all we could do for them. Then we marked the place with a broken spear and thought we were finished, but there was one more pitiful thing left to be tended to.

We did not know it until Kor went and caught himself a new mount. At a distance a fanged steed had been caught in gorse by its trailing reins. Kor strode over, untangled it and vaulted on with a fierce, set look on his face that silenced me when I would have cautioned him—I felt sure the half-wild mare would throw him or, worse, slash at him. But he rode it over to where Tass and I stood by the cairn, waiting, and he made his fanged mare stand while he cut at some fastening on the bearskin riding pelt at his far knee. Not until he lifted a shriveled trophy head into our view did I comprehend his haunted glance.

A dark-haired head, either Otter or Seal, with a contorted face telling how the person had died in pain even though it was so withered that little else could be told, whether it was man or woman, old or young, warrior or slave. Kor cradled the gruesome thing in both his hands, as if to somehow soothe it with his touch, then leaned down from his mount and gently set it atop the cairn. All the dignity of a king was in that gesture, and all his inborn comity, so that the thing seemed laid to rest even before Tass and I covered it with slabs of stone—I could scarcely bear to look at it, let alone touch it as Kor had done, stench of death clinging to his hands, and had it been a yellow-haired head hung to the bearskin by knotted braids I think I would not have been able to come near it.

What was this king, this Kor? It no longer seemed remarkable to me that the fanged mare, his new mount, obeyed him.

With a low, sweet whistle Tassida called Calimir to her, and in silence we journeyed on southward and eastward.

We rode until dusk, uneasy, anxious without reason to leave the strewn bodies of the Fanged Horse raiders far behind. The hot wind blew at our backs without ceasing. Tass suffered more than she would admit from her hurt head, and when we stopped at last she lay down at once, without eating. Heedlessly she went to sleep, though we were benighted in a place with no shelter of any sort—not even a juniper stood near us. There was nowhere to hide, not even a dry waterway or a ravine. I ate, and tried to talk with Kor but got not much sense out of him except that he would keep watch. That said, I also went to sleep.

Sometime in the moonlit mid of night I awoke and saw that Kor was gone. Half alarmed, I got up and went looking for him. At no great distance from the camp I found him sitting as if a demon rode on his shoulders, with his head bowed to his knees.

I sat next to him and waited.

"The toll is paid," he muttered after a while.

"I should hope so," I said fervently.

It did not occur to me that more troubled him than loss of life. He loved his folk, I knew that, and it hurt him to give them over to death. As for me, I had my own feelings to deal with. In my right mind, I had never enjoyed killing. . . . I sat by him, silent, glad of his presence, for a long time.

When the moon was low he lifted his head, faced me, and spoke. "I am in thrall," he said. His eyes were dry, so dry they seemed to burn, his face quiet and grave. "I am doomed, as doomed as was Birc at his first sight of the deer maiden. Tassida has enslaved my heart."

If it had been anyone else, a younger brother, a shy youth such as Birc, I would have smiled. But it was Rad Korridun, and I felt my own heart stop. The hot wind blew through the night with a sound like a sigh.

"Kor—"

"I will never be able to love any maiden but her."

"But Kor," I faltered, "how can you say that? You have only just today—met her. . . ."

"You know as well as I, what I say is true. It is fated."
He dropped his head to his knees again. "*Ai*, Dan, I am
sick and stupid with longing. I go hot and cold. I ache.
What am I to do?"

I laid a hand on his shoulder. "Court her," I said.

"I am afraid."

"Why fear? Only good can come of it."

As if to make a mockery of my words, something came
in the way of the moonlight. Three devourers rippled
through the night as we huddled to the ground in fear at
the sight of them. I had never felt so nakedly exposed to
danger. But they skimmed over us without a sound, flying
eastward, casting their shadows over our camp and over
the place where Tassida lay sleeping before they were gone.

Chapter Fifteen

"Three of them," said Kor heavily, in the morning.

"Three of what?" It was Tass, stumbling to her feet, still hazy from sleep.

"Devourers."

Her eyes snapped fully open. "Here?"

"Over the camp, last night." If he was smitten with her, he was not showing it at that moment. His mind was on peril, and so was mine.

"Things cannot be well with my father's tribe," I said, "if they have let Pajlat and his raiders range so near the Demesne. And seeing the devourers does not comfort me, either."

"So much for our thought that there might be but the one," Kor muttered.

Tassida was rolling her gear into her blanket with some haste. Her face was taut.

"Tass," Kor asked her suddenly, "what do you know of the devourers?"

She stiffened where she knelt with her bedroll, stopped what she was doing, and looked at him. The look showed nothing to me, but it must have to him.

"I can tell you have encountered them," he said very gently. "What was it that they tried to do with you, as you are a woman?"

A panicked, stricken glimmer in her eyes, though her face had not moved. Quickly gone, like the shadow of a flying thing, but Kor nodded as if she had answered him.

"Knives are of no use against them," he said.

"I know it." She turned back to her bedroll, tying it savagely tight.

"I would sooner die than be attacked by one again," she added in a low voice.

"Has it happened to you more than once?"

"No." She turned back to him, and this time her look was quiet—she had yielded a trust to him. "But I have seen the devourers as many as twelve at a time."

"Sakeema help us!" That sent him to his feet. "Where?"

"Over the western sea."

"It is my thought," I said, rising also, "that we had better come to my father in all haste." A child's hope was in me that he would somehow be able to help us, though I could not have said how. I always thought well and warmly of my father, those days, and I thought of him often.

Kor, I now know, expected no aid of Tyonoc of the Red Hart Tribe. But he was mindful of Pajlat and his raiders, and therefore quite willing to ride hard. So was Tassida. We rode, the three of us, with the hot wind at our backs like storm of passion.

Kor had little chance for courting that day. We rode for the most part in a trance of misery, the sun scorching us out of a sky that glared so blue we saw it as a white shimmer of heat, while the wind licked at us like flame. Sweat oiled our faces and salted our lips and eyes. We drank water as sparingly as we were able, but still we emptied waterskins, slit them open and gave our mounts to drink, threw the spent skins away. The horses lagged, their heads nodding low, the tender skin of their faces blistered and bleeding from sun and hot wind, even the fanged mares as sapped as we were. Kor's captured mare was a homely nag the color of yellow clay but for her reddish legs. Blowing sand had scoured the legs so that raw skin showed through the russet hair. Still the nag walked on willingly.

"You have not yet named your mare," Tassida remarked to Kor.

He shook his head at her, smiling in spite of his cracked and swollen lips. All his love for her showed in that smile, but if she saw it, she gave no sign.

"Name her! She will go even better for you."

"There is no time for a vigil," Kor said.

"And no need! Name her now, as we ride."

"Is that how you named Calimir?"

A quiet. There was only the clopping of the horses' hooves on stony ground.

"Would you tell us sometime, Tass, how you came by him? And where?"

She shook her head violently. "You people," she burst out, hot as the wind, "you believe nothing I tell you!" Then she put heels to Calimir's sides and sent him trotting some distance ahead of us, flinging her hair back in the proud gesture that already we well knew.

I watched her with rueful admiration. Kor rode silently beside me, and I could tell that he was watching her as well. "The mettle of her," he murmured. "It must take courage for her to play the boy among men."

"That, and a strong bladder!" I blurted. "She has never made excuses for a halt, gone off among bushes. . . ." Then I recalled how many times I had bared my cock before her as before the others and relieved myself against a trailside tree, and I felt flaming heat take my face, as if I had drawn too near a hearth. Kor was regarding me curiously.

"I have never known you to blush, Dan," he remarked.

"Mother of Sakeema!" It was a new-learned curse, and I was fond of it.

"Not even when Birc surprised you and Lumai up in the spruces, and teased you in front of Winewa."

"My modesty is of a different sort," I retorted.

I thought at the time that I was telling him the truth. Not until the second day did I let myself admit I had blushed for love of Tassida.

There were many passions in me, clashing like surf: sorrow for Birc and the others we had lost, longing for my father, worry about him and my people lest all did not go well with them. And the aching wound I could not name but had borne for months. And care for Kor. Above all, that fear and hope for Kor. If only Tass would return his regard . . .

So it was a new grief to me when I heard the song throbbing in my blood—I could no longer help hearing it—and knew that I myself might be his rival.

It did not have to happen, I told myself. I had known many women, and sometimes even denied myself one, or been denied, and all such passions had passed. I would say nothing, and this one would pass also.

The hot wind still blew.

"A day or so more of this," I told Kor and Tass, "and we ought to be out of sparse grass and into green again." Neither of them answered me—a day or two seemed all too long, at the time. Talu snorted, perhaps in scorn, then snorted again, surging forward, and this time I heard her rightly. It was fear.

"It is nothing but your own shadow!" I scolded her, for there was nothing moving anywhere near, not even the snakes that she and Kor's fanged mare hunted at night to sustain themselves. Asps liked the heat no more than we did. They went under rocks in the daytime, and sometimes when we stopped the mares would paw them out and munch them. . . . Calimir might shy from a serpent, but it would not be a snake that had frightened Talu.

As if he had heard my thought, the gelding took up the same tune, snorting and leaping in his turn. And then Kor's nameless mare. "Easy!" he exclaimed. He himself was not yet completely easy on horseback.

"Something is wrong," Tass said.

Then finally, stupid as I was with the heat and my own perplexities, I comprehended what it might be and turned to look behind us. Kor did the same.

The length of the horizon, something like a dark mist drifted into the sky.

"Is that smoke?" Kor asked, not wishing to believe it.

Still staring, I nodded.

"But—but it is immense! The whole of the steppes must be on fire!"

"Yes. Come, we must ride more quickly." I put Talu into the lope. She wanted to break into a hard, panicky gallop, but I would not allow that, or not yet. The others rode with me.

"The wind is swift," I warned. "The fire may well travel as fast as we do." Or faster. I had seen the charred carcasses of deer caught by such fires, but I did not speak that thought.

"Did Pajlat plan it so, do you think?" Kor asked, his voice grim.

I had not considered that. "Perhaps."

"Perhaps not," said Tass in her clear voice. "Such fires chance all too often. The shadowlands are dry, any spark can cause one. Even a spark carried by this wind."

I glanced back. At a distance, flames shot up from a lone juniper.

"Hotwind wildfire, folk call it," I said.

I turned Talu to place the wind behind my right shoulder. If we loped mostly southward, perhaps we would be able to outflank the fire. Perhaps not. We no longer rode directly away from it, and it drew closer behind us. I had no need to look back—I could smell the smoke, as Talu smelled it, snorting. But Kor looked back.

"Let us ride faster," he said in a voice carefully controlled. I heard the taut control. Such fire must have been as strange and fearsome to him as the rolling waves of the ocean were to me. Therefore he was afraid. For my own part I did not feel very much afraid, though there was no denying that we were in peril.

"No," I said, "save the steeds' best strength for when we need it worst. This is apt to seem a long day, Kor." We turned our backs to the wind again, cantering straight before the fire, and we did not gain on it.

"Is there nothing to stop it?" he called to me over the dry noise of hooves. "A stream? A ditch, even?"

"Not likely," I said. "Tass?"

She shook her head, riding silently, rocking as if she were a part of Calimir's smooth canter, long legs pressed around his barrel and her hair rippling out in lovelocks behind her.

We loped along for hours, sometimes veering southward, sometimes trotting straight before the wind to rest the horses, though they wanted little rest—they were plainly frightened, their ears tilted back toward the danger behind us, their eyes rolling whitely as they swung their heads from side to side, trying to watch it. But they loped on steadily and bravely, and from time to time Kor reached out to pat his mare on her sweaty neck—a gesture rare in him, for he was not much accustomed to horses.

"She has a name now," he told us. "Sora. The wild-fire. She runs as swiftly as the flames."

"So we hope," I said dourly, but Tass surprised us both with a smile.

"Her legs are red, like the heart of fire, and the rest of her is yellow, her mane like the tips of flame. It is a good name for her."

"To be sure, she is a beauty," I said, trying to jest, for Sora was every bit as ugly as Talu but for her color. May she carry you to safety, was my unspoken thought.

The fire dogged our heels, relentless, hungry, until it drew so close we could hear it licking and gnawing at brush and bleached grass. I looked back to see flames leaping as high as the horses' chests, flames scrabbling and hissing and swallowing blunderbrush in gulps, running toward us in bounds. If there were a gust in the wind, it might catch us all in a moment.

"Time for a gallop, flat out," Tass said.

I nodded. The horses were tiring, but that was perhaps to the good. Perhaps their weariness would keep them from running out of control. I wanted no panic. If Kor could keep the leash on his fear yet a while longer—I looked over at him and saw his face bone white even in the witch wind heat, and he was staring forward.

"But how—when—it cannot have gotten ahead of us!"

At my left side I heard Tassida fervently cursing. Fire confronted us to eastward, and our every stride brought us closer to it! Fire just as fearsome as the one behind us, fire that leaped to devour junipers at a single swallow, that leaped to blacken the shadowlands. We were trapped in the narrowing span between the two.

"It is not possible!" Tass railed. "Have we gone mad?"

"No need to save water any longer!" I shouted, and, letting Talu's reins lie on her neck, I untied the opening of my waterskin so that every drop of it spilled out and down

my legs, down even to my feet, soaking them. Already
Talu had lengthened her stride. I let her. By my side I saw
Kor struggling with his goatskin, trying to do as I had
done and not lose his seat, perhaps wishing that he had
been reared a horseman. Ashen, he looked as wild as the
fanged mares. Still I was not very frightened, for there was
no time for fear. One fire lay a few strides before us, the
other a few strides behind. . . . "Hang on by the mane!" I
shouted at Kor, and with a yell of despair or bravado I
kicked Talu to send her leaping through the flames before
us.

And just as she sprang I saw Kor fall. . . .

Hard on his back he fell, his head snapping downward
to hit against the rocky ground, and he lay still.

Now truly I was afraid.

Talu was through the fire and perhaps ten strides farther,
long galloping strides, before I could wrestle her to a stop.
And the whole world had gone mad: there were people
scattering before me, people flailing blankets about, Herders, where the Herders ought not to be. And Talu was fully
panicked at last, rearing and squealing and useless, and
Kor's mare Sora by her side, riderless and just as crazed
with fear. I never thought of borrowing Calimir, though he
and Tass stood quietly within arm's reach. Intent only on
saving Kor, I swung myself down by Talu's neck, threw
her reins at Tass and ran back the way we had come.

"Dan! Don't! Are you out of your mind?" I heard
Tassida's voice only faintly, and the words had no meaning to me. I reached the fire, threw my arms skyward to
keep them out of the flames and ran in.

The heat was searing, fearsome, reaching even to the
indeeps of my lungs, so that I could scarcely breathe. *Ai,*
if Kor was in this, lying in it, insensible, there was no
hope for him. . . . I at least was upright, and my leather
boots, my leather leggings, soaked with sweat and the last
of our drinking water, saved me from the worst of it. Pain
only speeded me. I leaped through the flames as the horses
had.

Kor lay—there was less than a man's footpace of un-
burned ground to either side of him. He lay sprawled

where he had fallen, the heat of the oncoming flames crisping his hair, his eyes closed and his face a frightened gray touched with orange flame light. If he had broken his neck—but there was no time to find out. I gathered him up quickly, if only to save his body for a fitting burial, and I hoisted him onto my shoulders, as far from the flames as I could manage. One step, and the fire closed around my legs.

I could no longer run and leap, not with Kor on my back. I walked through the fire. For only a few moments, perhaps a dozen steps, truly, but it seemed an eternity that I walked through burning pain and an orange blindness. I could not breathe or see, I stumbled, no longer sure of my direction. It was no use, I would fall—

I felt Kor stirring on my shoulders, felt the tremor as he groaned. He lived, and perhaps he would be well! Joy spurred me so that I staggered a few steps more, and before me I heard a clear call. Tass. In a moment I felt her hand on my arm, and the heat, the pain lessened, and I stopped and eased Kor to ground that, mercifully, did not burn. Then I also lay down, or perhaps I fell, and someone, the blessing of Sakeema on that someone, was pouring water all over me.

"Open your eyes," Tass ordered, wiping water away from them with her hand.

I did so, and saw her blurrily, then more clearly, scowling down on me. Beyond her Herders clustered around, staring, and beyond them, the fire—I sat straight up in alarm.

"Far better than you have any right to be," Tass grumped.

But fire was coming, I had to save Kor from the fire, I thought groggily. "Kor!" I cried.

"Right here," he said. His voice was labored, his face creased with pain, but he was lying by my side, looking up at me, speaking to me, and perhaps he would yet be well if the fire did not take us—

"The fire!" I exclaimed.

"You walked through it," Kor muttered. "You walked through fire for me." His eyes had closed, but his hand moved toward me before it fell to earth.

"No!" I blurted, meaning that he had not understood, I had not yet saved him, I must shoulder him or drag him or lay him over a horse before the flames flowed around us again. I struggled to get up. Tass pushed me back none too gently.

"Be still," she commanded, and she went to Kor, feeling his head and neck with her fingertips, then lifting his head in her hands. I watched, wild with impatience—what did she think she was doing! There was no time—but in a moment Kor opened his eyes again, and in the same moment my poor mind, stupid with smoke and fear, comprehended that we were no longer in danger, that the fire was somehow held at bay by all the people around me, and I looked.

A ditch of sorts had been scratched in the surface of the high shortgrass plain, and ranged along it stood Herders with blankets, beating back the flames that sometimes wandered across it. They had set a fire row to halt the wildfire, I later learned, but hotwind had roused their own small fire to wildfire as well, and it had turned on them, nearly rending them. Then wildfire had joined with wildfire in a burst, a storm, of flame. But the worst of the danger was past. Already the blaze leaped lower, for there was nothing any longer for it to feed on. I turned my head. At my back stood brown sheep, huddled into a dense, bleating flock, and gray burros, and the domed brushwood huts of the Herder village. Here, where it did not belong, with the thunder cones nowhere near.

The crowd around me parted, and old Ayol, the longtime king of the Herders, stood before me, scowling down on me, the richly figured ceremonial blanket around his shoulders. Scowling. Tass was mettlesome always, but old Ayol was gentle—why was he frowning at me?

"Tassida the Wanderer has ridden our way before, and we welcome her," he stated with ritual dignity. "Korridun King of the Seal Kindred we welcome as an honored friend. To Dannoc of the Red Hart Tribe we extend the aid due to one in need, as Sakeema would have done, but we do not welcome him. The Red Hart people have betrayed the trust of the Herders."

"What?" Surprise and anger brought me to my feet, where I stood swaying, the charred remnants of my leggings hanging in wet draggles from my legs. If I moved again, I would find myself naked. Not a fitting showing for one confronting old Ayol.

"Tyonoc of the Red Hart has turned against the ways of his forebears. Tyonoc of the Red Hart has violated the friendship of the Herders," Ayol chanted, his yellow eyes not on me but on the sky, showing me in that way his contempt. "Why, then, should the Herders welcome his son?"

I took a threatening step toward him, no longer caring if my clothing fell away and left me uncovered. "Tyonoc of the Red Hart has never showed you anything but honor!" I shouted. Unreasoning fury had hold of me, that he should speak evil of my father. It did not seem to matter, at the time, that I could not in fact remember what my father had lately done. Mind did not matter, for heart felt blindly and fervently certain that Tyonoc could do no wrong.

"Dan," said Tass coolly from behind me, "don't be an ass. Ayol speaks but simple truth."

I turned on her in astonishment. "Not so!" I flared.

"Tyonoc has driven the Herders from their lands," Ayol stated darkly. "Dannoc did not know? Then look around you, and believe. Why do the Herders crouch on the unfriendly steppes, in the way of Fanged Horse raiders, of wildfires?"

"You've gone mad, old man!" I raged at him. "You're muddleheaded in your dotage."

I said to him many things more. Plainly, for all to see, I was a madman, shouting and tottering, flinging up my hands. Ayol said no more to me, but stubbornly he stood his ground before me, scowling yet more deeply, and his twelve clustered around him, weapons in hand. Only my own fear of my own weapon kept me from drawing the great sword and joining in fight with them. That, and Kor, who had struggled up somehow and managed the few steps to my side. He held onto my arm, as much for support as to restrain me.

"Dan," he said quietly, "let it go."

"Let it go?" I was outraged. "I cannot! You heard what he said—"

"Dan, you walked through fire for me. It cannot be so much harder to grant me this one request. Let it go."

I stood panting with fury and staring at him. But I shouted no longer at Ayol, and when I spoke again my voice was soft and even. "Do you believe what he says of my father?"

"It is not a matter of believing for me, Dan. For your own part, believe what you must."

"And count yourself mercifully received," Tass put in crisply, "that you have not been killed, as many of Ayol's people were killed, not long ago."

I ignored her, my gaze fixed on Kor. An awful fear had me in a choking grip. "Kor," I insisted, "what he says of my father. Is it true?"

"Ayol has said it is. So has Tassida."

"But if you tell me . . ." I could not go on. Fear had overpowered me, and I saw only black, black of scorched and smoking earth, black of my charred clothing, black of benighted water and a nightmare.

"I will tell you nothing," Kor said, his words traveling to me distantly, as if through water. "I will tell you nothing, ever again. You must find your own way to truth, Dan."

But not that day. It was not to be borne, and I could not begin to face it or encompass it. My heart would have broken. Mind clashed with heart, and both shrieked inwardly, and I swayed where I stood. Tass reached out to steady me—I fell to the ground at her feet, I fainted. When I awoke it was after nightfall, and I was lying in one of the brushwood huts of the Herders, naked under a blanket of fine wool.

Chapter Sixteen

Nothing ailed Kor except a banged head and bruises. For my own part, I had some painfully scorched skin, especially where lappet and leggings should have met. They had let the flames at my groin, and to my blushing shame I discovered that Tassida had rubbed it with some sort of unguent while I lay unconscious. But by the second day, well fed and rested, I was going about in a breechcloth made of lambswool, and I remarked to Kor that we ought to be on our way.

"It seems to me," he replied, "that we are both far better healed than is in reason. Why, I wonder?"

I shrugged, for I shied away from thinking, those days. By mutual unspoken consent Ayol and I had said no more about the matter between us, as it was not in me to deal with it, not then, and he seemed content having had his say that first day. I dare say Kor or Tassida had talked with him about me. And if I remembered calling him foul names, it seemed part of a dark dream.

We took leave of him courteously in the morning. He and his folk had not much provision to spare us, but we were only a few days' journey from the hunting lands of my people, where I felt certain we would soon find food.

We rode long and late that day and the days that followed. The hot witch wind had at last abated, and once again we took joy in the journey as the land slowly turned from sere to faint green to the tall-grass green of the prairies where the badgers and blue hens lived.

If Kor had done any courting of Tass at the Herder

village, I did not know of it. And there was little chance now for any—we were always, the three of us, together. It would have been too dangerous to go separately even if I could have found an excuse. So I rode my dun gray Talu in the rear, and Kor took the fore on his homely Sora, the wildfire mare, and Tass rode between us for the most part, or beside Kor, on the handsome Calimir. Every day Kor rode more as a king might. And his passion for Tass sang in his voice when he spoke to her, showed in his glance and his gestures when he was near her, so that she must have seen it. I thought she could not help but love him when he was so afire with love for her, all warmth and beauty and comity as of gentle fire. . . . There had never been a more noble wooing. But if she saw it, she gave no sign. And it sometimes seemed to me that she spoke most often to me, though she had to call back over her shoulder to do so, for Talu would kick at Calimir if we rode abreast.

"That sword of yours," she called to me the first day out.

"What of it?"

"You are half afraid of it."

Kor looked around worriedly, knowing I did not much care to speak of the unaccountable weapon, but I grinned at him and at Tass. I quipped, "Indeed, I am entirely afraid of it."

"Why?" She swiveled on Calimir's back to peer at me, placing a hand on the gelding's rump. Her tunic tightened around her waist, her breasts tilted toward me, her thighs shifted, braced against the horse's back. I felt a warm tide rising in me, and I had to swallow before I spoke. Then I spoke more truth than I had intended.

"I am afraid—it might turn against someone I love."

"But why would it do that, as long as you wield it?"

The tide turned dark, black, a black terror pressing in on me, and though I withstood it—for I was accustomed to it by then—I could not find words to explain it to her. How to tell her that I was a madman and a murderer, if she had not heard it already? She must have known, so why was she probing my fears? Bitterness engulfed me. Feeling it, Kor reined in his horse to ride beside me.

"Tass," he protested quietly.

She turned her eyes away from me. "But there is no need to be afraid," she protested in her turn. "The sword has a name, a centering, a will for loyalty. It is not a feckless thing."

I recalled her tale. "Yes," I said darkly, "but I do not know the name."

"A pity," said Tass, "for if you did, it could never be turned against you or anyone you love."

I lowered my left hand and touched the sword, feeling the dread power of the thing that went through me every time I touched it, feeling the blade of it hard and keen inside the leather scabbard. It was hard for me to believe that it had been made and named by any man, even a man of legendary times, and not just born out of some nightmare, out of earth's uneasy dream.

"Where did you get it?" Tassida asked.

"I don't remember."

Kor surprised me. "Dan," he urged, "think."

"I don't know, I don't remember! Sometimes I dream—" I hated even to say it, but my fear had subsided enough so that I could. "I dream of black water and feel as if I am drowning. That is all I know."

"Water," Tass murmured. "That is odd. The swords were shaped in fire. Often the swordmasters gave them names borrowed from war or fire. Flamewing, Firefang, Blaiz . . ."

"Tass," asked Kor, his love for her soft in his voice, shining in his eyes, "who has told you all these things?"

"No one."

"Tass," I broke in, thinking she was being obstinate, "help us, help Kor! If there is a seer, perhaps we can go to him." A seer would know why the world seemed to be dwindling.

"There is no seer!" she retorted with an odd, plaintive undertone in her proud voice. "No one to help us. You think I have not searched?" She sent Calimir at a canter up a grassy slope, and we followed.

"There," I breathed when we topped the rise, and we all stopped our horses to look.

To southward and eastward lay the vast upland valley of my people, spread out like a great rumpled pelt furred with evergreens, mottled and spotted with streams, shallow lakes, wildfire meadows, and the clearings the beaver left behind. Deer, Sakeema's cattle, grazed openly in the meadows, and I smiled at the sight, though it seemed to me there were not as many as there should have been. . . . In the far distance rose the snowpeaks to one side, the thunder cone range to the other. But nowhere, near or far, could I see the skin tents or firesmokes of my people. That was as I expected, for they seldom camped openly. I would find sign of them soon enough.

We camped under the hemlocks by a singing stream, and we were all merry, for once again we had water in plenty and we were sheltered. Hidden from the eyes of devourers—even though we had only once seen some on the journey, that was my first thought. They seemed the worst of our enemies, though Pajlat's minions had attacked us and the devourers had not.

I went and shot a half-grown deer, and we shared the meat with the fanged mares. They ate ravenously, even the hide and some of the bones, and Calimir watched curiously, for there had been grazing enough for him for several days by then, and perhaps he could not comprehend their hunger. In the morning, strengthened, we rode on.

On the third day I found signs of my people, the small, neat hoofprints of their ponies and the pawprints of their hounds—for we used dogs in hunting, sometimes, to run the deer toward where the archers waited, small tan hounds as graceful as the deer themselves. I had thought my people would be near the marshy rivers to westward where the sweetroot grows at the time of year, and I was right. The trail seemed fresh enough, and we followed it as it wound down a wooded valley—

"Dannoc!"

A high, clear voice called from the slope to one side, and someone came thumping and crashing toward us. Only astonishment could have made a Red Hart hunter move so noisily. We halted. Joy had been in that call, joy that warmed me like a friend's cooking fire, and in a moment a yellow-braided woman in doeskin tunic and buckskin leggings ran toward me between the trees. I grinned and slid down off Talu when I saw her—it was Leotie.

"Dan! But how—what—" She flung her arms around me, and I kissed her and lifted her off her feet, hugging her, for I was very glad to see her, even though I felt Tassida's silent presence at my back, even though Leotie wore blue-dyed feathers in her braids.

"But you are pledged," I teased her when I released her. I twirled one of her braids. The indigo feathers tied to the end showed that she was in her first year of wedbed. "Who is the man so blessed?" I gave the braid a yank before I released it.

Her smile of delight turned to a scowl. "Dannoc, you know very well who, and if you insist on being a bear about it—"

"Leotie," I interrupted, "I don't know who. I woke up in a cave by the ocean, with the folk of the Seal Kindred, and I remembered nothing, not how I got there, not even my own name. Some of it has come back to me, but not all."

Her face, which had been flushed pink with pleasure, turned pale, and she seemed not able to speak a word.

Others of my people were hurrying down through the trees, drawn there by Leotie's cry, and a few of them had come close enough to hear this. And the nearest of them, a tall youth, nearly as tall as I, came and put his arm around Leotie as if to comfort her or support her. He faced me silently, his face a mask. It was my brother Tyee.

"You!" I exclaimed.

Leotie nodded, looking as if she were trying not to weep. Tyee did not move or speak. He looked thinner than I remembered him, and lean, as if he had seen trouble.

"And I held it against you?"

Leotie nodded again.

"Well, the more fool, I." Lifting my hands palms out in gesture of peace, I went to greet my brother.

Tyee's face crumbled as if the mask had cracked and fallen apart, and suddenly he looked as near tears as Leotie. "Dannoc, nothing has been right since you went away," he whispered as he returned my embrace, thwacking me on the back. "Why did you do it?"

"I don't remember," I told him, and then there were others of my tribe around us, ten or more of them, all young men and women close to my age, and they were all reaching to touch or hug me, gathered around me in a cluster of joy.

"Kor!" I shouted. "Tassida!" For I wanted them to be part of that joy-flower as well.

Kor left his mount and came over to me, looking nearly as shy as Birc. Tass stayed where she was, on Calimir's back, wearing her cocksure air once again. Let her sit, then, I thought.

"Tyee, Leotie," I told them, "this is Rad Korridun, king of the Seal Kindred and a friend such as few men ever find. Kor, this is Tyee, my brother. . . . How is our father?" I asked Tyee abruptly, and he looked at me with a very still face, as if the mask had come back.

"Much as ever. Where are your leggings, Dan? And why have you cut your hair?"

"It is a long story and not much worth going into."

They had it out of me anyway, or most of it, over the confused course of the rest of the day. We made camp where we were, very nearly, and there was an excited uproar and a busy bringing in of meat. They wanted to feast me.

"Where are Father and the others?" I asked Tyee.

"A day to the southward, near the place of many springs. I have sent a messenger to tell them the news, and we will go with you there tomorrow."

"But why are you out here, off by yourselves?"

"Scouting for deer . . . What tribe is she of, that maiden with the dark eyes?"

Tassida had gotten down off her gelding at last, stiffly, arrow straight, and no one was speaking to her, for my people did not know what to make of her.

"Sakeema knows," I told Tyee. Being with him, I

remembered what it was that had always annoyed me
about Tyee: for all that he looked like a tall, strong man,
there was no strength of spirit in him. He was good and
kind, but he bent like a reed before storm wind. Already I
felt that there were things he was not telling me, not
because he was dishonest, but because he was afraid. Well
enough. There were things I would not tell him.

"She is not of Korridun's tribe?"

Kor himself came up to me at that moment, sparing me
answer. "I am going to see if I can take Tass off somewhere," he said to me in a low voice, "to hear me out."

I nodded at him. "She would probably prefer that to
this. We will save you some meat."

Tyee talked on, but I no longer heard him. I saw Kor go
to Tassida, speak to her, place a hand on her shoulder, and
after a while, walking aimlessly so that no one was likely
to notice—though in fact everyone noticed—they wandered off.

I felt sure of the outcome, and I wished him well. By
the cooking fire in the midst of the camp I sat and talked,
but I cannot remember much of the talk, for in spite of
myself my mind was with Kor. Later I sat and ate and
talked. Leotie complained that we had no mead, but we
were all merry enough. We feasted. Dusk came, so that
the fire seemed to burn yet more brightly. By this time, I
thought, he will be lying with her. . . .

And there through the dusk came Tass, alone, striding
past the fringes of the camp, heading toward the horses. I
stumbled up from my place by the fire, my legs nearly
numb with sitting, and caught up with her just as she
reached Calimir.

"I am going," she told me curtly, swinging her bedroll
onto the gelding. "You cannot stop me."

She looked frightened and angry, as far as I could tell in
the half light. "I doubt if anyone could stop you," I said
to mollify her. She seemed hardly to have heard me.

"I will not lie in wedbed with any man, ever!"

It was her anger speaking, I told myself, but the words
struck me like hurled stones. She was tying the cordgrass
bridle and leather reins onto Calimir, her hands so harsh in

their movements that the gentle gelding flung up his head in protest.

"Not if it were Sakeema himself!" she shouted, turning and lunging a step toward me. "And yes, I speak also to you, Dannoc-who-cannot-remember."

My face must have moved. She seemed truly to see me for the first time. For a moment she stood still.

"I'll not be chivvied back and forth like a driven deer between you two—" She sounded uncertain.

"We have no notion of chivvying you!" I said hotly. "What have Kor and I ever done but show you courtesy? Tass—"

She turned her back. I caught at her arm.

"Tass, by all the powers," I appealed, "what is *wrong*?"

She snatched her arm away as if I had burned it, vaulted onto Calimir. I got hold of the reins before she could lift them.

"Tass, what is the matter with you?" I was angry now. "Kor is—noble, wise, merciful, they are only words, but he is—he is very truth of them, fire true. The love he would give you—"

"Let go of my reins," she said in a low voice between clenched teeth.

"Listen to me! And do not tell me you hate Kor, for I know it cannot be true. At least do not leave so churlishly. You will hurt him to the quick."

"Dannoc, you ass," she said in a strangled voice, as if she were choking with anger, and she pulled out her knife.

I stood stunned by the gesture. That she could draw against me! I never thought of the great sword that hung by my side, and I did not care if she hurt me, I did not move. "Please," I begged her softly, "think of Kor."

"You fool," she whispered, "I am thinking of him." And she slashed with the knife. She meant only to cut the reins from my grasp and gallop away without them. I saw that by the angle of her aim, and I moved to release my grip so that she would not put herself in such danger, riding a horse out of control. But Calimir had grown tired of our shouting in his sensitive ears, and as the knife swished down he swerved and shied, sending it hard onto my arm. It cut to the bone even as I let go of the reins.

"Mahela blast it all to perdition!" Tass swore, giving Calimir a kick, and as the horse leaped away I heard her sobbing.

It was some time before I gave up watching after her and turned around. Blood was running down my shield arm, and all my tribemates sat silent as the twilight, watching me, even those on the nearer side of the fire had twisted around to watch me. It seemed to me, thinking about it, that they had been silent for some time. I stared back at them for a moment, and some of those who had turned to gawk hastily faced back toward the food and the fire. But Leotie got up and came over to me with a strip of binding for my arm.

"What have you been doing with your nights of late, Dannoc?" she asked, smiling, gentle, trying to tease. "Much the same as ever?" But I did not answer her. She wrapped my arm tightly to stop the bleeding.

"Where is your friend?" she asked a moment later, still gentle, still teasing. "Has she taken the knife to him, too?"

"I trust not!" I found my voice, and I had to answer her smile. "If he is not back by moonrise, I will go looking for him."

In fact, he was back a little after full dark, and I met him at the firelight's reaches, for I had been watching for him. "She's gone," I told him.

"I know." He sat down where he was, wearily, and I sat beside him, and the others let us alone. Nor were they any longer very merry.

"Go after her, Kor," I said.

"When this other matter is done, perhaps."

"Never mind that!" I felt annoyed and disappointed in him, in his lack of courage. "I can go to my father alone, and you can come to him another time. Kor—"

"What has happened to your arm?" he interrupted mildly.

"Never mind that, too. Kor, you must go after her now, before she rides out of your reach!"

"Dan," he retorted with just a touch of edge to his

voice, "I have not gotten by entirely without thinking, out
there in the forest, and I myself have decided what I must
do. You were not there, and there is no need for you to
instruct me."

Once again, it seemed, I was an ass. I sagged, defeated.
"Sorry," I muttered.

"No need."

"I still cannot believe she would refuse you."

"It is not that she dislikes me," Kor said, something
wry in his voice. "We talked, we rambled. We were
friends. . . ."

He got up and touched my shoulder so that I also got up
and followed him. We walked out of the reach of the
firelight, wandering and looking up at the stars.

"Why did she hurt your arm?" he asked after a while.
"I would not have thought it of her."

"It was mischance." I remembered Tassida's sobs as
she rode away, and the memory sent a pang through me. I
longed to comfort her, to soothe away her anger and pain,
to heal whatever hurt was in her that had sent her away
from us—and then the guilt struck. I would never touch
her, never allow myself to touch her. She was beloved by
Kor.

"Dan," Kor said softly, "no need for shame. Sakeema
knows, you have given me my chance."

"Blast it," I whispered between clenched teeth. He had
felt—whatever warm song had flooded my veins—

"I know you love her. I have known for days."

"Curse it, Kor!" I cried out, turning on him, miserable
and angry, though not truly at him. "Why do you have to
know such things? It can only hurt you, and I would have
held my peace until it passed!"

"You think it will pass?"

I was no longer sure. It felt different, as—Tassida was
different. . . . Numbly I rested my head against a hemlock
trunk. "I hope so," I muttered.

"Perhaps you ought to take your own advice, and go
after her."

So Kor was not wholly without malice, after all. He had
said that to hurt me, I felt sure of it, and he had succeeded.

I nearly writhed with the pain of the knife-edge he had put me on. But there was this odd consolation, that whatever anguish he caused me, he felt as well. In less than half a heartbeat he groaned out loud and reached blindly toward me, meeting my hand as it lifted toward him. Hands met and gripped, hard, and that simple pain of the body helped both of us.

"Forgive me," Kor whispered, a catch in his voice. I heard his chest heave. "Dan, you are all honor, and I have hurt you—"

"Blast it, hush," I ordered him. There was no need for such talk. His goodness vexed me.

"You would have given your happiness for mine, and I am bitter."

"Would you bloody *hush!*" I snapped.

"In a moment." He had charge of his voice again, and I was glad of it, for above all things I did not want to weep. I was afraid of weeping—not that of others, but my own. I heard his breathing, hard and ragged, and flinched from that sound, then heard it steady and was glad of that as well.

"There is one more thing I must tell you," said Kor. "I owe it to you."

I waited.

"Tass more than half loves you."

A bubble of joy welled up in my chest and burst into sorrow. Great Sakeema, no wonder he was bitter. Let me tell you a merry-go-sorry. . . . I could not speak.

"I felt it in her when you greeted Leotie. But it was all a jealous surge, love and anger. The anger has sent her away."

I could not bear any more; I was spent. "Kor," I appealed to him, "what are we going to do?"

Grip of his hand tightened on mine. "I wish I knew," he said.

Chapter Seventeen

All seemed so hopeless in regard to Tassida that we did nothing, and I, for one, gave over thinking about her. In the morning we readied our fanged mares. Tyee and his hunting band caught their curly-haired ponies, and we all rode together through the day to the place where the main body of the tribe was camping.

"Your people, these ones of them anyway, are much to my liking," Kor told me privately as we went out to catch the horses. "And Tyee—I very much like Tyee. His is a gentle heart. But there is a trouble in them none of them will name."

I looked at him warily. "You have sensed this in them?"

"Yes. In Tyee most of all. He feels it plainly, but he will not face it."

"Well," I said mostly to myself, "as one who cannot even remember—something, I can hardly scorn him for that."

Kor nodded but did not answer.

I decided to try Tyee yet one more time as we rode. I noticed he seemed to be in no hurry, but set a comfortable clopping pace, and by afternoon, as we nodded along, the sun had lulled us so that we were almost asleep.

Tyee rode by my one side, Kor by the other. "Tyee," I asked him drowsily, "what are you doing out here, really?"

"We came out to get away from Father for a while," he answered, just as drowsy, and then his head snapped up as if his own words had startled him awake.

"What?" I could not believe that, I who remembered a

straight man with strong hands and quiet ways. "Why? If all is not well, you should be with him."

"And what of you?" he retorted sharply, as if my words had stung more than I had meant them to.

What of me, indeed. I looked down at Talu's scrawny mane and smoothed it with my hand. "Was he—was he much stricken after I went?"

"No," said Tyee, the one short word.

I glanced over at him in surprise. Perhaps he was jealous. "What was said? Was there a search for me?"

"Nothing was said. There was no search. You were just gone. As if you were dead." Four curt statements, torn out of him. And before I could ask him more he kicked his pony and turned it, trotting back to where Leotie rode.

Kor spoke softly from his place by my side. "Your father has changed from the way you remember him, Dan."

"The more reason I should go to him," I said fiercely. He was crazed with grief, perhaps.

"Since your mother's death," Kor murmured as if to himself. But the words called up such a storm of reasonless anger in me that my whole body tightened with it, and Talu reared and jumped forward between my knees. I checked her. Kor was staring at me.

"You still cannot remember."

"No!" The anger, whatever had caused it, was not at him. I had nowhere to go with it except homeward, and I did not want that. I puffed my cheeks and blew through my lips, sending it away.

"Tyee is your younger brother?" Kor asked after a while.

"No. Elder."

Kor glanced round at me in surprise. "But then—his would have been the leadership of the tribe, had there been need of a new leader?"

I did not wish to think what he meant. Also, he was wrong. "In the event, it would have been up to the tribe, which of us to choose. Tyee, Ytan, or me."

"Do you think the tribe would have chosen you?"

"How should I know?" I shrugged. "Leotie chose Tyee."

"You were too much for her," Kor said in a low voice. "She wanted a man she could mother and scold. So she chose next best."

I had never thought of it in that way, and I grinned at him in thanks. But he was somber, not looking at me, and he rode the rest of the day mostly in silence, very grave, his mouth sober and straight, his hands still, sitting lance-straight on his mount, as if he were centering himself for the most difficult of vigils.

I remembered it afterward, his silence, his haunted eyes. But at the time I thought only of my father. Soon I would see him again. . . . If there was a trouble, I knew the way to blot it out, and I bathed my mind with the warm memories. Tyonoc, who had made the half-sized arrows for me when I was young and showed me the ways of a hunter. Tyonoc, who had fashioned me bow after bow as I grew, and finally had showed me through weeks of patience how to make my own, strong, recurved, a man's bow, out of deerhorn backed with sinew. Tyonoc, the king who himself had braided my hair for my name vigil . . . When he saw me, home again at last, his proud face would light with joy and he would embrace me. My throat tightened and my heart beat hard, thinking of him.

A little before sundown we found the place where the deerskin tents were pitched, along the banks of the river that ran down from the place of many springs. The largest tent, the one with the Red Hart emblem painted on its walls in bright ocher, was my father's. But he was not there, for with leaping heart I had already seen him. He and all my people stood assembled on the river plain, and there was a great fire, and mounds of food for a feast.

He was standing at the fore of the tribe, a still, tall figure in the garb of a king, the quilled and beaded head-band over his yellowbright hair that shone like the setting sun, the cloak of white deerskin fringed with ferret tails, the scars of hunting and battle gleaming whitely on his bare chest, and in his braids the peregrine feathers of a king, and on his arms the armbands. He was tall and massive, as tall as I, and glorious in the sunset, and he stood with great dignity with his twelve of retainers, six men, six women, at his back. This was all fitting. With him also stood my brother Ytan. And many were the smiles on the faces of his people behind him, and some of them shouted their welcome to me. And on the face of my father also there was a smile as I came before him.

I had expected something more—tears, perhaps. Such was his stature in the eyes of my people, my father was not afraid of tears—they could not lessen him. But his smile was enough for me. There was no dignity in me, seeing him, and I did not care. I was off of Talu and standing before him in a single stride, and with ardor I embraced him.

His body, hard, did not answer my embrace.

Puzzled, I stepped back to look at him. Yet he smiled, but there was something I did not recognize in that smile, not on his beloved face. . . . "Dannoc," he said, and there was something odd in his voice, too. "You truly do not remember."

Kor had come up and stood silently at my side.

"No," I said, "I do not remember. Have I displeased you in some way, Father?"

He did not answer me. His smile grew, but it was as hard as his body. "Who is that with you?" he asked.

He knew well enough, for Tyee's runner had told him. But I spoke for the sake of ceremony. "This is Rad Korridun of the Seal Kindred, their king and the best of comrades."

My father's eyes glinted and he turned to his retainers. "Seize them," he ordered.

I stood stunned, unable to believe that I had heard him truly. A murmur of surprise and horror went up from my people. Most of the twelve stood still, their faces showing the horror I felt, unable either to obey him or go against him. But three of them strode forward, and Ytan came forward with them. On his face rode the same smile that had been on my father's, and on him I knew the name of it: gloating.

He went to Kor and cuffed him, and that shocked me

out of my frozen stance. With a shout of anger I started toward Ytan. But two of my father's twelve had grasped me by my arms, restraining me. Two more took hold of Kor.

"Listen, my people!" My father lifted his voice in the king's call, and everyone fell silent to hear. "This is the foreign sorcerer who has taken my son away and bewitched him."

"Father, no!" It was Tyee, stepping forward, as stunned and distraught as I. "Korridun and Dannoc have come here with good intent to honor you. They have braved danger—" But he was trembling, his voice faltering so that half the tribe could not hear him. My father silenced him with a single harsh glance.

"By his own saying Dannoc is not in his right mind! And you will see how he is enthralled and under the power of the sorcerer who dwells by the sea."

My father turned toward Kor and spat at him. Kor had not spoken a word or struggled. Nor had I—not yet. I merely looked at Kor, a look that must have been as wild as the swirling of my thoughts, and he met my eyes in a quiet way. And with a pang like a spear thrust I saw that he was not surprised. He had expected all that was happening.

"So shameless is this one, he has come here openly to flaunt my son's captivity before us," my father ranted.

I spoke, standing very still and tall. "My father, I have loved you since I was born." My words were firm enough to be heard by all and yet meant for him alone. "I have never wanted to go against you or defy you. I have fought Pajlat himself to come back to you. But this day I must say to you: You are wrong. Korridun of the Seal Kindred is all goodness and all honor. You do wrong to speak ill of him."

I met my father's eyes as I spoke, letting him see all that was in me, all hurt, all love. Anger I had left behind, for the time. . . . But in his stare nothing answered me, not even anger. Nothing. Tyonoc of the Red Hart might as well have been a stranger to me. And at my final words he smiled his hateful smile.

"Thus speaks a man bewitched," he told my people.

None of them believed him, I could see that. They all stood white and silent, cowed and shamed. But my father did not look to them. He strode over to stand before me.

"Sire," I tried again, "it does you dishonor to lay hands on one who has come in peace. And you dishonor your son Tyee who brought us here."

He reached out and pulled the great knife of strange substance from its scabbard at my side, lifted it in his hand. His people shrank back from the sight of him as he held it, blade flickering like lightning, jewel stone in the hilt gleaming like a yellow, benighted eye. . . . The sword glinted both dark and brilliant as he raised it. The sun was setting in a blood-red glow that shadowed the deep lines of his face.

Face I had loved, face I had dreamed of . . .

"Bind him," he said to Ytan. Kor already stood bound to a yew tree some ten paces away from me. My brother, still leering, came to me and passed the leather lashings around my wrists tightly enough to hurt, to cut, then kicked my feet out from under me and pushed me to the ground, binding my legs as well.

"I think I will see what this sorcerer Seal king is made of inside," my father remarked, hefting the sword whose name I did not know.

"Father," I whispered to him, a plea for his ears alone. Still the thought was in me, if only he would hear me truly, all might yet be well. If only he would hear . . . But there was no such hearing left in him.

He went to Kor and slit his clothing with the tip of the sword, flicked it off in like wise, leaving shallow gashes in Kor's skin. Blood trickled down, and Kor stood without a sound, his sea-dark eyes gazing. All was blood light fading to wounded dusk, my people watching as stricken as I, bound up in horror and helpless. Somewhere near me someone was sobbing, dry sobs. No, it was I, myself, making that hurtful sound, Dannoc with his heart breaking. I knew my heart was breaking because the agony was familiar. It had done so sometime before.

"Let me, Father." It was Ytan, and he had my own

arrows and bow, brought back from where they had been lashed in their leather cases to Talu's gear.

Tyonoc turned on him with force enough to make him step back. "No." My father's voice was harsh, ugly. "This kingling is mine."

Korridun king. "Kor," I breathed, and though he could not in any way have heard me at the ten paces of distance, his eyes turned to mine. There was a rapt look about him, as if he faced a devourer.

"I am sorry," I whispered to him, still knowing he could not hear me. Knowing by then that I had been a fool, accursed fool and a wantwit fool to have believed in my father's goodness. I had let us be seized and bound when we could have escaped. Even as they held my arms I could have broken away easily enough had I let myself be roused, and with my uncouth weapon in hand I could have freed us both. But supposing my father had come in the way of the sword—

Black, black horror, terror drowning deep . . .

Tyonoc twirled the tip of the sword and gouged out Kor's left eye.

I think I went mad, then, truly mad. Months past, Istas had threatened me with similar torments, and Kor had sworn he would far rather have taken them on his own body than stand by helpless. . . . He took them. His sea-dark eyes, gone, his beloved face slashed into a mask of blood, mutilated. And hands, heart, manhood . . . The many torments, he suffered all of them, in slow and brutal succession, and though I saw him cry out from time to time I could not hear him, for I was sobbing and roaring and tearing myself to the bone against the thongs that bound me helpless. Love of my father had bound me helpless, and he was a monster, he—he had—killed—

I remembered. Everything.

I grew suddenly still, still enough to hear Kor scream in mortal agony as Tyonoc hacked open his chest. And like a storm breaking in thunder, flame, and flood, all happened at once. I was free of my bonds, someone or something had freed me, and I was on my feet, moving, and I was myself but also—something more, larger, like someone

out of legend, self I knew yet did not know by name—but
I knew the name of my sword.

"Alar!" I called her.

Lightning, the name meant. Sky fire. And I ran to meet
her as she tore from my father's hand and lightly flew to
mine. The hilt met my palm like a friend's warm grasp.
My father's face floated before me, pale, mouth parted,
my father's face, it was he who had betrayed me, made a
mockery of my love, and I was in frenzy, I knew what I
wanted to do to him—

With a roar of grief I slashed him open from throat to
vent.

I wanted his guts to spill out at my feet so that I could
spit on them, and trample them, and curse his soul—I was
so anguished, so enraged. But no innards were there.
Tyonoc looked perplexed and fell, and out of the gaping
wound I had made in him there flowed something as gray
as guts, fish-gray, unfurling and rippling and flying away—

A devourer!

I heard my people sob, scream, gasp, but I did not even
look after it as it flew off westward. I turned to Ytan—I
had wanted to behead him, but now I knew I must deal
with him as I had with Tyonoc. Heart told me there was a
devourer in him as well. But already he was fleeing through
the crowd of my frightened people, and as I looked he
threw himself on Talu and galloped away.

All became for a moment very quiet.

My father lay dead at my feet, his body empty and
collapsed in on itself, like a broken shell. My father. I
dropped Alar where I stood. I had killed my own father. . . .

He would never hurt me again. He would never hurt
Kor again.

Kor!

Kor . . .

Leotie and Tyee were already there at the yew tree,
cutting the thongs that bound Kor to it, tears streaming
down their faces. And Kor sagged against their gentle
hands, lifeless. No, it could not be—

In a single stride I was by his side, and I took him into

my arms, feeling, listening, breathless, silently begging to
Sakeema, let there be life, any life. . . .

It was too late. He was dead. Bloody, mutilated, and
dead.

Too late, far too late even before I had lifted my sword,
I had struck too late, ass, dolt, fool, murderer that I was,
world-accursed wantwit madman and murderer, I had let
them kill him.

I sank down where I was and cradled his body against
me, the poor violated thing, held his eyeless, disfigured
head against my shoulder. More than half demented, I
rocked him as a mother rocks her child at the breast, as if
by rocking him I could somehow comfort him or myself,
and as I rocked I crooned—or moaned. . . . His blood
clotted on my fingers. All around me I heard my tribe-
fellows raising the keen for a fallen leader, not for their
dead king but for Korridun who had been king by the sea,
and my grief could no longer be contained in moaning. I
put up my head and howled and wailed as a wolf might
howl to a midwinter's moon and bellowed as a mother
bison would, mourning her slain calf. And then I wept.

May I never have to weep so again—the water ran down
my face like torrents off the mountains during a springtime
storm. I wept for my father, who had left me years before.
I wept for my friend. *Ai,* my grief—I felt as if I would
forever weep, there could be no end to my grieving. My
people had gathered all around me, I knew they wanted
only to comfort me, but they had no comfort to offer me,
and they were grieving as well. . . . *Ai,* Kor, Kor, if I had
known before I lost you how I loved you, more than any
father. . . . Pain was in me like a knife that could not be
withdrawn, and I ached and shook with sobbing.

Time is an unkind thing, a relentless thing; it will not be
swayed for the sake of any peril. Tarry but a little, mired
in heartache, and it is too late, the king is dead. . . . Time
flies away with joy or a friend's life, but it cruelly crawls
for agony. And that night when I wept over Kor, time
seemed to stand torturously still, so that I who yet lived
grieved through a lifetime that would never end.

Tears blinded me. . . . Time was just. Merciful, even. Forever was too short a time for me to mourn Kor.

Sometime in the midst of forever I blinked and saw someone kneeling before me, tears on her face, hands faltering out toward the lifeless body that lay cradled in my arms. Someone with dark eyes and a face of startling beauty. I looked on that beauty with indifference. Even Tass could not comfort me.

"Too—late," I told her, my voice choked between sobs.

"No," she said numbly.

"Dead."

"No," she said again, and her hands came out and fumbled at his chest, feeling for a heartbeat.

"Killed . . ."

"No," she said, "you are wrong. He breathes. Look."

It was not possible. His whole chest was laid open. But I looked, my tears falling down on him—and I saw his chest rise and fall, the terrible wounds closing before my eyes.

"Your tears—" Tass edged away, her hands bloodied.

My tears had fallen on Kor's face. And as I watched, trembling, the raw sockets where his eyes had been filled out, the lids closed smoothly as if in sleep. And his face, his mouth, were whole again, comely. And with my arms, with all my body, I felt his heart beating, faintly at first but more strongly with every moment. And I was weeping still, more than ever, but the tears were tears of joy.

"I am frightened of you," Tass breathed, backing away from me, still on her knees. "There is a fate in you. I am terrified of both of you." She got up and bolted.

I scarcely saw her go, scarcely comprehended any of what was happening, myself afraid, terrified of the hope and the joy, knowing that if it were somehow madness or an illusion, if Kor were taken away in the night, I could not bear it, I could not endure such weeping again, I would die. Or if his eyes under the smoothly closed lids were not his own . . . I could not bear it.

"Kor . . ." I jostled him in my arms. "Kor!" I begged.

"Please wake!" But he was sleeping so soundly I could not rouse him.

"He—he is breathing? Truly?" It was Leotie, beside me, coming close to look, and all my tribesfolk were crowded around, babbling to each other in a tumult of relief and joy. Then their voices fell to a whisper and trailed off into an awed silence. In that silence I felt a great peace, and my sobbing quieted, though from time to time my shoulders still shook.

"But he is sleeping so gently," an old woman said softly to her neighbor. "See, he nearly smiles."

"His skin, as smooth as a babe's."

It was true. All marks of wounds were gone, even the scars the devourers had put on him in vigils past.

"Very comely, for all that he is so dark," someone else murmured.

"And so brave. He never begged—"

"Yes. Hush. We are all shamed by what happened."

"Sakeema has taken mercy on us," a man's voice said, "that he is alive."

"He is as fair as Sakeema himself, sleeping there."

"Dan." It was Leotie again, coming up to me with an armload of pelts and fleeces and blankets. She arranged the things into a thick bed. "Here, lay him gently down, and come, let me see to you, those wrists—"

I did not yet feel that I could speak. I shook my head.

"Dan, please. Only for a moment."

But I would not lay Kor down. Whether more out of love for him or fear of losing him, I would not let go of him, even for the moment. I sat where I was. In the end, Leotie washed off of me what blood she could and put a blanket around my shoulders and around Kor—he was naked, but warm. Others brought food for me, but I would not taste any. I had no thought for food. And then they took down my father's tent, brought it and raised it over me, on the spot, to keep off the dew and nighttime chill and perhaps the rain. They built a fire near my feet—the smoke curled up through the vent at the tent's ridge. Then, leaving the food and the bedding and some firewood, they went away, for it was very late.

I sat holding Kor through the night as he slept. Sometimes he stirred in his sleep, and every time he did so my heart warmed with joy. Between times I was afraid or angry or grieving, my thoughts tossing and swirling like the waves around the headland, but slowly quieting like the sea after a storm. I steadied my anger, my grief, as I might steady a lathered horse, and on toward morning at last I was calm enough to truly think. And think I did, more deeply and plainly and well than I had ever thought in my life.

Dawn lightened the sky above the smoke vent, turning it the colors of a wild rose. All was still—my people were finally asleep after a troubled night. The small birds were just beginning to stir and sing in the trees, one soft note, then a pause, then another, soft as the dawn. The world was fragrant, quiet, peace lying on it as simply as the dew.

"Kor," I said, my voice sounding loud in the hush, "wake up." My arms were numb and aching from holding him.

He stirred, but still he slept.

"Sakeema," I said very softly, "please wake and speak to me."

His eyes opened, and they were his own, looking on me with amusement and love.

Chapter Eighteen

Kor sat up, gathered the blanket around his waist and looked at me. "You are calling on the name of Sakeema?" he asked gravely.

"I spoke to you," I told him levelly enough, though there was a catch in my voice. It unsteadied me to see him sitting there, after all that had happened, well and whole—with the merriment starting in his eyes.

"Dan, for the first time I begin to think you truly mad! You call me Sakeema? You, who brought me back to life with your tears?" His voice grew hushed as he said that, and his hand lifted toward me, but I could not quite touch it. I was almost afraid of him.

I said, "Only Sakeema could have done what you have done for me. You came here knowing what would happen, letting it happen so that—I would see—"

"Dan," he interrupted, "I knew only a little. I had some fool's thoughts of—interceding for you, somehow. Certainly I did not intend to be killed."

"But you meant for me to be well."

"Yes, body of Sakeema, what else? All of us who love you wish you well."

"You knew you would not be talking with my father. You knew what he was likely to do to you."

"No. I thought it more likely that he would try to hurt you. As he had done before."

I stared at him, startled. He looked down at his hands. "I heard your ravings," he said softly, "when we were in the pit. I learned some things. You have remembered, Dan?"

Very weary, not yet ready to speak of it, I merely nodded. Kor's expression sat oddly on him, god that I thought him to be, for he looked sheepish.

"I am properly befooled," he said. "I had thought I would—fend him off for you, save you, and in the end it was you who saved me—from death itself."

"But not from torment," I muttered.

"From Tyonoc? When you could not lift weapon against him for your own sake, even though he drove you out of your mind? But in the end you did it for me. . . ." Wonder in his voice. I could not think so well of myself.

"I killed my father," I said starkly.

"No. You unhoused a devourer. Hardly a deed of evil."

I stared anew. "How— Did you know about the devourer, also, before we came here?"

"No! I saw it! It nearly flew through me. I have never been so frightened, even in life. I—I badly wanted to come back to you."

Nothing should have startled me by then, but I felt faint, looking at him. He was speaking of the moment when he had been dead, and he looked frightened still.

"I saw—I saw everything, Dan. I was floating a small distance above the treetops, looking back, downward, and I saw you break loose at last—you were magnificent. And I saw—my body—"

He winced in pain at the memory and shut his eyes, as if by doing so he could stop seeing it.

"Don't," I whispered. "Don't speak of it anymore."

He seemed not to have heard me. "The poor, hacked thing," he murmured. "Odd, that I should cherish such a thing."

I felt a cold touch of fear. "You will come to hate me," I said, my voice very low.

"What?" He opened his eyes and blinked at me.

"You will come to hate me for what has happened." The torment that sickened me, remembering.

"Never." Kor gazed steadily at me, his bare shoulders calm and beautiful, but tears coursed down his cheeks. "Dan, you held me to your heart."

I wanted to hold him to my heart again. Only fear prevented me.

"All night you held me. . . ."

His hand lifted toward me, and this time, willy-nilly, mine met it, for I could sooner have changed my shape than stay away from him.

"I will always love you."

I seemed to see a bubble of amaranthine light, bursting open like a flower, leaving a fragrance as nameless as the nameless god. . . . My fears, gone as if they had never been. Like my weeping, done with. A hush, a peace far beyond any I had ever known had hold of me with the clasp of his hand, a joy fit to fill the world. He saw it, or felt it, and smiled like sunrise, though the warm salt dew still lay on his face. I shall always remember that smile.

"But it is all I have ever wanted," I whispered to him, as if something uncanny spoke in me, as if out of a self I scarcely knew. "All I have ever wanted. Love."

"Dan, you have it." He embraced me, the hard, clean embrace of a friend and a king, and I felt dawn's light swelling inside me, the dayspring of joy. My long night was truly over. I might never weep again.

"You *are* Sakeema," I told him huskily.

"Dan, you *are* a blockhead," he replied, and thumped my back as if to rouse me, and let go of me.

It was a dawning that could never be taken from us, a daybreak that would live in us for as long as we lived, that hushed, birdsinging time. Kor and I, beneath the fawn-colored light, sheltered by a tent of deerskin, talking. He lay back at his ease on the bedding Leotie had left him and let the tears dry on his face. I sat gazing at him, letting self know to the center of being that truly, indeed, he lived. . . . And though there were some things I was not yet ready to tell, to him or anyone, we talked deeply and well. I remember we talked about Tassida—it did not trouble us to do so, for neither of us could be touched by sorrow that dawning. How Tass had returned and seen Kor's healing, and fled again, afraid. She and Kor had not spoken of what I thought, or not entirely, that night at Tyee's encampment, when she had cut my arm and left us. Kor had told her what he knew of Tyonoc and me, what he expected to face. She had come back, I surmised, with some thought of aiding us—and found a mutilated body in my arms. Looking at Kor, lying smooth-skinned and barechested on his bed of pelts and fleeces, I could remember without sickening. The dusk before seemed but a black dream, gone with dawning.

When dawn had turned to sunrise, and sunrise to early morning, Leotie came and softly called to us from outside the tent, then entered and gazed at Kor with shining eyes.

"You are truly all right," she marveled. She carried his pack and bedroll from his horse in her arms, but she stood as if she had forgotten them.

At her back walked Tyee, stooping under the tent flap and coming in behind her, looking diffident. I stared at him, seeing what I had not noticed the night before—his face was swollen and bruised black, his shield arm wrapped in bloody bandages, and he walked stiffly, and gingerly sat down by my side.

"Where did you get those marks?" I asked him.

"I was—conversing with Ytan."

"He came back?" I half rose in my horror. Tyee caught my arm and pulled me down.

"No. Last night. While the—Korridun's bloody welcome was going on."

"So it was you who set me free!"

He shook his head. "Leotie. It was all I could do to—busy Ytan, a moment."

"And it took such a parlous long time," Leotie said, "for the others of the twelve to sicken and turn away so that we had our chance. . . ."

She was still gazing at Kor. We are sorry, her glance said. "Bygones," he replied.

Tyee wore a tunic. "What is under that shirt?" I demanded of him. "Were you stabbed?"

"Yes," he shot back. "Heal me with your tears?" His daring surprised me so, I laughed out loud.

"Sakeema, no! I've spent tears enough—I hope there are none left!"

"Tyee!" Leotie feigned shock, then remembered at last

the things she was carrying and took them to Kor. "That fanged mare you rode has left Ytan somewhere and come back," she told me. "I'll go get your gear." She went out.

"I hope she threw him hard," Tyee grumbled. "I hope she broke his churlish neck."

I leaned back on an elbow and looked at him, mindful that I had a bone to pick with him. Though what had happened could not have been easy on him, either. I would be gentle.

"Tyee," I said, expecting him to look at the ground, "you could have told me, you know. What things were like here. You let me walk into the arms of a murderer, deliver Kor up to him for slaughter—"

He shook his head, meeting my eyes in a calm way that was new to me, in him—he seemed quite certain of himself. "You had to know for yourself," he told me. "You would have called me a liar and bloodied my nose before you could have believed any harm of our father."

Blast him, he was right! It was I who lowered my eyes.

"Has Dan always been like that?" Kor asked my brother whimsically. "So pigheaded?"

"Bullheaded," I corrected with what dignity I could muster.

"Of the three of us, he has always been the favorite, and the one most like our father."

My glance shot up again, for I had not told him that I was a murderer as well.

"When he was himself," Tyee added. "True man and true king. I remember too, you know."

"Then there really was a change," I murmured.

Sudden, but so subtle . . . Tyee and I talked, trying to comprehend it and think when it had happened. Perhaps only Wyonet, our mother, had truly known. Tyonoc's words had been the same, gestures the same, duties attended to, and often he smiled. But heart was all lacking. Loving him as I did, I keenly felt the difference, but denied it in my mind. Others, perhaps, had not noticed until after our mother disappeared, gone one morning without a trace. Tyee and I had made search for her, then mourned her. But Tyonoc had not. And when whispers had begun, I had made excuses for him, saying that he was dazed by grief. I had even managed to still the whispering in my own mind.

Tyee said, "She must have noticed—the change—before anyone else. Our mother. They were close. . . ." He turned to explain to Kor. "She was a strong woman, though not very wise or even clever. I think she reproached him."

"Still, perhaps it was not he who killed her," said Kor. "Perhaps a devourer took her. There was one in him. Perhaps he invited another."

"No," I said, the single word.

Kor looked closely at me; Tyee turned to stare at me. He said hoarsely, "You know what happened to her? Truly?"

I answered him only with my eyes. The knowledge lay heavy in me. Tyonoc himself had told me, one horrible day.

"Can you yet tell us, Dan?" asked Kor very gently.

I shook my head. Later, my brother and I would walk somewhere, in solitude, and I would tell Tyee what I knew. I needed rest and time, one more day, and he deserved to learn first, and alone. . . . Soft footfalls outside the tent, and Leotie came in with my gear, laid it by me, and sat down. The talk took an awkward pause.

"You spoke of devourers, Kor," Tyee said at last. "It is they, then, who carry folk away in the night? They are the demons who take the children?"

"I think so. Yes."

"How, then, did—" Like me, Tyee was finding it difficult to say the name. "—our father—Tyonoc—how did he remain?"

Kor asked, "Have you felt the embrace of a devourer, Tyee?"

"No!" He shuddered, and Leotie drew closer to him. "No. We have heard tales, but to my knowledge none of us had seen such a creature before last night."

"They come most often at night. Weapons and blows are of no use against them. They try to take you in utterly, so that you are nothing anymore but part of them." Kor spoke slowly, hard put to describe this process that was more horrible than being eaten. "But if you are—well centered—it is not the same, exactly, as being strong or courageous—"

Tyee was leaning forward, intently listening.

"—then they cannot devour you, or not easily. And I think your father might have been such a one, when he was truly your father, if he was like Dan."

I said nothing. The others nodded.

"I think that he withstood the devourer for a while, and it tried a different mode of attack. It folded itself into a weapon and pierced him. As it could not take him in, it went within him instead, made itself part of him as he would not be part of it."

We would not have been able to believe it if we had not seen.

"Twice they have tried that with me," Kor added quietly, "and I think one once attacked Tassida in somewhat the same way."

"Then there is—one in Ytan, too." It was Leotie, a note of horror deep in her voice.

None of us answered her. There was no need. For a long moment we sat in silence.

"We need you here, Dan." It was Leotie, looking into my eyes as she spoke. "The game is growing scarcer, and the Fanged Horse Folk come and go as they will. And this other threat . . . It has been hard since you went."

"It was hard coming back," I retorted.

"Yes." She had the grace to wince and lower her eyes. "Yes, truly. But, Dan—"

"Let him be! He is dazed, exhausted, can you not see that?" It was Tyee, speaking with more force than I had ever heard from him. Leotie glanced at him with a surprise perhaps equal to my own, then turned back to me, contrite.

"I wasn't thinking. Dan, let me bathe those wounds of yours, and then I will bring you something hot to eat, and then you had better sleep." She rose to fetch water.

"No, wait!" I put out my hand to stop her. "Tell me first what this thing is about."

"Let it go," she said.

"I will not be able to sleep until I know."

She sighed and put it briefly. "We want you as our king, Dan."

Kor said afterward that it should not have surprised me, but in fact it did. Taken utterly aback, I floundered in astonishment and a vague doubt.

"But—I have been gone, my ways are no longer your ways entirely. My hair is cut. You no longer know me."

"We knew when you came back to us that things would soon be better." Leotie astonished me anew by kneeling in front of me and taking my hands in hers, the gesture of supplication. "Your hair will grow. Please, Dan."

The uproar in my mind made me say the thing that lay uppermost. "Do you not want the kingship for Tyee?" I blurted.

"I have never been made of the stuff of kings," Tyee cut in from his place beside me. "You know that, Dan, as well as I do."

I took my hands out of Leotie's and turned to look at him, certain of what I was going to say, as certain as he was. "Never before, perhaps, Tyee," I told him softly. "But now you are."

He gazed back at me in plain disbelief.

"You are. You have always had goodness, and now you have found it all: the heart, the courage, the strength of spirit—wisdom, even." I turned to Kor, knowing he could sense these things more surely than I. "Is it not so?"

"Yes," he said very quietly but so firmly that no one could doubt him. "Your homecoming has in a way been a blessing, Dan."

Leotie was looking at Tyee with new eyes. I got up, stooped under the tent flap, and walked outside.

Morning was young and sweet-smelling, dewy. I breathed deeply, bracing myself with the sweet air, aware that my steps were unsteady. Then a glint of sun color in the grass drew my eyes down from the sky—it was my great knife, Alar, lying where I had dropped her. No one had dared to touch her, even to clean her, and my father's blood still clotted her graceful body like dark flowers. I went to the sword, turned her over and over, then cleaned her in the forgiving grass and sheathed her.

Standing, I saw the place where my father had fallen. No body lay there.

Kor came up beside me and put an arm lightly around my shoulders. Had he, somehow, grown? His head was almost on a level with mine.

"What have they done with him?" I wondered aloud, meaning Tyonoc.

"They did not know what to do, Leotie tells me. They let the body lie. And during the night sometime, Tyee says, it disappeared as if it had never been. The searchers are out now, but I think they will not find anything."

I stood for a while breathing the clean air and looking around me. In the main camp, some small distance away, folk were tending their cooking fires. There would be food for me there, and comfort, if I wanted them. For the rest of my life, if I wanted them.

Yet there was in me the thought of an impossible journey. . . .

"Kor," I said finally, very softly, very low, "I must find him."

"Your father."

"Yes. I only now grieve for him, yet he has been gone for years. It is not as it should be. I must find him and make my peace with him. I must bring him back."

He nodded as simply as if I were speaking of a journey past the thunder cones, perhaps, to the pit village of the Herders at the edge of the plains. "I have long thought I should seek my mother and my father," he said. "I was afraid—that is why I did not seek my seal form, knowing it would let me venture. . . . But now I am no longer afraid. I will come with you."

It was the most heady of gifts, what he gave me—his presence, his constant love. I turned and seized him by the hand. Then, moved beyond words, I embraced him.

"You are swaying where you stand," he said. "You need food."

Indeed, I was ravenous, and so spent I could scarcely totter the small distance to the nearest fire. But there my people gathered around me and gave me every sort of viand I could desire, and the children clustered around Kor, large-eyed. Their hair shone nearly as white as the sun, the little ones of my tribe. I looked at them and smiled. They knew Kor, who or what he was, as well as I did.

"Why is it that the children always come to you, Kor?" I teased.

"Because they know I like them. And why do I like them? Because their passions are clean, simple, and brief. Mercifully brief." His tone matched mine, and he gave me an amused glance. "Are any of these little suntops yours, Dan?"

"Perhaps. How would I know, for certain? I have not been pledged."

"Dan . . ." He looked at me in a sort of joyous despair and shook his head. "Go to sleep."

The mist was burning away, the day turning clear and fine. I stretched out right where I was, in the sunlight. Kor took water and washed the caked blood from my arms and legs. Leotie brought bison grease and bandaging, and bound them up. Before she was done I fell asleep, and I slept the sleep of one blessed by Sakeema's touch.

Chapter Nineteen

Two days later, after a vigil, Tyee stood before the assembled tribe and put on the ceremonial headgear, wearing the antlers of deer gone since the time of Sakeema, used only for the making of a new king. Tyee had sworn two things: to drive the Fanged Horse raiders back from the Demesne, and to restore the Herders to their rightful lands. These were pledges the people found fitting, for they wished to redeem their shame. They cheered Tyee riotously, gifting him with their heartfelt loyalty. He belonged to them, now.

And I belonged to—what? Kor? My quest? I was not unhappy. There had been time for talk with Tyee. We had walked out, he and I, to see the curly-haired ponies, my own fair sorrel Nolcha grazing among them with a half-grown colt at her side. "Take her," my brother had told me. "Let the fanged mare run back to her steppes." But I had left Nolcha with the brood herd, choosing yet to ride ill-tempered Talu.

I was not any more entirely a Red Hart.

And three days after the kingmaking, days full of much feasting and good friendship, Kor and I mounted our fanged mares and rode. My people sent us on our way with gifts of food and new clothing, with good wishes and more than a little doubt—we had no notion of how we were to accomplish the thing I had set before them. But we did not turn at once westward, toward Mahela's realm beneath the sea, for there was another matter I wished to attend to. We rode southward, toward the headwaters of the Otter River.

We rode through the day in silence for the most part, but from time to time thoughts welled up and were spoken, breaking the surface as sweetly and cleanly as spring water welling out of the mountainsides.

"There is Tassida to be thought of," I said to Kor near quarterday.

"I think of her often," he replied.

"What will you do? Do you wish to find her?"

"That is as it comes." He sighed. "I am no worse off than I was before. I yearned for someone, anyone, then, and I yearn for her now. If it is meant to be . . ."

He let the words trail away, and we rode silently for a while.

"I think I am better off when I do not see her," he said finally.

"I loved Leotie," I remarked.

He nodded, unsurprised.

"I did. I was too much of an ass to admit it at the time. There had been other maidens. . . . But I was heartbroken when she went to Tyee."

"He needed her even more than you did."

I grimaced at him. "Blast you, yes."

"He suffered as much as you did from the change in your father."

"More. We wanted his love, but we learned to court his smiles instead—and there were more smiles for me."

Kor grew thoughtful. Talu nodded her head, trying to shake the flies away, and I reached forward and brushed one off her ear. The steady cadence of the horses' hooves made me feel blessed, as if I were rocked in the embrace of the world.

"You were more of a threat," Kor said after a while. "Tyee's lack of spirit saved him."

I stared at him, thinking it through. "Yes . . . Tyee could be managed, and Ytan—he had always been sour, but he grew hard, he began to smile in that same way—"

Looking back, it seemed as if it had all happened at once.

"What brought the broth to a boil?" Kor asked.

"I don't know! I was so heedless, how should I know? What does Tyee say?"

"That your tribesfolk loved you too well."

We rode until we were far up in the foothills to the west and southward, well out of the usual range of my people, though there was scarcely any place in these uplands where they did not sometimes come. At dusk we camped, and in the morning we rode on until I saw a certain mountainside, or knee of a mountain, all in points and pinnacles, jagged as a half-made spearhead. Then I cast about, searching, for I could not remember exactly the way we, my father and brother and I, had come.

"It was in the mid of winter," I explained to Kor. "And he—" It was hard for me to call him Father. "—Tyonoc—and Ytan asked me to come out riding with them to study the movements of the game. Or, rather, more ordered me than asked—but I was glad enough to go with them. I was the youngest, and I felt honored, and there was always the chance of—well, a smile. So we took some dried meat and flatbread and rode. By sundown we were still riding through the snow, though we had not brought our sleeping robes with us, and I did not dare to ask why. And at dusk my father led us—there."

I pointed. It lay below us. A tarn, a small pool hidden in a steep fold of the mountain's flank, very dark, midnight dark even in the morning of a bright summer day. We rode slowly down to it, wary of it for no reason. When we dismounted we stood well back from the brink.

"It must be deep," Kor said.

"It is, believe me." I winced. "Very deep. So deep the ice had formed only at the edges of it. And the stars came out, they were shadowed on that black surface—the pool might as well have been a bit of sky, shining deep and black. The only light came from the stars. I could barely see even the white of the snow. It was the blackest of all nights."

"Dark of the moon," Kor murmured.

"Yes. And we built no fire. When full dark had fallen, my father spoke to me. 'This is a pool where legends are said to live,' he told me. 'Look in it and tell me what you see.' And I, young fool, I was so excited and honored that he thought I might be a visionary . . .''

Kor turned and faced me, steadying me with his eyes. I took a deep breath and went on.

"So I stood at the edge of the pool and looked. 'Go closer,' my father said, and with a hard blow he pushed me in."

"Not just a nasty prank," said Kor in a low voice. "Not in the wintertime."

"No. The water was cold enough to freeze my blood, and they knew it. They stood on the verge, on opposite sides, he and Ytan, and mocked me, telling me how they had killed my mother, slitting her throat and bleeding her like a deer and hiding her bones under a nameless rock somewhere. Their voices came out of the night like the voices of demons. Standing over me, they were black places where the stars did not shine. And there was no bottom under my feet, not even close to the shore, so steeply did the pool drop away. And the water seemed to pull me down. I—may I never again feel so sickened, so helpless. I thrashed about and swallowed water and shouted, not believing what they were saying to me, and when I raised my hands to them for aid they struck at me with their knives.''

I paused, remembering how the stone knives had come at me black out of the blackness, so that I had not known until my arm was slashed, bleeding, had not believed— that I was meant to die. That he, my own father, Tyonoc, with my brother Ytan, had plotted to kill me. As they had killed Wyonet. And truth had chilled me worse than the wintry tarn water, that my father had held her by her honey-colored hair, placed his blackstone knife to her throat—

"Go on," Kor urged gently.

I blinked at him. The sunny day seemed darkened, as if a shadow of that night lay over it.

"It was a long time," I said numbly. "I went under—I do not know how many times. The cold water sapped my strength, and when I came up to gasp for air they kicked at

my head—'' My voice began to tremble. "They kicked at
me, or stuck with their knives, and drove me down again,
and waited for me to drown. I had always been afraid of
drowning. As a child I had dreamed of drowning, bad
dreams, they woke me shouting in the night. . . ."

"And he remembered," said Kor softly. "Yes. I see."

"It would have been so much simpler, faster, just to
have stabbed me along the trail somewhere. But they
needs must drown me, because they found that crueler."
My voice was shaking hard, but I did not bother to weep. I
was done with weeping. "They laughed, they laughed and
jeered at me, at my struggles. . . ."

I could barely speak. "Go on," Kor said.

"I struggled for a long time." I could feel the struggle,
the pain in my chest, the panic, black water drowning
deep—but this time it was a memory, not a madman's
dream. "Then—my strength was nearly gone. I wanted—I
am not sure what. To defy them, somehow, or get away
from them, hide from their mockery. . . . Perhaps I just
gave up. I let myself sink. I forced myself down, deeper,
deeper into the accursed tarn, searching for the bottom of
it. Down until I was nearly insensible, and there seemed
no end to it. But then there was a scrape, or presence, and
somehow the hilt found its way into my hand."

"The great knife," Kor breathed, for I had not told him
why I was bringing him to that pool. "The sword!"

"A weapon, was all I knew then. A way to save my
life."

"But of course." His eyes were sparkling. "I see it
now, what happened. How you must have put the fear of
vengeance into them!"

"Yes, they cried out." I had to smile at his fervor,
though for me the memories were far from pleasant. "I
shot up to the surface and came half out of the water,
sword first, and I heard them yell with surprise and fear. I
swung, and I broke Ytan's knife off to the hilt in his hand.
He backed away from me, and I clambered out on his side
of the tarn." I pointed at the very place, lying before me,
bright with sunshine. "Over there. I stood up—"

"Where did you find the strength!" Kor murmured.

"I—I was enraged. I wanted to kill them both." Even after all that had happened, the words shook me. "I wanted to behead Ytan, and—my father—you know what I wanted to do to—to Tyonoc. Ytan ran, but—Tyonoc—he came around the pool and lunged at me, trying to topple me back in, and I slashed at him—"

His face in the starlight. My father, whom I had loved, who had loved me once and later betrayed me. Grieving, as stricken as I had been that night, I could not go on, I could not think or speak. I stared at the tarn, my lips moving soundlessly.

Gently Kor took up the tale for me. "He gave you a gash on the chest," he said.

Frozen where I stood . . . No, not so. That was all in the past. With an effort of will I nodded.

"And great heart that you are," Kor said with a quiet passion in his voice, "you could not kill him or even strike back at him, though you badly wanted to cut him apart. You took a horse instead and fled, and came to me somehow over the mountains, half healed but still enraged. . . . Do you recall that journey? It must have been fearsome."

I found my voice. "I do not remember much of it," I admitted.

"I will be forever grateful to your father," said Kor, "for having sent you to me. I only wish he could have done it more kindly."

I sat down on the turf, laid Alar aside, started to strip off my leggings and boots. Kor crouched down and peered at me.

"Dan," he chided, "is it not enough to come here and look and remember?"

I shook my head, stood up and stripped off my doeskin breeching, so that I was naked. I took a long breath and stepped to the verge of the tarn.

All lay very silent. No bird called. Looking at the dark, smooth surface of the water, very still, shadowed, I seemed to see the ghosts of stars.

Suddenly, though it seemed a simple enough task I had set myself, I was unaccountably terrified, and I whirled around to look behind me. Kor was standing where I had left him, watching me, and as usual he knew what I was feeling. "I will not push you in," he told me. "You know that."

Ashamed—no, there was no use in shame when I was with him, for he had always felt what folly was in me, and still there was that—that love such as I had once before lost. Lost. *Ai*, but I was afraid.

"Kor," I pleaded, "what if a devourer were to find a way into you, too? How would I know?"

The question took his breath—I saw his face change. For a moment he stood as silent as the pool.

"Knives might be of some use after all, Dan," he said slowly then. "I think I would kill myself before I would let that happen."

Not much comforted, I turned and dove headfirst into the tarn.

Deep, deep, drowning deep, and so black that even in the daylight I could see nothing. And ice cold, even in summertime. And pressure, water pulling at me. It was all familiar, grim but no longer a cause for panic. I forced myself deeper, holding my breath and searching for the bottom—I did not find it. There was a singing and a pounding in my ears. When I felt as if I might faint, I faced upward and plunged back to the surface, breaking it with a gasp, thrashing—

Kor was there, kneeling at the verge, reaching out to help me. He caught me by the wrist with a strong grip. I smiled and let myself be borne up by him until my breathing quieted.

"Let me try again," I said, and with a faint frown he released his grasp.

I pushed my way down more calmly this time, more strongly, forcing my way hands first through the blackness, until at last my hands—touched. There were rocks on the bottom, but also other things, shapes I knew, blades and hilts, more than one. My hand closed around a hilt—and the sword jerked away, turned and cut me across my startled fingers. In a moment I realized how much worse it could have hurt me. Clearly, a gentle warning.

Back at the surface of the tarn, panting, I let Kor pull

me out so that I sat on the bank beside him. I held up my
right hand. A shallow slash cut neatly across the palm side
of all four fingers. The chill of the water had not let it
bleed, but as I looked it filled with bright red. Kor looked
as well and went rigid.

"Your sword is down there," I told him, "but she will
not come to me."

For once I had truly confounded him. He could scarcely
move or speak for amazement. "Bind that," he said finally, and he got up and pulled off his tunic and breeches
and boots. His plunge cut cleanly into the surface of the
pool. The seal in him, I thought sitting there.

I sat in the sunshine, shivering in spite of the midsum-
mer warmth, for what seemed a long time. I did not bind
my hand, but let it bleed. Just as fear took hold of me and
brought me to my feet, Kor came surging up, shaking the
water out of his hair and eyes, and in his right hand he
held his sword. On the pommel shone a glittering stone of
pure, true red, blood red.

When I had helped him clamber out he stood before me
with a rapt and thinking look, staring at the sword and then
at the cut on my hand.

"A beautiful thing, for all that it is a weapon of war,"
he remarked, hefting it, lifting it to the level of our eyes.
Sunlight gleamed on the soaring blade. "Very clean, that
cut it gave you."

"As clean as the one I put on your neck once." I
looked. "The scar is gone." All scars had left him in his
healing.

"Matching marks," he whispered to himself, and his
eyes shot up to meet mine. "Dan, you have brothers, but I
have none."

"You want one?" I asked softly.

He nodded. "Get Alar."

Ardor singing deep in his voice. I reached down where
the scabbard lay with my clothing and drew out the sword.
Blood on the hilt from my bleeding fingers. . . . I seemed
to feel the air tingle, Alar tremble in my hand. Kor put
down his blade and held out his right hand to me, palm up.

"Across the fingers, like yours." He looked at me with

a hint of a smile. "Stop shaking, Dan. I am used to scars, I feel naked without any."

"You are naked," I retorted. As was I. And the jest failed, for my voice quivered.

I took a deep breath to steady myself and made the cut. How he trusted me. . . . Sakeema be praised, it was all right. Shallow, but deep enough to bleed. The red drops welled up, shining bright as the jewel in his sword, and I laid Alar aside, turned to Kor and touched his bleeding hand with mine.

Fingers curled, clasped. Blood mingled. Eyes met.

"You have a brother now," I told him. "It is a pledge." And my voice was strong and warm as the sunlight, and I no longer trembled. There was a mist of tears in his eyes, like the mist over his distant home, but I saw his smile, full of strength and joy, and I knew that my smile answered his in kind—I felt tall with joy, and fearless. Kor held his head high always, but he lifted it yet higher. He must have felt that same surge of courage.

"The two of us together," he declared, "we can do anything. And that is my pledge to you, Dan."

We stood for a long time without moving, unwilling to let go of the moment. Until the blood dried on our clasped fingers we stood, and when at last we sighed, stirred, and loosened our grip, the cuts no longer bled.

Without speaking we moved about, softly, as if in a good dream, not wanting to mar it with clatterings or our uncouth voices. We washed at the tarn, put on our clothes. I cleansed my sword and sheathed it. Kor sat cross-legged on the turf with his in his lap, one finger tracing the long lines of the blade. He looked up at the odd spires looming above us, then at me.

"Let us camp here tonight," he said, and though we could have ridden half a day yet, I nodded. He had turned it into a place for me to love.

I went out and hunted us ridge chickens—they are easy meat, they run rather than fly, and sometimes they forget even to run. I took two of the birds back to Kor, and we built a fire near the tarn and cooked them at our leisure. We gathered mountain blueberries, we baked flatbread on fire-heated rocks, and then we feasted, and talked easily of many things, even of Tassida. And after a while we grew silent and watched the sunset colors fade over the snowpeaks and the stars come out.

Our campfire had burned down to embers. Somewhere a whiskered owl was calling. The stars burned white in a sky as black and soft as a sable's pelt, and in the pool their shadows floated. I remember a crescent moon. The night was fair, the breeze full of heady fragrance from the pines downslope, and Kor and I sat gazing for no reason at the shadow-stars floating on the black water of the tarn.

We must have been half in a trance. Before we were well aware of it the white, glimmering flecks shifted, gathered, took shape and rose like a mist above the black pool. Or like tall clusters of white flowers half seen at nighttime, or like two hunters sprinkled with snow—no. Thin as a mist, but faintly glowing and plain in every line, two men stood there, or two ghosts of men, or visions, stood as if on rock, though the tarn water hid their feet. And they wore clothing such as I had never seen, clothing fit for kings—or gods. Robe and tunic and baldric and cape, layer on layer, long, fanciful sleeves bordered with stitchery and glimmer, cloak trailing to the heels, shining cloth gloriously wrought, and it was all white, all starlight. But although I remembered it afterward, I scarcely noted the clothing at the time. The faces held me. They were faces of men, perhaps warriors, older than I but not yet old, and there was a passionfire in them, and a sadness, and a grandeur that awed and frightened me. I inched my left hand over to where Kor sat, grasped his arm, and I could tell by the hardness of his arm that he saw them too. Neither of us dared to further move, or speak.

The two men of starlight, the two visions, faced each other with a steady, half-smiling look, and softly they drew their swords. The swords of starlight looked much like Kor's and mine. . . . And the two kings, if kings they were, touched blades without a sound, touched the tips of their blades and raised them high overhead, still cleaving, in a gesture of triumph or—I was not sure what, an emblem like a mountainpeak. . . . Then they sheathed their swords and held out their right hands to each other. Their fingers curled, clasped. That grip, I knew it. Their eyes met with a look I also knew.

Then, turning, they looked full at us, at Kor, at me.

Their gaze—we felt it eerily, reaching us out of a distance we could not encompass, chill deeps of time. For a moment we looked into their grave, noble faces of starlight, and then we could look no longer. Terror took us, and we cried out and hid behind our arms.

"They are gone," Kor whispered. "I feel it."

Clenching myself, I looked up. The surface of the tarn lay still, with only the ghosts of stars floating on it like tiny lilies.

"They did—not mean to harm us—or unman us. . . ." Kor's voice was unsteady.

"Then why are we both quaking?" Mine was no firmer.

"Reach out your right hand to me," Kor said.

I could just as easily have hugged him around the shoulders with the left. But I did as he said, and he held out his own, touched the raw cut on his fingers to mine. And instantly I felt a surge of strength. I shook no longer. Nor, I saw, did he. And his face was alight with wonder.

"Dan! When we two are together, we have the strength of four."

"Who were those two on the pool?" I asked, my voice hushed.

"Sakeema knows."

We slept, for we were no longer afraid. I awoke at sunrise to see Kor also awake, studying the early light on the odd pinnacles above us.

"Men made that," he said. "The part on the knee of the mountain, there, that is different."

I blinked at him, for how could men ever have made such a massive thing? And why? But remembering Tassida's tales and the vision of the night before, I did not speak my doubt.

"Well, Dan," said Kor, as if bemused, "I have come a long way from my seaside Hold."

"We'll have a longer way to go to beard Mahela, and a strange trail."

So we set forth on it, two youths on heavy-headed fanged mares, upslope toward the eversnow and icefields and the passes that led toward sunset. The first day of an unlikely journey . . . We held the reins with our left hands only, and from time to time we lifted the others and smiled.

Glossary

afterlings: followers, usually on foot.

afterwit: hindsight.

amaranth: a healing flower that disappeared when Sakeema was killed.

awk: leftward.

blackstone: obsidian.

brownsheen: copper-colored.

brume: dense, gray fog.

cachalot: sperm whale.

carrageen: a dark purplish seaweed.

chough: a small, insolent crow.

comity: innate courtesy.

cracking rail: a short-billed landrail of drab plumage, shy habits, and excruciating vocal abilities.

dreamwit: a visionary person, a mystic.

dryland: the opposite of ocean. Refers to any land above water, not necessarily arid.

dulse: an edible seaweed.

erne: a sea eagle.

eye of sky: the dispassionate gaze of the nameless god.

fire true: true enough to be sworn to by putting one's hand in fire.

fogwater: condensation.

fry: recently hatched salmon just emerging from the gravel, the length of the first joint of a man's index finger.

fulmar: a stiff-winged, gliding seabird.

gair fowl: the greak auk, a sort of northern penguin.

gannet: a large, white seabird.

glimmerstones: agates.

graymaw: a shark.

graysheen: silver-colored.

greendeep: ocean.

grilse: salmon returning from the sea to their native
    river; "summer salmon."

gudgeon: a rather stupid-looking freshwater fish.

gutknot: navel.

highmountain: alpine (as, highmountain meadow).

indeeps: penetralia.

inwit: instinct.

jannock: unleavened oatmeal bread.

king: a tribal ruler of either sex.

kittiwake: a small, short-legged, gentle-faced gull.

lappet: a breechclout.

lovelocks: curling tendrils of hair.

merkin: a woman's pubic hair.

moonstuff: silver.

moon-mad: temporarily passionate or out of control,
    with emotions running high, as if influenced, like
    tides, by the phase of the moon.

nagsback: a shallow mountain pass.

noggin's worth: a little.

orichalc: a hard, golden bronze.

parr: young salmon still in the brown freshwater stage.

peal: salmon returning from the sea to their native
    river, turning from silver to red.

pickthank: a flatterer.

rampick: a tree whose top is dead or broken off by
    wind.

roughlands: the shadowlands.

scantling: a toddler, a very young specimen of what-
    ever species.

scarrow: high, thin cloud.

scarrow-fog: a thin haze high in the sky that lets the
    sun show as a white spot.

scooning: skipping over the surface of water as a flat
    stone does when properly thrown.

shadowlands: the arid high plains beyond the mountains, the steppes or shortgrass prairie.

slowcome: a slow-witted person or one who is slow to act, sometimes with a sexual connotation.

smellfungus: a grumbler.

smolt: salmon in the final freshwater stage, turning from brown to silver.

smurr: drizzle.

snow mote: snowflake.

stone-boiled: cooked in liquid into which hot stones are dropped to heat it.

stoup's worth: a lot.

sunstuff: gold.

swordmaster: maker, namer, and wielder of his or her sword.

sylkies: undersea folk who can take the form of humans or seals.

thunder cones: volcanoes.

tongueshot: the distance a voice will carry.

troating: bleating, as of a deer in rut.

tumblestone: a rock washed smooth by the action of water.

wanhope: a person who continues to hope against all common sense.

whimbrel: a brown wading bird, related to dowitchers, godwits, curlews, willets, and snipe.

whurr: to burst from cover with a loud flapping of wings, as a partridge or a grouse.

witch wind: hot wind that blows down from the landward side of mountains.

THE BEST IN FANTASY

☐ 54973-2 FORSAKE THE SKY by Tim Powers $2.95
   54974-0   Canada $3.50

☐ 53392-5 THE INITIATE by Louise Cooper $2.95

☐ 55484-1 WINGS OF FLAME $2.95
   55485-X by Nancy Springer   Canada $3.50

☐ 53671-1 THE DOOR INTO FIRE $2.95
   53672-X by Diane Duane   Canada $3.50

☐ 53673-8 THE DOOR INTO SHADOW $2.95
   53674-6 by Diane Duane   Canada $3.50

☐ 54900-7 DARKANGEL $2.95
   54901-5 by Meredith Ann Pierce   Canada $3.50

☐ 54902-3 A GATHERING OF GARGOYLES $2.95
   54903-1 by Meredith Ann Pierce   Canada $3.50

☐ 55610-0 JINIAN FOOTSEER $2.95
   55611-9 by Sheri S. Tepper   Canada $3.50

☐ 55612-7 DERVISH DAUGHTER $2.95
   55613-5 by Sheri S. Tepper   Canada $3.50

☐ 55614-3 JINIAN STAR-EYE $2.95
   55615-1 by Sheri S. Tepper   Canada $3.75

☐ 54800-0 THE WORLD IN AMBER by A. Orr $2.95
   54801-9   Canada $3.75

☐ 55600-3 THE ISLE OF GLASS by Judith Tarr $2.95
   55601-1   Canada $3.75

Buy them at your local bookstore or use this handy coupon:
Clip and mail this page with your order

TOR BOOKS—Reader Service Dept.
49 W. 24 Street, 9th Floor, New York, NY 10010

Please send me the book(s) I have checked above. I am
enclosing $_____ (please add $1.00 to cover postage
and handling). Send check or money order only—no
cash or C.O.D.'s.

Mr./Mrs./Miss _____

Address _____

City _____ State/Zip _____

Please allow six weeks for delivery. Prices subject to
change without notice.

ANDRÉ NORTON